CRITICS RAVE FOR AWARD-WINNING AUTHOR PENELOPE NERI!

"A marvelous storyteller who holds readers enthralled!"
—*Romantic Times*

"Fans of taut thrillers with romantic subplots will applaud [Penelope Neri]."
—*The Midwest Book Review*

"Penelope Neri has crafted a dark tale of romance and danger."
—Barnes & Noble.com on *Moonshadow*

"Neri is a genius at creating characters that readers will love, and spinning a magical tale that will leave readers longing for more."
—Writers Write

DEAD OR ALIVE?

"Liz, wait! Richard Harper isn't dead. He just wants you to think he is. Don't you see? You're playing right into his hands! C'mon, lady. Hear me out. Don't run," he coaxed in a last, desperate effort to make her see reason. "Please?"

She stopped, and stood very still, her back to him. "You're wrong—or lying! *Richard's dead*. He *must* be," she said desperately, still without turning around. "They did an—an autopsy on him, for crying out loud! I read about it on the Internet. The Honolulu M.E. matched Richard's dental records to the body they pulled from the car wreck."

She was trying to convince herself, to gather her courage. He could hear it, see it. Yet there was a quaver in her voice, nevertheless. Fear had turned her face a chalky white.

"They matched *someone's* dental records to Richard's," he agreed softly. "But I talked to the M.E. myself, right after she got through examining the remains. And you know what? She didn't buy it any more than I did! That's one of the reasons I came here. To warn you. *Harper's still alive!*"

DOUBLE PLAY

PENELOPE NERI

LOVE SPELL NEW YORK CITY

With love and thanks
to Pattie Conroy Vatalaro,
who makes the bad times better.

Ditto to all who work
at or visit Suite 412, Kuakini Medical Plaza.
Bless you, my friends!
P.N.

LOVE SPELL®

September 2005

Published by

Dorchester Publishing Co., Inc.
200 Madison Avenue
New York, NY 10016

ISBN 0-505-52645-X

DOUBLE PLAY

PROLOGUE

Chat room at TropicalConnections.com
Honolulu, Hawaii
November

LULU> Hello, Keoki.

KEOKI> Hi, Lulu. How's it going?

LULU> Oh, so-so. You know how it is. Look, I don't have much time today, so I'll cut to the chase. Remember what we talked about last time?

KEOKI> Sure. What about it?

LULU> I'm going to do it. Leave him, I mean.

KEOKI> Whoa! When?

LULU> Soon! Just a few more days.

KEOKI> Six months of cold feet, then—bam! You're going, just like that? What brought this on?

LULU> Nothing brought it on. It's just time. You said yourself, two years is way too long.

KEOKI> Yeah, but this is a big step, Lu. Final. No going back.

LULU> Going back's not in my game plan, so don't worry about that. Hey. Lighten up. A few words of support would be nice!

KEOKI> Sorry. Your announcement blew me away. I'm behind you all the way, Lu. You know that. You thought it through, right? Considered all the angles?

LULU> And then some!

KEOKI> I sure hope so. Guys like him go crazy when their partners leave. They'll do anything to get them back. That includes killing them, Lu. Are you willing to take that risk?

LULU> Stay or leave, either way I could wind up dead, right? So the answer's yes, I'll take my chances this way. Don't try to talk me out of it, Keoki!

KEOKI> I'm not trying to talk you out of anything. I just want you to go into this with your eyes wide open, knowing all the risks, considering all your options. If your mind's made up, I can put you in touch with a woman in Waikiki. She runs a halfway house for women who—

LULU> Thanks, but no thanks. I don't need counselors or halfway houses. I have a plan. A *good* plan. I just wanted to say good-bye before I left. This is the last time we'll chat, Keoki. I'll miss you.

KEOKI> Me, too. You be careful, okay, Lu? Take care of yourself. Be safe.

LULU> I will. Thanks, Keoki. For everything.
For listening to my whining, for your good advice, the whole nine yards. You've been a real
friend. I would never have found the courage to
do this without your support.
KEOKI> If you mean that, do me one last favor,
Lu. Wait a few more days.
LULU> I can't wait.
KEOKI> Why not? Has he hurt you again, Lu?
Is that it? Let me give you the number of that
shelter. If something falls through—
LULU> I don't need phone numbers. I told you,
don't worry about me. I have a place to go, and
someone to go with, okay? Be happy for me,
Keoki! Don't you see? I'm not alone anymore.
Wow, look at the time! I have to go now. He'll
be home soon. Adios, Keoki. Take care.
KEOKI> Lu, wait. Let's talk about this some
more.
KEOKI> Lu? Come on, Lulu. Write to me!
KEOKI> Lulu? Are you still signed on?
Lulu . . .

Jack McQuinn, a.k.a. Keoki, sat and stared at
the blank computer screen for several minutes after Lulu had signed off, but she didn't log on
again.

Had he done the right thing by urging her to
leave her abusive husband? he wondered. He
hoped to God he had! Her life might depend on it.

He logged off when it was clear that Lulu wasn't

coming back. But long after he'd left the Department for the day, her parting words continued to bother him. *I can't wait,* she'd written. *I have a place to go, and someone to go with. Be happy for me. I'm not alone anymore. . . .*

Was it his gut instinct working overtime, or did her words have an ominous ring?

"Elizabeth."

At the sound of his voice, her hands froze on the keyboard, stilled by panic. She didn't turn around. Didn't look to see who'd said her name. She didn't have to. God, no. Despite the countless nights she'd prayed it would be someone else, it was always him.

Richard. Her husband.

Immediately she felt as if an oppressive weight were crushing down on her, slowly squeezing the life from her. Her shoulders drooped. A throbbing headache beat like a drum in her temple.

"You're home early, Richard. I—I wasn't expecting you yet. How was your day?" She tried to sound light, welcoming, but knew her voice sounded strained, unnatural.

"So it appears." Colorless eyes narrowing, he frowned. "What were you doing on my computer, Elizabeth?"

His tone was cultured, clipped, cold. On his lips, her very name became a weapon, a punishing blow. An obscenity.

"Recipes." She blurted out the first thing—the

4

most innocent thing!—she could think of, knowing even as she spoke that it would not be enough. Would not save her from the inevitable. Nothing ever had, not in the two years she'd been married to this man. No excuse or explanation ever satisfied him.

"I was looking for a recipe," she added quickly, breathless with fear. "The—that chicken breast with the white wine sauce? The one you liked so much?" *Or claimed to like, the last time you almost killed me!* He was always very charming, very complimentary, almost *loving* in the aftermath of his explosions. So charming, she sometimes found herself falling under his spell all over again.

Don't fall for it, not this time. This time's different, she reminded herself.

From somewhere she found the courage to press her bare toe to the OFF switch. From where Richard was standing, he couldn't see the monitor.

There was a click, then her link with the outside world ebbed. The screen faded to gray. For the time being, all traces of Keoki and the Tropical-Connections chat room vanished.

She was alone.

"You're avoiding the real issue, Elizabeth."

He said it in a matter-of-fact, mildly annoyed way that was chilling, knowing him as she did. He sounded like a schoolteacher admonishing an incorrigible student, prior to meting out some suitable punishment. But she knew better. Oh, yes.

There was nothing mild about him. His disguise as a brilliant doctor, a cardiothoracic surgeon who had given the gift of life to countless patients, concealed a monster.

Despite the deceptively mild tone, this "schoolteacher's" punishments were never suitable. God, no. They were excessive. Cruel. Terrible.

Dread crawled through her veins like an insidious cancer, spreading despair, destroying hope, eroding dignity wherever it feasted. Turning courage to cowardice.

"The issue being," he taunted softly, menacingly as he came to stand behind her, his elegant surgeon's hands kneading her narrow shoulders, "that you aren't permitted to use my computer, for any reason whatsoever, unless I'm here. I thought I made that perfectly clear to you the last time, Elizabeth. But apparently not, hmm?"

"But—I have to do *something* with my time!" she exploded recklessly, leaping to her feet, shrugging off his punishing hands. "You're a brilliant man! Surely you can see that?"

Against the building holocaust of his cold rage, her small protest was weak, no stronger than the puny flare and fizzle of a damp firecracker. Nevertheless, she bravely continued, whirling to face him with her gray eyes blazing.

"I've done everything you've ever asked me to do. *Everything!* I left my family to live in Hawaii with you. I don't call or write to them anymore, because you asked me not to. Remember? You said it would make the separation easier to bear. Easier for whom, Richard? Not for me!"

Her voice broke, but she set her jaw and managed to go on. "I resigned from the hiking club, at your request. I quit the gym, again because you insisted! If you won't let me go back to nursing, I—"

"Enough! Quiet, you stupid bitch! I told you how I felt about your precious nursing! The head of the Cardiothoracic Surgery Department's wife doesn't need to work. It doesn't reflect well on me, as your husband, for you to be working. It's not as if we need the money!"

"No? Then what am I supposed to do with myself all day? *All week!* Tell me!" she demanded, hurling the question into his face, knowing she had nothing to lose, not anymore. She was leaving, as soon as she could. Her mind was made up. Either he would kill her, or she would go.

But even as she defied him for what could well be the very last time, a tiny part of her still hoped, still clung to her foolish dreams. A part of her wished, just this once, that things would end differently this time. That tonight, her defiance wouldn't end in pain and terror. *Not tonight, please God. Not tonight!*

Instead of hurting her, perhaps by some miracle he would come to his senses. He'd smile and say he was oh, so sorry. He'd had a difficult case that day—a child who'd coded, perhaps, despite his Herculean efforts to save its fragile life. It was wrong of him, very wrong, he knew, to take his

7

own grief, his failure, out on her, his beloved wife, he'd say. Could she ever forgive him?

He would take her in his arms and hold her tenderly, as he'd done during their whirlwind courtship in Miami, where she'd been a surgical nurse, and he the godlike chief of cardiothoracic surgery.

From then on, she would have a happy, normal life. A life like other women enjoyed, with a loving husband. Children. She would have the family she'd craved for most of her life as a child in the Florida foster care system before the Scotts finally adopted her. They had made her dream of belonging to a family a beautiful dream come true.

She'd lost that precious normal life, that happiness, that happy family, all over again when she married Richard, and moved with him here, to the 50th state. To an island paradise he'd made into a living hell.

Little by little, he'd alienated her from everyone and everything she loved: her family, her friends, the things she liked to do, *everything!*

Abruptly the fragile bubble of hope inside her burst. The spark fizzled and died. Nothing would change, not tonight, nor any other night, because *he* wouldn't change. He was what he was. A control freak. An abusive, violent man. Tonight, like every other night, would end in pain, in terror—perhaps even in death.

Her death.

She couldn't let that happen. Not now, when she

had so much to live for! If he wouldn't change, then she must.

"Do you really expect me to sit home all day, doing nothing? Seeing no one? Just—just twiddling my thumbs 24/7 while I wait for you to come home, like a—a Stepford wife?" she raged.

"Yes, Elizabeth! That's exactly what I expect!"

"What kind of life is that for an intelligent woman? For God's sake, we're not living in the Dark Ages, Richard!"

His lips tightened. Irritation flared in his pale, empty eyes. An unhealthy red flush rose up his throat. "Caring for your husband and his home should be enough for any decent woman!" He frowned. His ice-blue eyes narrowed in suspicion. "But *are* you a decent woman, Elizabeth? Sometimes I wonder. What were you doing on my computer? Surfing the Net?" he suggested with a sneer. "Looking for men to whore with? Is that what you do while I'm gone? Answer me, you filthy slut! *Is it?*"

His handsome face was mottled now, the fair skin blotchy and red with rage against close-cropped blond hair. Hair so very fair it was almost white.

Once, she'd been so attracted to him! He'd seemed so sophisticated, so worldly, so protective and caring. She'd been drawn to him like a moth to a flame, flattered by his attentions, dazzled by the knowledge that a respected Miami surgeon, older, important, sought after, wealthy, had noticed her. *Loved* her.

9

Oh, what a naive, trusting fool she'd been.

He towered over her now, his fists clenched at his sides, his fury barely controlled. She recognized the signs. It was only a matter of time before he struck out. Before his cold fury became a raging inferno.

"May I remind you that you already have a man, *Ms.* Harper?" he demanded in clipped, angry tones. "Like it or not, you have *me.* Now get up to our room and wait for me there."

He was already unbuckling his belt as he said it. He never used his hands on her. Oh, no, the almighty Dr. Harper never risked injury to his precious surgeon's hands. Those hands were his livelihood. His pride.

"*No.*" She said it so softly, so defiantly, she wondered afterwards if she'd really spoken at all, or had just imagined her lips forming the word. Where had she found the courage? Had her secret fueled it? Was that it? It must be! It was the only explanation for her bravado.

"*No?*" he echoed in disbelief. "You'll do as I tell you, dammit, you stupid, worthless little bitch!"

"No, Richard! Not anymore. I won't let you hurt me again. *No! No! No!*"

She flung her long black hair over her shoulder and planted her fists on her hips. Smoky eyes blazing, she glared him down without flinching.

He laughed in her face.

His arm shot out. Those skilled, tapered fingers snared her delicately boned wrist like a manacle before she could spring out of reach. He wrenched her arm up behind her, forcing it against the joint.

As if from a distance, she heard a popping sound as delicate bones snapped, as tendons tore. Immediately a clammy sweat sprang out on her brow. Pain roared like a freight train through her useless arm. She felt light-headed. Wanted to be sick. *Oh, God—oh, God—*

"Go ahead, Eliza-beth," he taunted in a hoarse whisper that had an almost Southern lilt when he was angry, as he was now. His hot breath fanned her cheek. "*Make* me," he murmured silkily in the voice of a lover.

"Please." She didn't want to beg, but couldn't help it. Couldn't help herself. Oh, the pain!

"Please what, Elizabeth?" He applied more pressure to her damaged arm. "Hmmm?"

"*Please. Don't. P-please don't.*" Red filled her vision.

"Say it, bitch! Say my name!"

"Richard. Please, Richard. Please don't," she whimpered as he shook her violently. "Oh! Stop! Stop! Aaaah! Please don't hurt me!"

He laughed. "That's better. I think you're finally learning, Elizabeth. I'm the one calling the shots here, not you. Never you! Now get upstairs! We'll continue your discipline there."

He wetted his lips, his empty eyes shining, eager.

Like a puppet, she started up the stairs, knowing as she went that, one way or another, this time would be the last.

ONE

Honolulu Police Department,
Specialized Services and Missing Persons Division,
Hawaii
Two weeks later

"Today, a sixty-member search team made up of police officers, firemen, K-9 units, and members of the Specialized Services and Missing Persons Division resumed their search for missing hiker Elizabeth Harper," Detective Tom Pacheco read aloud.

"A former member of the Outdoor Hawaii Hiking Club, Harper disappeared three days ago while hiking alone in the Kahana Valley State Park.

"According to club treasurer, Mitsuko 'Bea' Watanabe, 57, of Kaimuki, Harper was a member of the group for only a few months, but was already considered an experienced hiker by her fellow members.

"'Kahana Valley got some pretty challenging trails, you know?'" Watanabe told this reporter.

13

"'That's why we always hike with a buddy, yeah? Never alone,'" Tom continued.

"Harper apparently broke this unwritten hikers' rule."

"Dogs with HPD's K-9 division found Harper's car keys and water bottle at the top of a steep cliff late Tuesday afternoon, the day following her disappearance. The recovered items were some distance from the marked trail. Hikers speculate that Harper lost her way and became disoriented. It is also possible she fell off the cliff and was injured. Club members are assisting the search parties in locating her. However, bad weather, dense vegetation, and difficult terrain make the search a daunting task.

"Last year, German tourist Franz Schmidt was recovered alive after being missing for six days in the Kahana Valley. On day seven, members of another hiking club located the missing man on a cliff at elevations of between 2,200-2,300 feet. Schmidt's right ankle was badly fractured. He had numerous bruises and scrapes from a fall, and was suffering from exposure. His rescuers credit a mirror the injured hiker used to signal his location with his eventual safe recovery.

"A Kaneohe Marine who disappeared last April has never been found.

"Experienced hikers carry whistles, cell phones, mirrors, and flashlights with which to signal in the event they become lost, according to Watanabe. It is not known if Harper had any of these items with

14

her at the time of her disappearance. Despite helicopter flyovers, no signal flashes have been spotted from the valley.

"Unless additional evidence is recovered or sightings are made during the coming week, the search for Harper will be called off on Wednesday.

"Harper, 27, is the wife of Dr. Richard Harper, chief of Cardiothoracic Surgery at the Kamehameha III Hospital, Honolulu. She has lived in Hawaii for only two years.

"Dr. Harper declined to make a statement for this reporter. Harper has, however, offered a substantial reward for information that leads to his wife's safe recovery. Her family is expected to arrive in Honolulu from the Pelican Point area of Tampa, Florida, today.

"Harper's car, a silver Lexus, was found in the Kahana Valley State Park's parking lot. All doors were locked. There were no signs of foul play or suspicious circumstances at the scene, although police have not ruled out the possibility of foul play. Ms. Harper's credit cards and other personal papers were found intact in the locked glove compartment."

"Kahana Valley!" The detective sighed and shook his head. "It's like looking for a needle in a haystack. A *big* haystack," Tom Pacheco declared, shaking his head as he tossed the *Honolulu Star Bulletin* onto his desk. "And a very pretty needle!"

"Yeah? Hand it over," Jack McQuinn said. "Let's take a look."

15

Pacheco was right, Jack saw as he unfolded the newspaper. The missing woman *was* very pretty, with long dark hair and big dark eyes. He couldn't tell what color they were.

Tom grinned. "Forget it. She's not in our league, Jack. Mrs. Harper and her old man live on Diamond Head Drive. Very high *maka-maka*."

Snooty, Jack translated the Hawaiian expression.

He frowned as he looked down again at Liz Harper's picture. Her eyes were so damned sad. *Haunting*, if you wanted to get poetic about it. He'd always been a sucker for women with big beautiful eyes.

He continued to see those eyes in his mind's eye long after he'd tossed the flyer aside. And, although he tried to work on other missing persons' cases, his thoughts kept returning to the Harper woman.

"Give me what you've got on the Harper case, Pacheco," he offered casually. "I'll look it over, see what I can come up with, okay?"

"Oh, gee, thanks, Jack. And you'd do the same for anyone, right?" Tom joked. "Your interest in this particular case is purely professional, right? Nothing to do with the fact that the missing person just happens to be a beautiful *wahine?*" He grinned and rolled his eyes.

"Oh, yeah?" Jack quipped as if he hadn't noticed. "Hey. You're married, Tommy. What do you care?"

"So's she, wiseguy. Watch yourself," Tommy warned, flipping McQuinn the Missing Persons folder. It was labeled with a case number and the name HARPER, ELIZABETH ANNE in large block letters.

Missing Persons, a branch of the Homicide Division, routinely investigated the husband, wife, or significant other when someone disappeared, unless the circumstances of the disappearance, or a cast-iron alibi, clearly excluded the spouse's involvement. Ditto the parents whenever a kid vanished.

It was a sad fact of life that many Missing Persons cases eventually became homicide investigations. An even sadder fact was that most homicides were committed by assailants their victims were either related to or knew well, not strangers.

Jack opened the Harper folder and quickly scanned the information it contained.

Several members of the hiking club had given statements to Detective Pacheco. They confirmed everything hiker Bea Watanabe had told the newspaper reporter, adding that Elizabeth was a well-liked but somewhat shy, reserved young woman. An experienced hiker who took safety precautions seriously.

Experienced, huh? So why'd you go hiking alone, Liz? he wondered.

He ran a quick computer check with the state Department of Motor Vehicles but didn't turn up

17

anything new, other than that Richard Jerome Harper was the Registered Owner and the Owner of Record of both the silver Lexus his wife had driven, and a metallic pale-blue Porsche.

The result of his computer search of the Criminal Records database was more enlightening. It appeared that, while still a med student in New Orleans, Louisiana, the future surgeon had been arrested for vicious assaults on two female prostitutes. The women had later dropped all charges.

Since then, on the surface at least, Richard Jerome Harper and Elizabeth Anne Scott Harper had been model citizens, pure as the driven snow. Which could mean something—or nothing at all.

It had been Jack's experience that men who got off on beating women—their wives, their girlfriends, their hookers—rarely reformed. They got worse. More violent, as opposed to less.

"Yo. I think I'll pay the distraught husband a friendly visit," Jack said aloud. "Offer my condolences, maybe. He's had almost a week to think about things. I'd say it's time someone had a little chat with him."

"Tread softly, Jack," Tom warned. "The meatcutter's got friends in high places."

"Hey. I'm quaking in my boots," Jack tossed over his shoulder with an evil grin. "You don't like him, I'm thinking, Tommy?"

"Hell, no. You want my take, the doc's an Ice Man. A real control freak."

18

Jack nodded thoughtfully. Maybe the elusive Mrs. Harper wasn't lost at all. Maybe she'd done a vanishing trick for reasons he'd yet to discover. Or—more likely—maybe her meat-cutter husband had murdered her.

"Catch you later, Tom."

The Harper home on Diamond Head Drive was a sprawling Casablanca-style residence with red-tile roofs and dazzling off-white walls. Jack whistled under his breath. The lot on which the house was built must be well over an acre—a valuable chunk of prime real estate on an island where land, precious land, was counted by the square foot.

The long, narrow Olympic-sized lap pool around back was enclosed by a white stucco wall that had spring-loaded wrought-iron safety gates, all up to safety codes. Every few feet there was a column topped by a white cannonball. Cold, but classy.

The pool deck was tiled in slate. Both pool and wall were later additions to the property, he guessed. Squat sago palms in circular planters offered shade for pool parties and barbecues, with verdigris umbrella tables and chairs set in their fronded shade. Neither the pool nor the deck looked used.

The grounds didn't match the house's architecture somehow. They were landscaped, tropical, and fastidiously manicured—not a dead leaf or a weed anywhere that he could see. Or a single flower, either, come to that. Graceful fronded areca and royal palms, leafy monstera, and giant birds-of-paradise grew from planter beds of white coral, each bed sculpted from lawns of plush green velvet. It was beautiful, but way too perfect for his taste.

While flipping channels to find his favorite sports shows, he'd watched enough *Trading Spaces* episodes to know the place needed color in a big way; splashy scarlet geraniums in big earthenware pots or half barrels, maybe. Sunflowers. Bright pink hibiscus. A dog. *Something*, for crying out loud! He couldn't imagine a setting more at odds with the lovely, vivacious woman in the posters than the one before him. Then again, could be he was way off.

When leaning on the intercom-doorbell brought no response, Jack circled the house again.

He was walking down a flagstone pathway that led around the property when he caught the bright silvery flash of sunlight off metal from one of the Phoenix palms.

Curious, he stepped into the planter bed. White coral scrunched underfoot as he reached up between the palm fronds. With difficulty, he pried a small shiny object from the natural pocket between the palm's thorny fronds and its sturdy ridged trunk.

He looked curiously at the object—a silver earring—in his palm. It had been intentionally hidden there, he decided. It was wedged too tightly for it to have simply been snagged from an ear by the palm frond.

Made of cast silver, set off by tiny round turquoise stones or beads, at first glance the earring appeared to be a Hawaiian petroglyph—the ancient stick figures found etched onto rocks here in the islands. The small, bent-over figure was playing what looked like a flute. The little guy's hair stuck up from his head in sparse, wiry strands.

Jack was no jeweler, but to him, the figure looked more Southwestern than Hawaiian. Drawing a small evidence bag from his pocket, Jack tucked the earring inside, sealed, then labeled it, before continuing his stroll around the Harper property. Who would hide an earring in a tree? he wondered. And why?

The neighbors had a tennis court, and had just finished a singles match.

"Beautiful home you have there, ma'am," Jack called over the stucco wall, smiling. "You must be very proud of it."

"Thank you. We are." The wife, an older woman wearing a flirty tennis skirt, bright red sleeveless top, and white visor, mopped her glistening face with a towel. Her makeup had run a little in the heat. "Were you looking for someone?"

He flashed his badge.

"Ah. Of course. Detective . . . McQuinn, is it? If you're looking for Dr. Harper, I saw him leave this morning at his usual time."

21

"Which would be?"

"Six-forty-five, regular as clockwork. You can set your alarm by the man," the husband supplied. "That's when I go out to get the morning paper. That darned kid never throws it to the front door. Always too far to the left or the right."

"Do you know where Dr. Harper goes at that time?"

Husband and wife exchanged glances. "Well, we assumed he went to the hospital, Detective. Where else would the man go every morning? He's a heart surgeon at Kamehameha III, isn't he?"

"You're not sure?" Again, the exchange of looks between husband and wife. "How long have the Harpers lived here, Mrs.—"

"Van Hoorn. Amy Van Hoorn. This is my husband, Derek."

"Nice to meet you, sir, ma'am."

"And you, Detective. Do I detect a New York accent?"

"Yo." Jack grinned. "I'm from Brooklyn, ma'am. How long have the Harpers been your neighbors, Mrs. Van Hoorn?"

"Ohhh, almost two years, I believe. That's when they moved in."

"Yet you're not on speaking terms with them?"

"It's not so much a case of that as . . . well, we don't really *know* them, Detective. They keep to themselves, you see, and so do we. You know what they say about good fences!" She smiled apologetically.

"I do, yes." He smiled back, turning on the Mc-Quinn charm his Italian mother claimed he'd inherited from his Irish father, a Navy man turned New York cop. "Were you aware that Mrs. Harper disappeared a week ago while hiking in the Kahana Valley?"

"Yes, of course. To be honest, we didn't know anything until we read about it in the papers. Some of the other neighbors have been talking about it, too. So very sad! Mrs. Harper always seemed like such a nice little thing. A bit shy, perhaps, but always ready with a smile and a little wave. Is it possible they might still find her alive, after all these days?"

"We hope so, ma'am. Are you also on waving terms with Dr. Harper?"

"No. The doctor's not nearly as friendly. I've waved to him, but he turns his head and pretends he doesn't see me."

Amy Van Hoorn looked as if she'd like to say more. Clearly, she didn't approve of Harper, and Mrs. Van Hoorn didn't strike him as a fool. He made a mental note to talk to her alone at some point. Women often picked up on subtleties that went clear over men's heads, but didn't want to seem gossipy. He'd be willing to bet that Amy knew more than she realized.

"What my wife is trying to say, Detective, very tactfully, of course, is that Harper struck us both as a cold fish," Derek Van Hoorn said.

"Yes," Amy agreed eagerly. "That's it exactly.

Cold. To be honest, we were stunned that Dr. Harper would go to the hospital every morning as if nothing had happened. Business as usual! That poor girl. She's much younger than he, of course." She shook her head, making her expertly lightened blond pageboy swing to and fro. "I certainly wouldn't want to be one of his patients, not with all he has on his mind. He must be preoccupied, at the very least. Far too preoccupied to do heart surgery."

"Did you ever see any indication that the Harpers weren't getting along? I apologize if my questions seem insensitive, but it's standard practice to ask when there's a disappearance."

"Yes, yes, of course. We quite understand. We watch all those police programs on the Discovery Channel, don't we, Derek?" She frowned. "So frightening! That's why we moved to the islands when Derek retired. It's a slower pace of life here—"

"To answer your question, Detective, we wouldn't have noticed anything, because we hardly saw either of them," her husband cut in. "But then, that's how it is on Diamond Head Drive. People tend to keep to themselves, except for the old-timers like us, who've been here from the beginning."

Van Hoorn's unspoken implication was that people who could afford to live in lavish homes in exclusive neighborhoods with four- or five-million-dollar price tags didn't wash their dirty linen in public. If the Harpers hadn't been getting along, Jack doubted he would hear about it from these two.

"We all grieve in different ways, ma'am, sir," Jack said carefully. "I'm sure Dr. Harper is confident that everything is being taken care of by the HPD and the Fire Department. It's possible his business of saving lives takes his mind off his troubles."

Van Hoorn, a deeply tanned, chubby man with a receding hairline, snorted. "That's very charitable of you, Detective. But if my Amy went missing, you wouldn't catch me slicing and dicing! No, by God, I'd be too busy helping the search parties to do any damn surgery!" He slid an arm around the waist of his beaming wife, and winked at Jack.

Jack silently agreed with Derek Van Hoorn as he drove back into the city, headed for the Kamehameha III Hospital. If Liz Harper were his wife . . . hell, he'd be tearing his hair out by now, scouring the Kahana Valley on hands and knees, armed with a machete to hack down trees and level mountains until he found her. He sure as hell wouldn't be coolly operating on unsuspecting patients.

At the hospital, a quick check of reserved physician parking stalls showed that the doctor was indeed "in"—and how! A custom ice-blue metallic Porsche sat smugly in Doc Harper's stall, as shiny and pretty as the day—less than a year before, if he was any judge—it rolled off the factory floor.

25

Squelching the urge to key the vehicle's gleaming paint job, Jack rode the parking elevator to the third floor.

When the elevator doors slid smoothly shut behind him, he followed a dozen signs leading down pale green-and-cream halls painted with dark green monstera leaves to wards named after flowers. Hibiscus Ward, Plumeria Ward, Orchid Ward, and so on.

The cardiothoracic ward where Harper performed his magic tricks was called the Lokelani, or Rose Ward.

A photograph of Harper, unsmiling, looked down its thin Aryan nose at passersby.

Jack shook his head. If anyone ever needed a heart transplant, it's this joker, he thought. Harper's eyes were pure ice. Did he operate with or without anesthetic? Jack wondered idly. To him, the doc looked like the kind of guy who'd enjoy it more without.

He waited the better part of an hour for Harper to finish surgery, catching him as he came out through the swinging doors of the operating room into the doctors' locker room. There was blood all over his pale blue scrubs.

"Yo. Doc Harper?"

Harper reacted as if he'd been shot. His head snapped around. "What the hell are you doing in here? This room is off limits!"

"Your scrub nurse let me in, sir. She thought you'd want to speak to me. I'm Detective Jack Mc-

Quinn with Missing Persons, HPD. I'm here about your wife, sir." He phrased the statement deliberately, curious to see Harper's reaction.

There was none.

A loving husband, fearing the worst, hoping for the best, would have responded immediately, eagerly. *What about my wife? Have you found her? Is she all right? Tell me she isn't dead!*

Harper didn't betray his emotions by so much as the flicker of an eyelash.

"Well? Carry on, Detective. What about my wife?" he demanded, sounding impatient as he peeled off his scrubs, his cap, the blue surgical booties that covered his shoes.

"Tell me about her. What's she like, Doc?"

"What's she like—? I'm not interested in playing games, Detective," Harper snapped. He pulled on a pale blue golf shirt with a tiny polo player on the left chest.

Once out of his scrubs, Harper looked more like a successful drug lord than a surgeon, Jack decided. Or an SS agent in civvies. Despite the classy veneer, there was something coarse and backwoods lurking just below the slick polished surface.

"You're supposed to be out there, finding my wife. So, what the hell are you doing here, Detective, nosing around my operating room, asking stupid questions?" the doctor demanded.

Pushing your buttons, Ricky boy, Jack thought. *Finding out what it takes to melt the Ice Man and bring him to a boil. Not that much, from the looks of it. Did your Elizabeth threaten to leave you? Was that it? Did you follow her, kill her, then dispose of her body to make it look like she'd disappeared? Is that what floats your boat, Doc? Controlling people? Controlling women? Hurting them?*

"I'm doing my job, Doc. Just like you. And a big part of that job involves learning about your wife. So tell me, Doc. What's Elizabeth like? What kind of woman is she? For a start, do you call her Elizabeth, or Liz, or is it Beth? Or—hey, maybe she's a Lizzie? I had a girlfriend once who—"

"I called her by her given name, Detective. *Elizabeth*," Harper ground impatiently through clenched teeth.

Past tense, Jack noted. "Called," not "call."

"Of all the stupid questions to ask! As if it makes any difference what I called my wife! Your questions are ridiculous! I have another surgery in less than an hour. I have no time for guessing games!"

"On the contrary, sir. This is a very serious part of my investigation," Jack said mildly, taking a seat at a small aluminum table that held a coffeemaker, its carafe filled with black sludge. "Getting to know everything we can about a victim is an important part of any missing person's investigation."

"My wife is not a victim, Detective. She is merely . . . lost." He sounded annoyed, as if he'd mislaid his car keys somewhere—and blamed the keys.

28

"That remains to be seen, sir. Perhaps you'd like to pour yourself a cup of coffee while we talk?" he suggested, indicating the coffeemaker. "It must be tiring, on your feet all day, up to your elbows in . . . well, blood. And other bodily fluids."

He smiled, knowing from Harper's murderous expression, the way those elegant, long-fingered hands knotted at his sides, that the Columbo "dumb cop" act was working.

"Now, where were we? Ah, yes. Did—er, did Liz—have many friends?"

"Her name was—is—Elizabeth." Harper's teeth were clenched. Jack decided he enjoyed needling him.

"Yes, sir, of course, sir. A slip of the tongue," Jack said insincerely.

But he didn't say whose slip.

TWO

Richard Harper had added very little to what Jack knew about the surgeon's wife that day at the hospital. He'd volunteered even less in the days that followed. What few leads and possible sightings the public had given HPD had either fizzled out or been proven false. And, according to the airlines, nobody using Elizabeth Harper's I.D. had left the state.

It was as if she'd vanished into thin air.

When her family arrived from Florida, pale and drawn, anxious, yet pitifully eager to participate in the massive search of the Kahana Valley for Elizabeth Anne Scott Harper, Jack had had the unenviable job of breaking the bad news to the Scotts: No trace of the daughter and little sister they loved had yet been found.

And, after several agonizing weeks without find-

31

ing her, either alive or dead, they'd eventually had to leave the islands without her, their hearts broken, their questions unanswered, their anguished faces burned into his memory.

As the days, weeks, months, then finally an entire year went by, the case had gone cold. Wherever Elizabeth Harper might be, alive or dead, Jack, like the Scotts, had been forced to accept that she would probably never be found.

It was a long time before he'd been able to put her haunting eyes—gray eyes, according to her mother and her driver's license—out of his mind when he fell asleep at night. And even when he succeeded, each morning those same eyes had greeted him whenever he walked into his office. They'd smiled down at him from the poster pinned to the Missing Persons bulletin board. *Find me,* they'd seemed to say to him. *Don't give up on me!*

A seven-day Christmas fishing trip to Alaska, where he'd met up with some old buddies from Brooklyn PD, had been the key to ending the old year on the right note. He now had a freezer full of salmon and halibut and a raging hangover to show for his troubles. Despite it, today was his first day back at work, and he was raring to go.

Here's to another year, Jack thought, taking a hefty swig of sweet black coffee from the Styrofoam mug as he locked his car and headed toward the building that housed the police department. *A new year, and a new beginning!*

Monty Ishikawa, the Honolulu Police Department's forensic computer specialist, hurried up to him the minute he showed his face in the department.

"Hey, Jack! Welcome back! Say, you remember the Harper case?" Monty asked him. "About a year ago?"

"Yeah. Yeah. What about it?" Jack demanded, rubbing his jaw.

He scowled. Of course he remembered the goddamned case! His failure to find her continued to rankle from time to time, mostly when he'd had a few.

"You need to take a look at what I've turned up," Monty insisted, brown eyes pleading behind the thick lenses of his glasses. "It's important."

"Later, Sherlock," Jack growled, towering over the much shorter man.

Truth was, he was still feeling the aftereffects of the rowdy farewell party the evening before. Saying good-bye to his old NY buddies had involved substantial quantities of beer. He shook his head, wincing. Hell! He never learned. His damn head was still throbbing.

"No, Jack. I mean it. You really need to take a look at this," Monty persisted, trailing after Jack with a stack of computer printouts in his hand.

Jack sped up, taking sadistic pleasure in using his longer legs to outwalk the computer geek. Monty was short of breath, and almost running after him. Jack hid a grin. *That'd teach him.*

"I've transcribed some of the material we retrieved from Dr. Harper's hard drive," Monty explained breathlessly when he caught up, "including Mrs. Harper's visits to a chat room. The TropicalConnections chat room." He paused expectantly, bushy brows cocked, clearly expecting a reaction.

He wasn't disappointed.

Jack's head snapped up. He stopped dead in his tracks. The sudden halt sent pain ricocheting through his aching skull like a pinball bouncing off the bumpers. Bloodshot brown eyes narrowed. "TropicalConnections, huh? No shit!"

Monty nodded. "Um. Right. Er. No-er-shit! You see, you can delete unwanted files from your computer, but they still exist in the vacant spaces on your hard drive until the files are written over, so—"

"What was that about TropicalConnections?" Jack demanded, pouring himself a mug of coffee as black and thick as oil. He added a generous amount of sugar.

"Wasn't Special Investigations monitoring that site a while back?" Monty asked. "Remember? That case you worked about a year ago? A teenage girl made a date with a boy she met in a chat room, then disappeared? Turned out the 'boy' was a forty-year-old sexual predator using the chat room to lure underage girls to his apartment for sex—"

Jack snapped his fingers. "Got it. The perp's name was Frankie Ong. His case just came to trial. Yeah. Yeah. What about it?"

"Doesn't that particular chat room ring any bells, Jack?"

"So what if it did?" He shrugged. "Get to the point, Monty. My head's killing me!"

"Hangover, huh?" Monty grinned knowingly, sounding more than a little envious. Although shy and awkward, the little guy wanted to run with the big dogs.

Jack scowled. "No way. Cluster migraines," he lied. "They go with the . . . er . . . with the high IQ. You were saying?"

"Elizabeth Harper visited that site, too! She used the screen name Lulu. *Lulu.*" Ishikawa grinned expectantly. "Does that ring any bells, Jack? Or should I say, *Keoki?*"

It rang bells, all right. A whole damned carillon of them.

"Lulu?" Jack stopped stirring his coffee. He stared at Monty in disbelief. "No joke, Sherlock?"

"No joke. Here—see for yourself." Monty shoved the sheaf of printouts under Jack's nose. "I thought I'd show these to you before I showed the lieutenant. I think you'll find the top page especially interesting," he hinted slyly.

Jack did.

Flipping through the printed pages, he reread line after line of typed conversations between himself, as Keoki, with the missing woman, Elizabeth Harper, who'd apparently called herself Lulu during her dialogs with him in the TropicalConnections chat room. Dialogs in which she'd confessed that her husband was physically abusing her, he recalled. The ache in his head was pounding like a jackhammer now. And he—as Keoki—had responded by urging her, time and time again, to leave the bastard.

There'd be no more Sarahs, he'd promised himself at the time. No needless deaths, not on his watch.

And Ms. Harper—a.k.a. Lulu—had subsequently disappeared. Dropped off the face of the earth.

He swallowed, his throat suddenly dry from more than the hangover. He could almost feel Internal Affairs breathing down his neck. Nosing around. Asking questions he wouldn't be able to answer.

And what, exactly, was your relationship with the missing Harper woman, Detective McQuinn? they would ask.

Did you ever meet with Elizabeth Harper in person?

Were the two of you having an affair?

Come clean, McQuinn. Isn't that why you encouraged her to leave her husband, Dr. Richard Harper?

He swallowed.

"What made the department pull Harper's hard drive?" Jack asked. "Do you know?" A search warrant specifying Harper's hard drive would have been needed. For that to fly, there had to be probable cause.

"Oh. That's right." Monty grinned. "I forgot. You were gone all week! How was the fishing, anyway?"

"It was just fine, dammit! Give it up, Monty. Cut the crap. *Why did they pull Harper's hard drive?*" he repeated.

Despite a thorough investigation that had included searching Richard Harper's palatial home, and his pretty ice-blue Porsche, no trace of Elizabeth Harper's whereabouts had ever been found. Nor had any skeletal remains been recovered from the Kahana Valley in the thirteen months since she'd disappeared. But then, hikers who vanished into the valley had a way of staying missing forever. The terrain was just too overgrown, too inaccessible, to make finding them—or their remains—a likelihood. Like many other similar cases, her case had been relegated to the back burner, unsolved but active. Further investigation would be made if—when—fresh evidence surfaced.

Apparently, in his absence, it had.

"They've reopened Harper's Missing Persons case," Monty supplied triumphantly, seeing the question in Jack's eyes. "A fax came through from Scottsdale P.D., see?"

"Arizona? What's Arizona got to do with it?"

"There's an APB out on him! Apparently, Dr. Harper was married before. His first wife drowned—under suspicious circumstances."

"*First* wife, huh? Son of a bitch!"

"Anyway, I—"

37

But Jack was gone.

Within seconds of reaching the Special Investigations room, he had the Arizona flyer in hand.

"Goddamn!" he muttered as he read the lines print. It was an APB, an all-points bulletin, just as Monty had said, with a pic of a younger Harper front and center. It had been faxed to police departments in all states, seeking the whereabouts of white male suspect, Richard Jerome Harper, DOB 01-19-1966, LNA (last known address) Scottsdale, Arizona. Harper was wanted for questioning in the death of his first wife, Ellen Cohen Harper, four years earlier. In light of fresh evidence that had surfaced only recently, the Scottsdale police had issued a warrant for Harper's arrest.

"Son of a bitch!" Jack exclaimed. He flung the paper aside and leaned forward over his desk, his palms braced on its scarred surface. He felt sick to his stomach, as if someone had slammed a piledriver into his gut—and this time, the feeling had nothing to do with drinking too many beers.

There was a better-than-even chance that his well-intentioned advice to an unknown innocent woman had placed her on a collision course with a killer. *Her own abusive husband!*

Or had it?

I have somewhere to go, and someone to go with. Be happy for me! Lulu, a.k.a. Elizabeth Harper, had written confidently, refusing his offer of help or contact numbers. Her statement had stuck with him. That "someone," he'd guessed, was probably a lover. A boyfriend. Tired of being her old man's punching bag, the pretty lady had simply found another guy. And more power to her, he'd thought at the time.

So. Was she dead—or on the lam? Jack asked himself. There was a damned good chance he'd never know, unless . . .

"Hey, Monty. Little buddy. Got a minute?" he asked, clamping a hand over Monty's shoulder. "I need more printouts from Harper's hard drive. Can you help me out?"

"Sure, Jack. Say, I was thinking, next time you go on one of your fishing trips, maybe I could come along?" Monty suggested hopefully, trying to keep up with Jack's long, easy strides.

"Sorry, Sherlock. Not a chance. See, the fish in Alaska are bigger than you!"

THREE

Sangre de Cristo Foothills
Near Santa Fe, New Mexico
January

Jack eased the rental car into the last guest stall and killed the engine.

Just a few feet from the parking lot, piñons and cottonwoods began their long, jagged climb into the dark foothills of the Sangre de Cristos. Riding high above their ridges, a milky moon and a billion frosty stars cast ethereal light over the world below.

The night smelled of snow.

Cooling metal pinged and ticked in the silence as Jack made a quick visual check of the two-story adobe apartment building called Los Piñons, noting secondary escape routes. After fifteen years on the force, the habit was deeply ingrained.

According to the rental agency, Lisa Scott, a.k.a. Elizabeth Anne Harper, lived in 6B, a second-story walkup. Each unit had its own wrought-iron balcony off the living room. The squat, rectangular building had red-tile pathways and stairs. Its cappuccino-colored adobe walls were set off by iron lamps, arches, and cactus in red ollas. In the fading light, Los Piñons looked like a pretty nice place to live, although there were no showy features that would attract attention to the place.

Smart lady, Jack thought approvingly as he left the Jeep and headed for the stairwell. But then, she'd played it smart all the way, he had to give her that. If someone wanted to lie low, the Santa Fe area and nondescript Los Piñons was a pretty good place to do it. He doubted his pretty fugitive missed her ritzy house on Honolulu's exclusive Diamond Head Drive. Peace of mind was more precious to Liz Harper than fancy real estate—he'd bet hard money on it.

Taking the stairs two at a time, Jack reached the door to 6B. One palm braced against the wall, he rang the doorbell, passing a free hand through dark hair that badly needed a trim as he waited for someone to answer. A shave wouldn't hurt, either, he thought, rubbing his scratchy jaw. He hadn't shaved since Hawaii.

He knew someone was home—he'd been following her ever since she got off work that morning—but there was no answer to his ringing.

"So be it," he muttered. Fishing a business card from the pocket of his leather jacket, he slipped it under the door, then left the building.

Going through the motions of heading back to his rented Jeep, he turned right at the last stall instead of left. Hugging the shadows, he kept his head down and sprinted around to the rear of the building.

Hardy zeroscaping grew against walls as pale as bleached bones in the wintry moonlight. Juniper bushes cast dark blots of concealing shadow.

In back of the building, a quick glance told Jack that most of Los Piñons' residents were home, or else had left their lights on to deter burglars. He counted balconies. Apartment 6B was halfway across the second, or top, floor.

The unit was dark now, but there was a dull glow in one of the rooms in back—a nightlight left on, maybe? Or had she given him the slip and gone out the back entrance? There was only one way to find out. What he needed to tell her had to be told sooner, rather than later. If the place was empty, he'd wait.

Using a wrought-iron patio table as a step-stool, Jack reached above him. Grasping the icy rail of the second-floor balcony, he pulled himself up and over it.

He was breathing hard by the time he hooked numbed fingers over 6B's sliding glass door. Shaking his hands to get the blood moving, he silently cursed the balmy climate he'd left only forty-eight hours ago. Island winters had made him soft, he thought as the door glided sideways with hardly a sound. *Bad slip, Liz. Always secure the back door.*

The drapes were closed. Burrowing between their bulky folds, Jack stepped into a darkened living room.

The air smelled faintly of lemon polish and a fragrance he recognized from Hawaii, an airy blend of jasmine, plumeria, and tuberoses. There was another scent he recognized, but couldn't place.

Eyes adjusting, catlike, to the gloom, he made out a futon pushed against one long wall. On the far wall was a rustic bookcase of cinder blocks and wooden planks that held a small TV. There wasn't much else.

Bingo! The glow of a nightlight spilled into the hallway from the bedroom. Liz must be in there, asleep. Would she awake to find him standing over her, fearing her worst nightmare had come true? Or was he already too—

The thought popped like a burst bubble as pain exploded through his skull. With a startled grunt, Jack folded to the floor. Once down, he stayed down.

He came around to find Liz Harper standing over him, her fists on her hips. The face was the same lovely face that had stared out at him from the Missing Persons flyers, only angrier. The long, curly black hair was history, though. In its place was straight, silky golden-brown hair, streaked with blond highlights, cut in an edgy shoulder-length bob. The eyes hadn't changed, though. They were still gray. Gray eyes that smoked with anger.

The toe of her hiking boot tapped the tile floor. It was scant inches from his throbbing head, and well within kicking distance, he noted gingerly.

"Jeez, woman. That's a helluva way to greet a guest!" he grumbled.

"Yeah? I'd say you got what you deserved, mister, climbing over my balcony like that! A damn cat burglar!" she shot back. "What did you expect? The welcome wagon and coffee cake? Here. Let's get a better look at you."

She flipped on the nearest wall switch.

Jack recoiled as 150 watts flooded the room, scorching his eyeballs. He scrunched his eyes shut and groaned again.

"Aw. Did that hurt?" she asked sweetly.

"Hurt?" He snorted. "Whatever gave you that idea, lady?"

She shrugged. "Maybe I'm psychic."

"Or psych-o!"

Her lips tightened. The soft gray eyes hardened to slate. "Whatever. Headache?" When he nodded, she shrugged. "Good! Maybe you'll think twice before you break into another house."

"I might—if I survive this break-in. What in the hell did you hit me with? A two-by-four?" he demanded indignantly. That this small woman had taken him out so easily stung his pride more than it hurt his head. He hoped to God Tom Pacheco and the other guys back at HPD never found out about it. His rep as a tough New York cop would be toast.

"An omelet pan. Crude, but effective, don't you agree? Now—is there any reason I shouldn't call the Santa Fe cops to come get you, Mister"—her delicate brows lifted—"excuse me, *Detective* John Fitzgerald K. McQuinn?" she read, looking down at the small blue card he'd slipped under her door. Her eyebrows arched in disbelief. "J.F.K McQuinn? Oh, puh-lease! This is a joke, right?"

He winced, but it had nothing to do with the pain in his head. He loved his mother dearly, but what in the hell had she been on when she named him? "It's Jack, okay? Just Jack. On what charge?" he demanded in answer to her question. "Breaking and entering? Burglary? Unlawful trespass?"

"How about stalking, for starters? You were at Santa Fe General this morning. In the cafeteria," she accused. "Don't bother denying it. I saw you. And outside the ice-cream parlor this afternoon."

"You noticed me. I'm flattered."

"Don't be. You're about as big as a moose— pretty hard to miss."

"You could try a charge of stalking," he agreed, ignoring her insult. He gave a nonchalant shrug that was next to impossible, flat on his back. "And you could probably make it stick, too. But hey, do you *really* want the Santa Fe cops nosing around? Asking questions like, Who are you, really, Lisa Scott? Or was it Lulu something or other? Or maybe I should call you Elizabeth Harper? And then there's the biggest question, of course."

Her delicate dark brows cocked. The boot closest to his head tapped faster. "Which is?"

"Aren't you dead, lady?"

She flinched, but didn't rise to the bait, although the color drained from her face. "I don't know what you're talking about."

"Yeah, right, and I'm Elvis. If you'll let me up, I'll show you the Missing Persons poster. It's right here, in my pocket."

From his present position, he could almost believe she was as innocent as she looked.

In that oversized pale-pink sweater and black jeans, she looked younger, more innocent, more vulnerable than she had on the Missing posters. More like a delinquent sophomore who'd been sent to the principal's office. A sophomore who had, nonetheless, successfully staged her own disappearance.

Jack tried to stand, but found his ankles were taped together. Ditto his wrists. *Oh, jeez!* He could only have been out for a few seconds. But in that brief time, this delicately boned, tiny woman had trussed him up like a pig ready for the Hawaiian *imu*, the underground oven.

Delinquent schoolgirl, hell! She was more like Pippi Goddamned Longstocking, he amended, wincing as, two-handed, he felt the extent of the lump she'd raised on his skull. And *he'd* pitied *her?*

He swore under his breath.

Liz Harper made a prissy face. "You cut that

swearing out, or I'll tape that dirty mouth, too. Relax, Jack! The headache will go away, eventually. Hey. I doubt you'll even have a concussion."

"You're all heart, lady. A regular Florence Nightingale. I'm touched," he growled back.

He'd already decided he'd live. Barely. Still, she probably knew more about that side of things than he did. She'd been an operating room RN when she met Harper in Miami three years ago. For the past year, she'd been a trauma nurse in the ER at Santa Fe General. Neither job was for shrinking violets.

He shot her the scowl Sarah'd once described as "pure evil." The one that promised hell to pay when—if!—she cut him loose. But Liz Harper was immune. She glared right back at him, her arms folded over her shapely chest.

"If that look's supposed to intimidate me, give it up, Jacko. I've handled guys who were blind drunk, or flying on crack, and ten times more intimidating than you are right now."

"'S that so? It's a damned pity you didn't handle Harper like you handled them."

She flinched as if he'd struck her, and he immediately regretted his wisecrack.

"Aw, c'mon, Elizabeth, honey. Cut the damned tape off and let me up, okay?" he urged in a gentler tone. "I'm no threat to you. Honest. Hey. You might even *want* to hear what I've got to say. How about that?"

"I doubt it," she retorted without turning

around. "Oh, and by the way, *J.F.K*, my name's Lisa Scott. Or you can call me Liz. Just don't call me Elizabeth again, okay? I don't like it."

While he clumsily explored the swelling on his head, she ran her hands through her damp hair. The edgy pageboy cut made her look twelve going on sixteen—and sexy as hell! Which, come to think of it, made most of his thoughts about her illegal.

He scowled. What the hell was he doing here anyway? The woman had been nothing but trouble from the very first. He should have left well enough alone.

Because of her, he was now jobless. As he'd feared, the advice he'd given Harper in the chat room had not seemed so innocent to Internal Affairs, nor to Police Chief Harvey Lee.

The prevailing theory in the department was that, at Jack's urging, the Harper woman had prepared to leave her husband, only to be confronted by him and killed.

That was one of the reasons he'd come to New Mexico. It was in Jack's best interests to locate her, and bring her back alive, if only to prove to the world at large that, as he'd suspected, she was still very much alive and kicking.

Trouble was, nobody else in the department had shared his hunch. So he'd turned in his badge and weapon, and stepped down voluntarily. A temporary state of affairs—or so he hoped. The second reason was—

What the hell was she doing now? He craned his

head to watch as she marched back and forth around the small apartment, stepping over his long legs each time.

Oh, Christ! She was carrying armfuls of clothes—which could mean only one thing: The elusive Lulu or whatever she called herself now was getting ready to bolt. Again.

He struggled to sit up, but was briefly overcome by a wave of nausea. Despite what she'd said, he had the mother-and-father of all headaches. A hangover headache with none of the fun that preceded it.

Groaning, he leaned back against the wall and watched her through half-closed eyes.

On the futon lay a zip-up bag. Her back to him, Liz/Lisa/Lulu/Elizabeth was packing, exactly as he'd feared. He heard the rasp of a zipper as she closed the bag.

"Is this what you really want, Liz, or whatever you call yourself?" he challenged. "To spend the rest of your life running from Harper? Living out of a suitcase?"

"Some detective you are, Jack!" she shot back, taking a down-lined jacket from a peg by the front door. The color of eggplant, the hood was lined with faux fur of the same smoky gray as her eyes. She slipped on the jacket; zipped it.

"Didn't you hear the news? Richard was killed in a car crash on Tantalus six days ago," she continued. "So, if he hired you to find me for him, Detective McQuinn, or whoever you are, you're about five days too late. Adios!" She waggled her fingers in farewell.

Turning away from him, she went into one of the bedrooms. When she came back out, she was carrying a bundle of fuzzy blankets and a denim shoulder bag. Going over to the futon, she swung the other bulging duffel bag over her free shoulder, stepped over his legs, and headed for the door.

Her scathing comments brought him to the second reason he was here . . .

"Liz, wait! Harper isn't dead. He just wants you to think he is. Don't you see? You're playing right into his hands! C'mon, lady. Hear me out. Don't run," he coaxed in a last desperate effort to make her see reason. "Please?"

She stopped and stood very still, her back to him. "You're wrong—or lying! *Richard's dead.* He *must* be," she said desperately, still without turning around. "They did an—an autopsy on him, for crying out loud! I read about it on the Internet. The Honolulu M.E. matched Richard's dental records to the body they pulled from the car wreck."

She was trying to convince herself, to gather her courage. He could hear it, see it. Yet there was a quaver in her voice nevertheless. Fear had turned her face a chalky white.

"They matched *someone's* dental records to Richard's," he agreed softly. "But I talked to the M.E. myself, right after she got through examining the remains. And you know what? She didn't buy it any more than I did! My money says some other poor stiff is lying on that slab. Someone with Richard Harper's I.D. tag on his big toe, and Richard Harper's name on his dental records. That's one of the reasons I came here. To warn you. *Harper's still alive!* In fact, my money says the son of a bitch is either right behind me. Or he's . . ." He paused.

"What?" she snapped.

"—or he's already here. In New Mexico. Either way, he's coming after you, Liz, and you know it. You know what the man's capable of. He won't let you go. Ever! As far as he's concerned, you're his property. The son of a bitch thinks he owns you."

Her head drooped a little at this, like a lovely, weary flower on its stem. Then she straightened up and squared her shoulders.

"Okay. For the sake of argument, let's say I believe you. What about you? If Richard didn't hire you to find me, who did, *Detective* McQuinn?" she demanded.

Her voice sounded hoarse and strained. Fear had a way of doing that.

"The Honolulu Police Department?" she continued. "I don't think so. And how did you know where to find me? Come to think of it, how did you know I wasn't . . ."

Dead, too?

"Kokopelli," he murmured before she could finish her sentence. "Kokopelli, the Flute Player. That's how."

52

He tried to fish the earring he'd found from his pocket, but with his hands taped, he couldn't reach it.

"Check the damn business card I slid under your door. I was with the Honolulu Police Department until three days ago, when I quit. I came here on my own dime.

"See, I had a hunch you'd gone into hiding, but nobody in the department agreed with me. They were betting Harper killed you. I was sure you were still alive—and that he'd be coming after you. So I had to—to find you and warn you. In case I was right."

"You're saying you quit your job on a—a hunch? To find a woman you didn't even know? You really expect me to believe that?"

He pressed home. "There's more to it than that. When you disappeared, we filed the case as a Missing Persons case. Then about a month ago, the Phoenix Police Department contacted us."

"The Phoenix Police? What do they have to do with anything?"

"They'd uncovered fresh evidence in an old murder case—a four-year-old cold case from Scottsdale in which one Dr. Richard Harper was the prime suspect."

He heard her gasp.

"So, our Homicide Division reopened your Missing Persons case. They started digging into Richard Harper's past, too. They got a search warrant for your home. What they uncovered there suggested that he might have killed you, then made it look like you'd disappeared."

"What . . . what did they uncover?" Her voice was so faint he could barely hear her.

"Bloodstains in the bathroom. Among other things."

Something—a painful memory?—flickered in her eyes. She closed them. "You—you said Richard is the suspect in an old murder case?"

"That's right."

"Who—who is it they think he killed?"

"His first wife. Her name was Ellen."

"His first wi—? Oh, my God!" Her hand flew up to cover her mouth.

Jack nodded. He'd been right. She hadn't known about Harper's prior marriage. "So, thanks to the Phoenix PD, the entire focus of our investigation shifted. We reopened the case, and geared our efforts to gathering evidence that would help to prove Harper murdered you, too. I was the only detective who disagreed—the only investigator who thought there was a better-than-even chance you'd faked your disappearance. But then, I was the only one who knew you." He hesitated. "Does the name Keoki mean anything to you?"

She frowned, then nodded. "Ye-es. Yes, it does. He—he was someone I met in a chat room a few times. A friend."

"Keoki advised you to leave your husband before he hurt you again. You told him Richard was abusing you."

Surprise sprang into her eyes. Indignation followed. "That's right. How do you know that?"

"Because *I* was Keoki! Keoki was my screen name, just as yours was Lulu. HPD subpoenaed your computer hard drive when Phoenix P.D. contacted them. They recovered most of the data you'd tried to erase before you booked. When I realized you and Lulu were the same person, I was pretty sure you'd staged your own vanishing act. I asked myself, Where would you go? How would you support yourself on the run? Where would you feel safe? Once I had the answers to my questions, tracking you down was pretty easy."

"Easy?" She sounded incredulous.

"Yeah. See, I made it my business to know everything about you, Liz," he explained softly. "*Everything.* It's part of my job, and I'm damn good at it. Everything I learned pointed Southwest. To Santa Fe. I decided to start at the hospital, and—bingo!"

"There I was," she said, sounding bitter and angry.

"Right."

Monty Ishikawa had recovered several files on Harper's hard drive that she thought she'd erased. Visits to numerous travel sites, all of which pointed to a move to the Southwest, particularly the Santa Fe area. Finding the turquoise-and-silver

Kokopelli earring had served to confirm his hunch. So had vacation pictures of her and her family, which indicated she was familiar with the area.

"Why in the world would the police think Richard murdered me?" she asked with a short laugh, but her laughter was brittle and false.

"Because he hurt you, didn't he?" he asked softly. His brown eyes searched her face, remembering the luminous glow of those telltale bloodstains in the Diamond Head bathroom of her ritzy former home. Sprayed with Luminol, the place had lit up like the proverbial Christmas tree. Not enough blood, perhaps, to prove that a homicide had been committed, but enough to prove that something very bad had happened in that spot, perhaps more than once. "We already had a warrant out on Harper when he totaled his car."

She half turned toward him. Her eyes had narrowed now, he saw the hurt, the anger driven out by shock and confusion. "You said he killed his—his first wife?" she echoed faintly.

He nodded. "Yes. Did you know he was married before?"

"No," she confirmed.

"That figures. There's a lot you don't know about the man you married."

"So it appears. Then again, maybe I don't want to know. Maybe I don't give a damn anymore. Maybe I just want to get on with my life!" she flared, visibly shaken.

The outburst was more a protective mechanism than true anger toward him, he thought.

"Okay. Then what've you got to lose?" he coaxed softly. "Let me up. Hear me out. Give me five minutes to convince you you're in danger. Just five, that's all I ask. Then if you're still not convinced—hey, I'll leave. Okay, Liz?"

But he was talking to thin air.

Liz Harper was gone, leaving behind that faint fragrance he hadn't been able to define earlier.

Straining against the masking tape, he raged, "Way to go, McQuinn, you damn fool! You've lost her."

FOUR

Liz left her friend Trini Alvarez's ground-floor apartment at a run, looking neither left nor right as she dashed across the deserted parking lot to her car.

Despite her bravado, McQuinn had scared her, scared her badly. What if he was right? What if Richard *had* followed her here from Hawaii? What if McQuinn was really working for him, and not a detective at all?

The parking lot was deserted. Several cars were parked beneath the amber lights. Her car, an ancient Chevy, sat in the farthest row of stalls, the one painted with her apartment number, 6B.

Fingers numb with cold, she fumbled to fit her car key into the lock, only to discover it was already open. She frowned. *Careless.* She must have forgotten to lock it earlier when she'd carried up the groceries.

Sliding into the driver's seat, she keyed the engine. For once, her ancient charger behaved like a thoroughbred. The engine roared to life.

"Thank you, God!" she muttered.

Shifting into reverse, she glanced quickly in her rearview mirror—

—and froze!

Richard's soulless eyes stared back at her from beneath the black bill of a baseball cap. A cap he would never have worn in their former life together, she thought irrationally. Caps were too "hillbilly tacky" for a cardiac surgeon's refined tastes, he always said.

The eyes that should have been ice-blue were instead so dark brown they were almost black. Empty, emotionless black stones against a colorless complexion.

"No, I'm not a ghost, Eliza-beth," Richard taunted softly. "More like your worst nightmare."

His lips split in a thin, mirthless smile that never warmed his eyes. "So. Did you enjoy your year of freedom, you two-faced whoring bitch? I sure hope so, because it's the last taste of freedom you'll ever enjoy!"

He grinned. "Uh-oh! What's wrong? Why the face? Don't tell me you're *afraid* of me, Eliza-beth, darling?" he jeered. "Afraid of your own adoring husband?"

"No. Not anymore," she ground out, the words bleeding from her, drop by painful drop. "Not of you. Never again."

"Liar!" he rasped. The single word exploded in her eardrums.

She stiffened, gasping as he snaked an arm around her throat. He dragged her back against the seat, his forearm crushing her windpipe.

She fought for a precious breath of air, his grip so tight she was lifted up off the driver's seat.

"If you're not afraid of me, then why's your heart beating so goddamned fast? Tell me that, *Mrs.* Harper! You're like a frightened rabbit—and we all know what happens to rabbits. *Boom!"*

Stark terror became blind, reckless fury as he jabbed the icy barrel of a gun beneath her jaw. She closed her eyes.

This was how she was going to die! Here. Now. He was going to blow her brains out!

But, nuzzling her damp hair, he crooned, "Isn't this fun, Eliza-beth? It's been a year since we played our little games together. I've missed them, you know, darlin'. Missed *you.* After you vanished, I used to lie awake night after night, just aching for the feel of you." His hand clamped over her breast, squeezing painfully even through the down jacket. "Wondering where you were, what you were doing—who in hell you were doing it with, you cheating little whore! You faithless dirty slut!

"And what about you, hmm? Did you miss me, too, Eliza-beth? Did you miss your old man, huh? Did you? *Tell me, damn you!"*

"No! Not even for a second! Not for a—an instant! Every day without you was a gift! Let me *go, damn you!*" she ground out. Her fingers clawed at his hand, his forearm, fingernails shredding as she tried desperately to pry his forearm from her throat.

"Nooo, Eliza-beth. No," he purred silkily. "Don't fight me!" He caressed her cheek with the back of his gun hand. "Remember how angry I get when you fight me? Accept it. You've come to the end of the road. You don't know it yet, darling, but *you're already dead!*"

Her skin crawled, but she forced herself to go limp in his arms.

"That's my good girl. Do as I say, and I'll make it quick." He nuzzled her hair again. "Give me a hard time and"—he shrugged, implying a world of hurt with the careless gesture—"you'll wish you'd never been born."

She licked dry lips, apparently compliant, resigned to her fate. "All right," she whispered. Her voice was hoarse. She had too much to live for to die like this! "Wh—what do you want me to do?"

"Back out of this stall. Drive slowly to the exit, then turn left onto Los Piñons Drive. Head south."

South? There was nothing in that direction. The finished road petered out into rolling foothills, mountain meadows, and pine forests. Trails for horseback riding and hiking that led deep into the New Mexican wilderness. Places where screams would never be heard—and a body would never be found. "The city's north of here."

"Shut up, bitch!" Harper ground out. He jerked her back so roughly she gagged and retched, unable to draw a proper breath. "I need a quiet place to teach you a lesson. You'll never make a fool of me again, Elizabeth!"

His grip slackened a scant second before she passed out. Greedily gulping air, she clawed her way back to consciousness. A hasty glance in the rearview mirror showed Richard's pale complexion, mottled red in the light of the streetlamp. His empty eyes blazed.

Her own face was chalk white. Her throat bore the angry dark imprints of his fingers.

Anger revived her. That, and adrenaline. The bastard. He was enjoying this. He was excited by his power, by the control he had over her, a woman less than half his size.

Yet again, the icy gun barrel prodded beneath her jaw. "What are you waiting for, bitch? *Drive!*"

Hands trembling, she did as he ordered.

Keying the ignition, she backed carefully out of the stall, turned right, then drove slowly toward the parking lot exit.

Less than fifty feet from the exit, she suddenly yanked the steering wheel around and floored the gas pedal.

The Chevy's engine gunned.

Richard swore as the vehicle shot forward, hurtled up a steep grassy mound, then slammed into the streetlamp at the top of it with the force and momentum of a small tank.

For an endless moment, the Chevy hung there, braced on its rear wheels, defying gravity for an instant, before it flipped heavily onto its right side— the passenger side, thank God!

The violent momentum flung Richard forward, over the front seat, headfirst into the windshield. When the car turned over, he flopped back against the passenger door like a rag doll, and huddled there, unmoving. Blood hid his features, but he was still breathing. Unconscious, but not dead.

It was now or never—

With a strangled whimper, she pushed up the driver's door, clambered up and out of the smoking car, then dashed across the parking lot to the second-story stairwell. Beyond rational thought, she fled toward the sanctuary of home.

Ignoring her deepest instincts, she forced herself to keep going, past Trini's apartment. Taking the stairs two at a time, she reached 6B and threw herself inside.

Slamming the door behind her, she leaned against it, her chest heaving, her gray eyes wild, her breathing labored and panicky, her thoughts in chaos. It took every ounce of willpower she possessed to keep from screaming, from wailing like a banshee in her terror.

"Back so soon, honey?" McQuinn drawled, scowling. "How come? Forget your car keys?"

No. But she'd completely forgotten McQuinn.

He'd freed himself, she saw. The remnants of

her masking-tape handcuffs dangled from his wrists.

She nervously wetted her lips, pacing back and forth.

Tall and broad-shouldered, McQuinn was much more intimidating standing than he'd been flat on his back, when fear had lent her courage. Dare she trust him? Should she accept his offer of help?

No way!

She couldn't trust anyone, not yet. She didn't dare. She had too much at stake. Too much to lose.

Oh, God! What should I do?

"I said, what's up?" Jack asked again, frowning when she didn't respond. The blankets and baggage she'd been carrying were gone, he noted. She was trembling uncontrollably, and there was a shocky look about her that he didn't like. He frowned. His expression softened.

"Hey—are you okay?" he asked. Reaching out, he placed a hand on her shoulder. Searched her face. His brown eyes narrowed. "What in the hell happened to you?"

Liz snarled something incoherent, shrugging him off before the concern, the gentleness in his gesture proved her undoing. Quickly she brushed past him. Plunging between the living room drapes, she stepped out onto the balcony.

It was a second or two before Jack realized

she'd climbed over the railing, and wasn't coming back in.

"Whoa! Wait up there!" Both feet still numb with pins and needles, he followed her out, only to discover she'd already reached the ground floor.

"What the hell are you doing?" he demanded, dropping to the ground floor beside her.

"Get lost!" she hissed. "Quit following me."

"Hell, no! After what I went through to find you, I'm sticking to you like glue, honey. So, where to?"

"I don't know where *you're* going, McQuinn, but *I'm* getting out of here."

"Oh, yeah?" He grinned knowingly. "Starting to think I'm right about Richard?"

She shook her head but wouldn't look at him.
Bingo!

"Need a ride?"

That got her attention. She shrugged. "Maybe."

"How come? Where's your car?"

"It's . . . well, it's on the fritz, kind of."

Despite her warning, he'd followed her to the corner of the building that overlooked the parking lot. He peered past her. "Ah. Let me guess. *That's* your car, right?"

He cocked an eyebrow at the overturned Chevy in the parking lot. The same smoking wreck he'd trailed all day was now on its back, ringed by Los Piñons residents who'd heard the impact and come running.

A broken streetlamp was showering sparks over the Chevy's belly. Just one stray spark, a small puddle of spilled gasoline, and there'd be one hell of an explosion. The apartment manager was ordering everyone back, out of the way.

Liz nodded in response to Jack's question, then ducked back out of sight, flattening herself against the building wall. "Ye-es."

"Hell of a time to have an accident!" He shook his head.

She set her jaw. "It wasn't an accident."

He grinned. "Let me guess. Insurance fraud?"

She shook her head, too overwhelmed by fear and exhaustion to laugh, or even answer. Instead, her eyes suddenly filled, brilliant with unshed tears in the starlight. Making a valiant effort to compose herself, she muttered, "Something like that. I really have to go now, McQuinn—"

"Oh, jeez. *Harper?*"

Jack wasn't smiling anymore. His eyes had darkened, turning almost black. Those generous lips had thinned, too. It struck her, suddenly, that McQuinn would be a dangerous man to cross. As dangerous, perhaps, in his own way, as her husband.

Mouth working soundlessly, she nodded. The words tumbled from her lips. "He—he was sitting in the back seat when I got in. Just—just sitting there. *Waiting.* He—he told me to drive, so I—so I—"

"So you rolled the car?"

She nodded.

"Good girl. Way to go!" he approved. Taking on her brutal husband had taken guts.

"Maybe, but I won't get far without a car." She closed her eyes and leaned against the adobe building. "Richard hit his head on the windshield. He was out cold. So I jumped out of the car and ran back upstairs. I didn't know what else to do. Where to go. You were right." She shuddered. "He's not dead. Oh, God! He came here to kill me!"

Other residents had heard the Chevy's violent impact with the light pole. They trickled out of their apartments to gape at it, some carrying children wrapped in blankets, others wearing pajamas or sweats under heavy outdoor coats.

The front of the overturned Chevy was completely caved in. The hood gaped in a drunken grin. Steam—or more likely, smoke—belched from the wreck.

Richard squatted on the curb, clutching a bag of frozen peas to his bloody forehead and nose. He'd dyed his white-blond hair since the last time she'd seen him. It was dark now. The gold-framed glasses were gone, too—probably traded for dark-colored contacts, she thought, holding her left hand with her right to keep it from trembling. His eyes had been almost black in the rearview mirror—not the icy blue of her nightmares. Black, but still soulless, still empty.

The front of his white windbreaker was covered with blood. Although head wounds always bled profusely, she was pretty sure he'd broken his nose in the accident.

"Goddamnit, I don't need an ambulance!" she

heard him scream. "What's wrong with you people?"

But Liz could hear the thin wail of sirens in the distance, growing louder, shriller, by the second. Dogs in the buildings began to howl. Like it or not, someone had called 911. The paramedics wouldn't let Richard walk away anytime soon. Their arrival would buy her the time she needed to get many miles from Los Piñons.

"I have to go!"

"My rental car's in the last stall," McQuinn offered as if he'd read her mind. "The Jeep. Here. Take it."

She looked down, surprised, as Jack pressed car keys into her hand.

"When the ambulance turns into the parking lot, everyone will be distracted. That's when you make your move. You're in no condition to drive, so as soon as you're in, I'll follow you. Is that okay?"

"What's to keep me from driving off?" she challenged him.

"Not a damn thing."

Their eyes met. Quickly she looked away. It was as if he could see deep down inside her. As if he knew what she was going through.

Despite everything, something hurt and needy inside her melted in response to that fierce, sweet warmth. She'd been wrong about McQuinn. He was far more dangerous than Richard. He could make her feel again.

"How do I know you're not working for him?"

she challenged huskily. She jerked her chin toward the injured man and the tableau beneath the sparking streetlamp.

"You don't. I'm not, but . . . well, I guess you'll have to take my word for it. It's okay, Liz. You can trust me. I'm not like him."

"Trust you? I don't even know you!" Their eyes met again, hers darkened to charcoal, dilated by terror; his a deep warm caramel brown, flecked with gold and green. They were kind eyes, she noted reluctantly. Compassionate eyes.

Before she could say more, an ambulance careened into the parking lot. The siren's dying wail ebbed to a sulky whine as the vehicle screeched to a halt. Its revolving light continued to wash the pale adobe buildings with red.

"Go!" he rasped.

She dashed across the parking lot to the Jeep. After a second's hesitation, she opened the door, climbed into the back, then risked a peek out the window.

She recognized the two EMTs as Wendie and Steve from Santa Fe General, where she'd worked in the Emergency Room. Richard was sitting on the steps of their "bus" now. He was fighting Wendie as she tried to examine the bloody abrasions on his forehead and nose. Steve was busy taking his vitals, pumping up the b.p. cuff.

All eyes were on the injured man, the emergency crew, the ambulance, the revolving light, the sparking streetlamp. All backs were to the parking lot. "Was anyone else in the car with you, sir?" she heard Steve ask.

Perfect!

She ducked back down as the driver's door opened. Jack slid into the driver's seat. Although a tall, broad-shouldered man, he moved like a cat. "Stay down. This is gonna get hairy."

Casually Jack backed the Jeep out of the stall, his right arm resting across the back of the passenger seat, apparently alone in the vehicle. He drove slowly toward the parking lot exit.

All eyes were on the injured man. Nobody gave the cruising rental car a second glance. No one, that was, except Richard Harper. He watched the silver Jeep roll past the little tableau through slitted eyes.

Peeking out the Jeep's rear window, she felt the hairs rise on the back of her neck.

At the parking lot exit, Jack made a decorous left turn, heading north on I-25, like the proverbial little old lady on her way to church on Sunday morning. But the instant Los Piñons was out of sight, Jack put his foot to the metal and let her rip.

A yellow fire truck and a Santa Fe Electric Company truck met them at an intersection, but made the turn and barreled off in the opposite direction, toward Los Piñons. Jack gave both drivers a breezy salute.

"You okay?" he asked.

"Fine. Thank you," Liz murmured.

He grinned as she buckled her seat belt. Apparently, she was nervous about his driving, despite her assurance. Hence the seat belt.

He drove several winding miles in silence, the foothills and the countryside streaming past them in a dark blur. The Jeep gathered speed as Jack pushed his luck to suicidal limits on narrow roads that snaked back and forth between the mountain foothills and the Pecos River like a giant roller-coaster.

Catching a flare of light some distance behind them, Jack checked, then rechecked his rearview mirror. *Goddamn!* Someone was coming up fast behind them. An SUV, by the looks of it. The other car's huge headlights were blinding in Jack's rearview mirror.

Harper had thrown off the paramedics to come after them!

"Liz. Ms. Harper?" Jack said over his shoulder.

"Call me Liz," she said from the back seat. Her eyes met his in the rearview mirror. "I guess I owe you that much for getting me out of there."

"Yeah, well, it may be a little early to thank me."

"Why? What's wrong?"

"We're being followed. Keep your head down, okay?"

The road unwound before them in an endless black ribbon, twisting back and forth, up and down, hill upon hill.

Again, Jack checked the rearview mirror. His last burst of speed had left the other vehicle in the dust, for the time being. It had also bought them precious time. Temporarily hidden in the dip of one of the hills behind them, the SUV had disappeared. And, for a few precious seconds, the Jeep would be similarly hidden from the other car!

Without warning, Jack killed the headlights and swerved off the main road, wrenching the wheel around in a hard left. The Jeep straightened out, then bounced down a potholed dirt track, its entrance half hidden by rocky outcroppings and leafless trees.

The sudden sharp turn jerked Liz across the back seat, despite the seat belt.

"Stay down!" He killed the engine, then let the rental car coast, bouncing and bumping its way to a shuddering halt on the rocky side road.

"Sorry about the rough ride," he murmured, ducking down himself. "Just pray we lost him on that last hill, okay?"

No sooner had he said it than the headlights of the SUV arced across the road they'd just left. For one heart-stopping moment, its monster headlights flooded the interior of the Jeep, spotlighting the surrounding bushes, trees, and rocks for several yards in all directions. Then they were plunged once again into inky darkness as the vehicle continued on. It thundered on down the same highway they'd traveled just moments earlier.

They both sighed in relief.

"He bought it, thank God!"

"Richard?"

Jaw tight, he nodded.

"You're sure it was him?"

"Yeah," Jack confirmed with only a moment's hesitation. "Listen, I took a wrong turn back there at the intersection. We should have gone north, to the city, not south. While Harper's chasing our shadow, we'll head on back to Santa Fe, okay? The sooner there's an APB out on that s.o.b, the better."

"Shouldn't we wait, in case he doubles back to look for us?"

"No. We'll turn back now, while Harper still thinks he's chasing our tails south. First stop, the Santa Fe police department. I've already filled them in about him."

In the starlight, she was deathly pale, he saw, shivering despite her down-lined jacket. He guessed she was coming down from an adrenaline rush brought on by fear and her body's response to her narrow escape. "Hey, you need to get warmed up. Climb on over into the front seat," he urged. "I'll turn on the heater."

"All right." Her teeth were chattering.

Moments later, she was seated beside him. "Good. Buckle up, now."

"I'm buckled."

"Ten four. Time to rock 'n roll." Shooting her a grin, he turned the key in the Jeep's ignition.

Nothing.

There was only silence. No hollow click, no magical growl, not even a sickly cough or whimper as the Jeep tried to start.

Jack's grin slipped. He tried the key again. Growled, "C'mon, baby! Do it for papa!"

Still nothing.

Goddamn! The engine was as dead as the proverbial doornail. He slammed the heel of his palm against the steering wheel in frustration.

Liz flinched as if he'd physically struck her instead of the wheel.

"Whoa. Sorry about that. I . . . jeez, I didn't think! Liz, I'm sorry."

If he'd had a single doubt in his mind, he now knew exactly what kind of husband Richard had been. What the son of a bitch had done to her. Over a year had gone by, but her immediate flinch away from him, the stark terror that leaped into her eyes, confirmed his suspicions.

"It's okay," she insisted, yet quickly averted her face. "Really, Mr. McQuinn, I'm okay."

"If you're really okay, call me Jack."

"All right. Jack it is."

"Do you have a cell phone?"

"Yes."

"Thank God! Where is it?"

"At home. On charge."

"Shit!"

Between the bushes and leafless trees, Liz saw the headlights of the SUV, coming back down the winding road they'd just left. It was traveling more slowly now as it retraced its path. Searching. Circling like a predatory hawk, it was hunting its prey, preparing to strike.

Jack swore again under his breath. "That son of a bitch! He doesn't miss a trick!"

"He's backtracking, looking for us!"

"Oh, yeah."

"Oh, my God! What do we do now?" There was rising panic in her voice, stark terror in those incredible smoky eyes.

"With any luck, he'll miss the turnoff and drive right on past us," he lied. "Soo, we'll sit tight, and wait." He didn't buy it himself. Would she? he wondered.

"What if he sees the turnoff? What then?" she asked.

"Then I'll handle him." Jack frowned. "Unless—"

"What?

"You said he was carrying?"

"A gun, you mean? God, yes!" she shuddered. "He held it to my head!"

"That changes things." He wanted to avoid a shootout with Harper, if possible. The chance that Liz might get hurt, even killed, was just too high.

"But—you're a cop! Aren't you armed?"

"Officially, no. I handed in my service revolver when I resigned. Unofficially?" Reaching inside his leather jacket, he curled his fingers over the comforting handgrip of the 9-mm Glock he wore, tucked into its shoulder holster. He never drew his weapon unnecessarily, but would do so without hesitation if he had to. "Just call me Rambo."

His soldier-of-fortune grin, intended to reassure,

to make her smile, instead sent chills dancing down her spine. She wetted her lips. Shrugged. "Okay. So what's your problem?"

"I don't want any shooting unless he instigates it. That's how innocent people wind up dead."

"Then I think we need to get out of here, don't you? Right now!"

Jack nodded grimly. "I'm right behind you."

Snow was falling as they spilled from the car. The soft flakes swirled like feathers from the starlit sky as they scrambled off the dirt track, into the vast wilderness that bordered it.

On impulse, Jack caught Liz's hand in his, and hung on. She darted him a startled smile, but to his relief, she made no effort to pull free.

In seconds, the night swallowed them up as if they'd never been, leaving only the darkness and the wintry hush—a silence as deep as it was deafening.

FIVE

With only starlight to guide them, they stumbled along a rough track that was swiftly disappearing beneath a layer of new snow. Their goal: to put distance between themselves and the broken-down Jeep before Harper showed. *If* he showed, Liz amended silently, hanging on to Jack's hand for dear life.

In two years of marriage, nothing Richard did had ever touched her as profoundly as this stranger's outstretched hand, and the offer of help implicit in the gesture.

In her emotional state, that strong hand was almost her undoing. *I won't fall apart,* she told herself, setting her jaw and planting her feet, one after the other, on the snowy ground. *I can do this. I have to!*

They followed the uphill track for about a half mile, new snow yielding softly underfoot, until the trailhead opened into a clearing. There, a sizable log cabin crouched beneath dark pines. Behind it, two smaller outbuildings or sheds hugged the deep shadows.

Add a wolf howling at the moon, a tethered horse, and you'd have a Southwestern Christmas card, Liz thought, warm breath congealing on the frigid air. *Yippee-ay-oh-cay-ay and a Merry Christmas from New Mexico, Li'l Buckaroos!*

According to the signs, they were now entering the Pecos Wilderness National Park. No ATVs, trucks or other vehicles were allowed beyond that point. She heard Jack snort in disgust.

"Pecos as in Pecos, Texas? What the hell is this place? A spaghetti-Western set?" he muttered.

"Pecos, New Mexico, not Pecos, Texas," she explained. "And this is a national park. The Battle of Glorieta Pass was fought somewhere around here. That, in case you didn't know, Detective," she added with an impish grin, "was the westernmost battle of the Civil War. The historic town of Pecos is also nearby, population . . . around 1,500."

His dark brows lifted. He gave a low whistle. "Jeez. Did you swallow a guidebook or what?"

"Not quite. There's a huge sign behind you," she admitted, grinning.

Jack turned, saw the massive sign, and grinned back. "Ah. A wiseass, huh? Well, I'll say this for you. You might be down, but you're not out, Ms. Harper—not by a long mile."

"It's Liz," she said with a smile. "And you're right. I'm not!" She brought her chin up. If she acted as if she had it all together, perhaps at some point she would.

"Good for you."

The same sign announced that the Rangers' Station was open to the public year-round, 363 days a year, but would be closed until eight the following morning.

"Eight?" She groaned. "Then we've got"—she glanced at her watch—"twelve hours until the cavalry arrives."

McQuinn snorted again. Had she dented his ego by not thinking of him as the cavalry?

"A park ranger's not my idea of reinforcements," he explained, "unless we're stealing picnic baskets." He shot her an evil grin. "A SWAT team with Kevlar jackets, tear gas, and battering rams—now, *that's* the cavalry."

"Can we get out of this wind? I'm freezing," she said with a shudder as another gust sent snowflakes swirling all around them like feathers. "That jacket can't be warm enough. Aren't you cold?"

She stared at his leather bomber jacket as if seeing it—and the man inside it—for the first time since he'd broken into her apartment. As, in a sense, she was.

Things had happened so fast after she hit him, taped him up, and ran down to the car. She hadn't had time to take proper stock of her "intruder" until that moment. She decided she liked what she saw.

She'd met dozens of cops at the courthouses she'd passed through while growing up. They'd been the scary side of the Florida Family Court and Foster Care system. Authority figures to be hated and avoided at all costs, like CPS Social Workers and Family Court judges—or so she'd believed as a frightened foster kid. Cops were the ones who carted kids off to Juvey Hall.

Along with custody and placement hearings, physicals, new schools, and a never-ending line of new foster parents—some good, others bad, a few downright terrifying—cops had played a big part in her childhood.

McQuinn—tall and dark, with a five-o'clock shadow and shaggy black hair—looked more like a tobacco model than the uniformed cops she was used to seeing. A bad boy with a past—and, she suspected, an attitude to match.

"Okay. What's with the inspection, lady?" the bad boy in question growled, shooting her a dark scowl.

She reddened, embarrassed at being caught staring at him. "Sorry. I was just . . . thinking. Um, aren't you cold?"

"Damn right I'm cold! A little B and E is called for here. These are 'exceptional circumstances,' right?"

Letting go of her hand, he flexed his fingers—trying, she guessed, to get his circulation moving. New Mexico's winters were a far cry from Hawaii's endless summers.

She danced from foot to foot to keep warm while he rummaged through his pockets. Without the body heat generated by movement, she was freezing, despite her down-lined jacket.

Although he'd claimed he was cold, too, McQuinn—Jack—gave no sign of it. A real Mr. Macho, she thought, hiding a grin as she asked innocently, "B and E? Is that anything like S and M?"

He cocked a dark eyebrow at her. "Hell, no. It stands for Breaking and Entering. Unless our friendly park ranger left a door unlocked?"

He sounded hopeful, but they were soon disappointed. A quick tour of the station's perimeter confirmed that all doors and windows had been securely fastened before the park ranger left for the day. Ditto the doors to the two outbuildings or sheds, which were padlocked.

"Too bad."

"Yeah." He sighed loudly. "But about what I expected. Okay. Here goes nothing."

Using one of several odd-looking tools that dangled from his key ring, Jack forced the lock on the rear door of the Visitors' Center with an ease that would have alarmed her, under different circumstances. As it was, she felt only relief when he murmured, "We're in!"

"Way to go, MacGyver. Thanks."

"Any time, sweetheart." She heard amusement in his voice as he pushed the door inward. "After you."

The Park Rangers' Station/Visitors' Center was

a huge log cabin with high ceilings and rough-hewn rafters. Moonlight streamed down from a glassed-in skylight, turning everything silver and gray. The solid walls of the building immediately made her feel less vulnerable, less exposed. *Protected.*

"Did they leave the power on?" she wondered aloud, fumbling for a light switch.

"Probably. But let's not advertise where we are, okay? Make our friend Harper do his homework."

As he spoke, he dragged a heavy wood-framed armchair with loose leather cushions across the plank floor to the door they'd just entered.

She quickly moved to help him jockey the chair into place.

"Will that really keep him out?" she wondered doubtfully, breathing hard as they wedged the massive chair beneath the lock.

"Hell, no. But it might slow him down. Buy us some time. Give us a chance to go out the front door, say, if he comes in through the back."

"Right." Dry-mouthed at the thought, she swallowed, then flashed him a quick grin. "Sounds like a plan to me."

Being flip, joking around, was her way of dealing with stressful situations. It was a coping mechanism she'd learned as a part of the ER's trauma team, where life-and-death situations were the name of the game. You either rolled with the punches, found a way to deal with the critical injuries, the stress, the trauma victims, and managed to see a lighter side to even the darkest situations, or you cracked. Humor beat thinking about what could happen if Richard managed to get in. If she let herself go there, she'd fall apart.

It was several degrees warmer inside the station. The room had a rich woodsy smell. Pine resin, smoke, leather, and wet wool, she decided, sniffing. The wood box beside the fieldstone hearth was stacked with dry pine logs. Fire-starters and long matches were stored close by.

"I'll build us a fire," she offered, stifling a yawn that came out of nowhere as she unzipped her jacket. "If we have to be holed up in here, at least we'll be warm."

"Good idea. The smoke won't be visible in the dark."

They probably didn't need a fire, now that they were out of that cold wind, but it was something to do. Busy work to keep her hands from shaking, and her mind off Richard. Off memories of his abuse, both verbal and physical. Off the feeling of that icy gun barrel, jammed beneath her jaw. Just thinking about what would have happened if he'd pulled the trigger made her sick to her stomach.

Soon it was much warmer inside the station. Her face went from numb with cold to glowing with warmth in seconds. Her hands tingled almost painfully as feeling returned. Again, she caught herself yawning. God, she was sleepy!

It wasn't surprising, though, when she thought about it. When she'd woken to the sound of her sliding glass door being opened, she'd been asleep for less than twenty minutes, according to the clock-radio on her nightstand. And she'd been up almost 24 hours before.

Instead of going straight home to bed after pulling a crazy graveyard shift in the ER, she'd been up all day. And what a busy day it had turned out to be.

The morning she'd spent running errands. Dry-cleaners. Groceries. Laundromat. In the afternoon, she'd helped her friend Trini Alvarez with her little boy's second birthday party. With Cody's soldier daddy, José, far from home, serving in Iraq, she and Trini—also an R.N. at Santa Fe General—spent much of their free time together, or with Trini's family.

Remembering, she smiled. What an afternoon they'd had. Cody and seven sticky, screaming infants and toddlers, and a couple of chatty kindergarteners, all on a sugar high. Cherubic faces and tiny hands had been sticky with strawberry ice cream and squishy chocolate cake. Wiggles, SpongeBob SquarePants, and Blues Clues toys were everywhere, along with balloons, animal party hats, and streamers. It had been a mess, but everyone—grandmas and mommies included—had had fun.

At the time, she'd never dreamed that in a matter of hours her life would be turned upside down, all over again. After the huge adrenaline rush of McQuinn breaking into her apartment, being held at gunpoint, then having to roll her car to escape

Richard, it was inevitable that she would eventually crash. Her sleepiness now, along with the start of a mean headache, said that time had come.

She rocked back on her heels, arching her back, which was achy with tension. The three or four hours of sleep she'd been getting lately just weren't enough. What little sleep she'd had since hearing of Richard's car crash had been filled with nightmares. Terrifying images of Richard engulfed in flames, his face a grotesque melting mask as he lunged at her from the inferno of his blackened Porsche.

Remembering what McQuinn had told her about the charred remains in Richard's car, she swallowed. If Richard wasn't dead, whose body had they found? Had her husband really murdered an innocent man, a stranger, just to stage his own death, as the detective claimed?

"You sure know how to build a fire. Girl Scouts?" Jack asked, abruptly cutting into her grisly thoughts.

"Hmm? What was that about the Girl Scouts?" she asked, admiring the silhouette McQuinn cut in the moonlight that streamed through the skylight above him, painting everything in chiaroscuro, like a scene from a black-and-white movie.

And a very attractive silhouette it was, too, come to think of it. Tall. Broad across the shoulders, lean across the butt, with sexy dark eyes, a generous mouth, a strong nose and jaw. On him, the five-o'clock shadow and too-long hair looked good. In fact, he was the kind of man Trini laughingly called a "babe." Someone Liz would have been attracted to herself, before her disastrous marriage. She'd always been a sucker for bad boys with puppy-dog eyes that hinted at a tragic past.

She frowned. Would she ever be able to trust a man, love another man, after Richard?

"Sorry," she apologized. He was, she realized, waiting for an answer. "What was that again? I was miles away—"

"I noticed." He grinned. "The fire. I asked if you were a Girl Scout?"

"No. Not even close!" She sighed. "I was never in one place long enough to join anything while I was growing up. I was too busy being shuffled from family to family."

"How come?"

"I was a foster kid," she said, as if that explained everything. "My birth mom died when I was six. I never knew my father." She shrugged. "You're a cop. You know how it is. Nobody wants to adopt the older kids. They're too much trouble. *Babies*. That's what everyone wants. Newborns. Blank slates. You can't blame people. So I ended up in a foster home. The first of many."

He continued to prowl while she talked, probably trying to get his bearings in the gloom. But he didn't comment on what she said, and for that, she was glad.

Did McQuinn resent quitting his job to find her?—*if* he really had quit his job—she wondered with a pang of guilt, one that she immediately shrugged off. Too bad if he had. She hadn't asked him to quit on her account, or for him to come looking for her, she told herself defiantly, the old street-wise Liz reasserting herself.

Nor had she asked for his advice when she'd been desperate for someone—anyone!—to talk to, and had believed he was Keoki, her chat-room friend. *You didn't have to ask,* a little voice reminded her, *because Jack's a good guy. He has a conscience. He did what he thought was right— and he did it for you.*

Shrugging off her uncomfortable thoughts, she knelt on the wide fieldstone hearth, stacking logs with brittle angry movements.

"So where *did* you learn to build a fire? Juvey Hall?" he asked casually. One dark brow lifted. "Arson 101? Pyromaniacs R Us?"

"Very funny." Her laughter served to defuse her anger, loosened the tight, cold knot coiled in the pit of her belly. Not that she could bring herself to relax completely, under the circumstances. After all, what did she really know about McQuinn? Not enough to trust him completely. Not yet.

"If you really want to know, I learned to build fires by going camping with the Scotts. That's the family that adopted me when I was thirteen."

"Adopted? 'S that right?" The dark brows lifted in feigned surprise. "But I thought older kids didn't get adopted."

There was a challenge in those dark bedroom

eyes. Was he teasing her? She wasn't sure, so she shrugged again. "I guess I got lucky. Fire-lighting was the first thing my new brothers taught me. Not that it's hard to light a fire with matches and fire-starters. It's much easier than rubbing two sticks together!"

"Or disappearing off the face of the earth?"

Her chin came up. "Yes."

She tucked the fire-starters between the logs, then struck a match, nostrils flaring as it sputtered to life. She touched a flame to the dry kindling as if she were in church, lighting a candle.

"There! And now we pray," she said softly, fanning the sparks with her hand.

She hadn't meant that they should pray for the fire to catch, he knew, but for deliverance from Harper.

Amen to that, Jack added silently.

Despite her efforts to be upbeat, he could hear the strain, exhaustion, mistrust underscoring her voice now. He'd also caught her in a yawn. It was no surprise to him that she was tired. She'd worked a busy 11-to-7 shift in the ER last night, caring for a steady stream of patients.

Parked in the hospital parking lot, slouched down in the driver's seat of the rented Jeep, he'd watched the county ambulances roll up to the ER's automatic double doors and unload several times. There'd been m.v.a. victims, the bloodied combatants of a fight at a local cantina in the custody of Santa Fe PD. A senior citizen with heart problems. A kid with asthma. The list of patients was a long one.

But, instead of going home to bed when she finished her shift, Liz had grabbed a cup of coffee from the hospital cafeteria and run all over Santa Fe doing errands.

The afternoon she'd spent at an ice-cream parlor, surrounded by squealing rugrats. He knew, because he'd followed her there, too.

He knew from personal experience that you couldn't work all night and play all day without paying the price. Sooner or later, the need for sleep caught up with you—just like your past.

He shook his head. He had to give her credit, though. Against all odds, and despite the statistics stacked against her, she'd found the courage to escape an intolerable situation, by methods that were unorthodox, to say the least.

She'd plunged into the dense rain forest of Oahu's Kahana Valley, and apparently never hiked back out.

In the process, she'd successfully escaped Harper—and none too soon, either. The son of a bitch would have destroyed her if she'd stayed.

As far as he knew, she had taken nothing with her into her new life but the clothes on her back, and her fierce will to survive. She must have spent a harrowing year trying to rebuild her life from scratch, always looking over her shoulder, always wondering if—when!—she would find Harper behind her.

Each day she must have wondered if this would be the day he found her and brutally ended her life. And she'd done it all alone, only for it to end with Harper doing the old double play, and staging his own death, exactly as she had done. There was, however, one very important difference between the two. Harper had killed to make his escape.

Harper's apparent death had temporarily put the brakes on her husband's arrest and extradition to Arizona for the Scottsdale murder of the first Mrs. Harper. The authorities couldn't arrest a dead man.

According to the reports Jack had read prior to his resignation, after four years' silence, an unnamed witness had come forward with information on the Ellen Harper cold case. The terrified witness—an unnamed R.N.—had apparently seen Harper take phials of a powerful muscle relaxant from the drug locker of the Phoenix hospital where he'd been an up-and-coming cardiothoracic surgeon four years ago. The R.N.'s fear of Harper, the negative consequences to her career if she testified against a physician, had ensured her silence, until her conscience began to nag at her.

On exhumation of Ellen Harper's body, traces of the same substance had been found in the tissues. A needle mark in her neck that could not be explained by either a doctor's visit on the day of her death, or by attempts to resuscitate her, indicated that the substance had been injected shortly before Ellen's death, causing a massive seizure while the victim was swimming in the pool of her ritzy Scottsdale home.

Her death had not been the tragic drowning accident the coroner had ruled at the time, but cold-blooded murder. But since both the police and insurance investigators had failed to incriminate him, Richard Harper had been released. He had become the beneficiary of Ellen's 4.2-million-dollar life-insurance policy. Free to leave Phoenix. Free to marry again. And marry he had.

Then in Honolulu, with everyone convinced he was dead, the victim of a fiery car crash, Richard Harper was free again; this time free to hop a plane, leave Hawaii, and go after his missing second wife without fear of pursuit or arrest.

He'd subsequently hunted her down, held a gun to her head, and threatened to blow her brains out. A nice change of pace from his usual means of self-expression—beating the crap out of a woman.

His friend, Detective Tommy Pacheco, had once called Harper "the Ice Man"—and not without reason, Jack recalled, shaking his head.

That Liz was keeping it together as well as she did was nothing short of a miracle.

He scowled. What had happened to the so-called friend she'd told him about in the chat room? The "someone"—probably male—who meant she'd "never be alone again"? The guy must be a real loser, Jack decided, because here she was again, facing the same damn nightmare. *Alone.*

"Now who's staring?" she accused. Her tone jerked him back to the moment. Long-lashed smoky eyes glistened in the shadows as she looked up at him. "A penny for 'em, McQuinn!"

"All right. I was just wondering how you did it? Escaped Harper, I mean," he covered.

"Yeah. Right." Her incredulous expression said she didn't believe him. "What were you really thinking?"

"Like I said. How'd you get from the Kahana Valley to the airport?" Talking would take her mind off Harper. Besides, his curiosity was genuine. You didn't stare at a beautiful woman on a Missing Persons poster for the better part of a year, search her home, go through her belongings, her most intimate possessions, without wanting to know more about her. In his case, a whole lot more.

"It was no big deal. I hitchhiked, Detective. Some surfers in a rusty Subaru picked me up on the side of the road about a quarter mile from the entrance to Kahana Valley. They took me as far as the Swap Meet at Aloha Stadium. From there, I caught a bus to the airport."

"Why didn't the surfers come forward?"

"Beats me. They didn't seem the type to watch much TV." She grinned. "Then again, when they picked me up, I guess I didn't look much like my photos."

"Why was that?"

She shrugged. "I had on a blond wig and big

94

shades. Different clothes. I got everything from Goodwill, including the backpack. Thirty minutes after planting the car keys and my water bottle, I was halfway around the island."

"I checked the flight lists. You weren't on them. How'd you buy the ticket?"

"Fake I.D. A driver's license in another name."

"Lisa Scott?" he guessed.

"Yes."

"Where'd you get it?"

She shrugged. "I learned a lot from hanging out with my big brothers."

"Like what?"

"Like how to get a fake I.D. I hung out on the U.H. campus for a day or two. Asked around. It didn't take long. I pawned my wedding ring for the airfare."

"Thank God for big brothers, huh?" He grinned. "How many brothers?"

"Three. Rob, Jim, and Steve."

"Aah. So you're the kid sister. Teased mercilessly, I bet?" He grinned.

"Hmm. Spoiled rotten, too."

"Hey. That's what little sisters are for. Teasing and spoiling. Admit it. You love it!"

"I do," she agreed warmly. "Who—what about you?"

"Four sisters and a brother. Gina, Michaela, Sabrina, Maeve, and Joe. All older. I guess I'm the spoiled baby, too."

She laughed, as if she found the idea of him being someone's baby brother funny.

The smile lit her face and warmed her eyes. She should smile more often. She would, if he had his way, he promised himself, grinning back like a fool.

"A big Italian family." She sighed. "That sounds like fun."

"Italian? What makes you think I'm Italian? No, don't say it. Let me guess. It's my dark good looks, right?" He grinned.

"That was some of it, sure. I just assumed . . ." She shrugged.

"Well, you're only half right. I'm Italian on my mom's side, Irish on my dad's. Some combination, huh?"

Her smile deepened. "Unbelievable. Is that a New York accent?"

"Ninety-nine percent Brooklyn, with a dash of Long Island and a pinch of Hawaiian thrown in. Hey—you can't live in Hawaii for long without picking up the local *da kine* talk. You know how it is?"

She laughed out loud. "Oh, I know! I loved it there. I've missed the island people. The Aloha spirit."

It was one of the things he liked about Hawaii, too. Getting to understand the local pidgin—or broken—English was like being given the keys to a secret island society. It meant you were an insider. That you belonged.

He guessed that was why Liz had loved the islands so much. Most foster kids spent their entire lives trying to belong to something. To someone. To *somewhere*.

"What were you doing in the islands, anyway? You don't seem like the surf 'n sun, beach-bum type to me."

His dark brows lifted again. "That obvious, huh? You're right, though. I'm not. I'm an . . . oh, I don't know . . . an Alaskan-salmon-fishing-ice-hockey-beer-drinking-New-York-cop kind of guy."

She laughed. "Phew. So, what were you doing in Hawaii?"

He shrugged. "Beats me. What does anyone do in Hawaii? The islands are where you go to heal, right? So, that's where I ended up."

He could have kicked himself the moment the words left his mouth. He hadn't given much thought to how they would sound to her.

For Pete's sake, can it, McQuinn! What the hell are you doing, running off at the mouth, spilling your guts like that, huh? Talking about the islands and "healing," for crying out loud.

"You needed to heal." She said it softly, more statement than question. "How come? 9/11?"

"That was a big part of it, yeah," he admitted, clearing his throat. "But there—uh—you know, there was . . . more. Other reasons."

"Want to talk about it?" She was staring at him again, staring long and hard. Her cool, compassionate, *interested* gaze unnerved him. It was as if she could see right to the heart of him. He wasn't sure how he felt about that.

"Maybe. One day," he hedged. "But not now, okay? Whoa! Your, uh, your fire's going out," he observed, clearing his throat.

Right now, she needed to believe in him. To trust that he could get her out of this jam.

Time enough later to tell her he'd screwed up, big time. Or that his screw-up had cost another woman her life . . .

Richard Jerome Harper parked the black SUV alongside the abandoned silver Jeep.

In the moment before he switched them off, the headlights revealed a rutted trail, littered with rocks, stark leafless bushes, and a light blanket of snow. Two pairs of dark footprints led directly uphill to where a line of dark pines stood silent sentinel.

For the first time since that little bitch rolled her crappy car and broke his nose, an ugly smile thinned his lips. It revealed a chipped tooth and a split lip that was bloodied and swollen.

Assholes! he thought. They thought they were so fucking clever. But they'd as good as handed him a map to their hiding place. This would be just like old times, going rabbit hunting with his daddy.

"Here I come, Eliza-beth," he crooned in a sing-song bayou drawl that harkened back to his childhood. "Ready or not! You cain't hide, sweet thing. Not from good ole Ricky Boy."

Reaching into the SUV, he took out two battered red-and-yellow gasoline cans, some rags, and a trouble light. He stuffed the rags into his pockets, tucked the cans under one arm, and switched on the emergency light with the other hand.

The broad beam lit the dried bloodstains splattered across the front of his white jacket, ugly as inkblots, as well as a swath of wintry landscape for several yards in either direction.

He jabbed the remote to lock the SUV's doors. Then, rifle in one hand, the gas cans still tucked under his arm, he trained the trouble light on the footprints and set off.

He followed the tracks uphill, through the snow, as he'd so often followed the tracks of deer or other game as a boy.

This would be easy, he decided—as easy as killing ole Coop, his handyman-gardener, had been. "Ain't that right, Coop?"

A reformed alcoholic with bad teeth, no dental benefits, and the IQ of a lab rat, it'd been easy to talk ole Coop into getting badly needed dental work done in his "benefactor's" name.

It had been just as easy to make him forget his precious Twelve Steps, get him liquored up, and belted into the driver's seat of that same benefactor's pretty blue Porsche, before sending it and Coop over Tantalus lookout in a fiery explosion.

Pity about that Porsche.

He chuckled. Thanks to a little extra gas, George F. Cooper, formerly of Oakland, California, was now toast—literally—while he, for all intents and purposes, had gone from being a wanted man to a dead man.

Elizabeth wasn't the only one who could play possum, no siree!

Getting rid of his whoring wife would be just as easy—like shooting fish in a barrel. She and her cop lover would hunker down in some cozy little bolt-hole, expecting him to break in, like the big bad wolf comin' after the three little pigs. But he didn't intend to huff 'n puff their house down. Hell, no! Those fools would never know what hit 'em. It would be the last lesson he ever taught that bitch and the nosy detective she'd been humping on the sly.

McQuinn had sniffed around, pretending to "investigate" his missing wife's disappearance when he'd known all along where the little whore was hiding.

Well, she'd soon learn the same lesson his liquored-up daddy had hammered into his momma every Friday night, regular as clockwork, before he started in on li'l Ricky.

Sharp as a well-honed skinning knife, craftier than a fox, Ricky Boy—as he'd been known as a snot-nosed kid—had been a few months shy of ten, and already no stranger to CPS workers, when he finally figured it out.

If he played his cards right, he could use CPS and the whole goddamned welfare system to get himself out of that life, and out of the state of Louisiana, both of which he hated, and far away from his daddy. He was smart, and as a hunter, he'd learned the value of patience.

As a ward of the state, that lesson had come in handy. He would bide his time, and make something of himself. Get himself far away from the bayou shack where he'd been raised, and become somebody important. Somebody folks looked up to, like a lawyer, or a doctor. All he had to do was play the game by their rules for a few short years.

And play them he had.

He'd changed overnight from an incorrigible truant, a discipline problem, to a compliant, motivated student who'd done his various foster parents proud. He'd excelled in the public schools he attended, winning enough scholarships and grants to get a free ride through college, and finally, medical school, from which he'd graduated at the top of his class. *Richard Jerome Harper, M.D.* He'd become one of the welfare system's shining success stories.

Hell, yes. He'd been smart. He'd been quiet, low-key, unfailingly polite. He'd worked hard at losing his bayou drawl. While other students partied or chased tail, he took speech lessons, studied, made good grades, kept to himself, ultimately parlaying his love of hunting, of dressing out his kill, into becoming a cardiothoracic surgeon.

"Such a nice, quiet young man," teachers, professors and little old ladies had cooed. "Mr. Harper's no trouble at all."

He'd distinguished himself in the medical field, first by landing a plum position at a prestigious Scottsdale, Arizona, medical center, then by marrying wealthy Phoenix socialite Ellen Cohen—

Ellen, her body floating in the pool, eyes wide and staring up at the bright blue desert sky, mouth wide open in an endless silent scream.

—against her rich daddy's wishes.

Her long black hair floated on the chlorinated water like a black Spanish fan, its long strands separating into snaky Medusa locks, like a nest of writhing water moccasins.

In the beginning, there'd been no outward signs. No clues that he'd taken with him into his new life the hard lessons of the old: the teachings his daddy had beaten into him as a snot-nosed kid, week in, week out, with a belt strap or a two-by-four, or whatever came to hand.

What a man owned stayed his, come what may, his daddy had always said, until he was good and ready to rid himself of it. And that included his woman.

No whoring bitch left a Harper man, not for any reason. No cheating whore ever let another man get inside her drawers. Not without paying the price tenfold.

Ain't that right, Miz Ellen?

Horror had widened Ellen's cheating baby blues

when he told her he knew all about her plans to leave him. They'd bugged from the sockets again when he plunged the needle into her neck, sending a lethal dose of muscle relaxant swirling into her bloodstream. Within seconds she'd seized and drowned.

He smiled to himself. And tonight? Hell! There was gonna be a hot time in the old town tonight, as the saying went. *Ain't that right, Eliza-beth?*

He stood in the deep shadows cast by the sheds, staring up at the darkened Visitors' Center in the clearing, the red gasoline cans at his feet.

And—when his wife and McQuinn were both dead—or just wishing they were—he had another score to settle before he disappeared forever. He felt for the object he'd tucked inside his jacket.

One last, very small score, he thought as he flung it to the ground.

SIX

"Oh, no! Don't go out!"

While Liz fussed over the fire, coaxing tiny flames from a handful of glowing embers, Jack continued to scout around, relieved she hadn't insisted on an explanation.

For a moment there, she'd reminded him of Sarah. Sarah, with her quick grasp of any situation, her ability to sense other people's problems, and know what to say or do to make them feel better.

But unlike Sarah, who'd been up-front about everything, including the ex-boyfriend who'd stalked and threatened her, Liz played her cards close to her chest. She probably felt it was safer that way. If you didn't talk about yourself, your secrets couldn't turn around someday and bite you in the ass.

Her game plan didn't surprise him. Growing up the way she had, passed from foster family to foster family—hell! Who could blame her for not trusting anyone? Kids needed a stable home. A family they could depend on. Parents like his, who'd given their kids unconditional love and guidance, set boundaries, consistently yet gently enforced rules. That was how kids learned to trust. By living with it, day in, day out.

Shaking his head to scatter the cobwebs of the past, he resumed his exploration of the Visitors' Center.

One corner was set aside for informational leaflets and guidebooks. Racks held glossy paperbacks, activities pamphlets, and travel brochures. *New Mexico*, he read by moonlight that was almost as bright as day. *Land of Enchantment. What to Do in the Santa Fe National Forest. Hike the Pecos Wilderness. The Battle of Glorieta Pass: A Timeline.*

A back door was set in the far wall.

The third side held a long desk. A giant map of the park was thumbtacked to a cork bulletin board on the wall above it. Hiking and riding trails, fishing spots, ancient ruins, the infamous pass, and the old Santa Fe trail were all clearly marked. So was the small town of Pecos, New Mexico, to the northeast.

Jack traced I-25 north and west in the bright moonlight that flooded the map.

According to the scale, as the crow flew, they were less than twenty-five miles from Liz's lowrise apartment complex. Two miles from the little town of Pecos to the north. Eight or ten miles south of Las Vegas—L.V., New Mexico, not Nevada.

He frowned. He thought they'd driven farther than that. The snaking black road, with its twists and turns in and out of the Sangre de Cristo foothills and around the Pecos River, was deceptive.

The door behind the information desk opened into a small office/lunch room. Beyond that was a private restroom. He went into the office. A metal flashlight winked at him from a pegboard, along with bunches of keys, all neatly labeled: *Snowmobiles. Tools. Cleaning Equipment. Office Supplies. Public Restrooms* He took the flashlight and turned it on.

A broad beam of light cut across a small microwave oven and a coffeepot. Mugs, condiments, and other lunch items neatly lined the countertops along one side of the room. A filing cabinet and a desk with an ancient computer, a phone, and a desk calendar were on the other side.

He'd dialed 911 before it hit him. *No dial tone.* Nothing but dead air. Swearing under his breath, he replaced the receiver, then tried booting up the computer. Ditto.

A power-outage? he wondered, replacing the receiver. Had the snowfall downed a line somewhere? Or . . . had the power lines been cut? It was a chilling thought, but his money was on the latter.

Once again, he swore under his breath. How

had that son of a bitch found them so damned fast, at night? Harper was more dangerous than Jack had given him credit for. Crazy like a fox. Or maybe a hunter?

There was still hot water, he discovered, running the restroom faucet, so the power had been on until fairly recently. Filling a mug, he sweetened it heavily, added two heaped spoonfuls of instant coffee, then carried it through into the other room.

A long leather-cushioned sofa with a rustic wooden frame faced the fieldstone fireplace. Alongside it was a matching armchair to the one they'd pushed up against the door. Moonlight poured over the sofa from the skylight, bathing everything below—including Liz—in its silvery light.

She sat with her booted feet tucked under her, watching new flames curl golden tongues around the logs like hungry dragons. The firelight flickered in her golden-brown hair and washed her pale face with rosy color.

Although she was outwardly calm, her thoughts had to be chaotic after his break-in, being held at gunpoint, then the car chase that had ended with them stranded here.

"Room service!" he sang out. Placing the mug between her hands, he folded her icy fingers around it. "Drink up! That's an order."

His throat constricted when she looked up at him. Strain and fear darkened her smoky eyes.

Lilac shadows ringed them, lending her a haunting beauty that he knew went more than skin deep.

If he lived to be a hundred, he'd never understand how bastards like Harper could abuse women like her. *Like Sarah.* Like thousands of other women across the country. *All over the world.* Well, maybe it was too late to help his former partner, but he'd be damned if he let Liz suffer the same fate.

He'd begun his search out of guilt, initially, convinced the well-intentioned advice he'd given Liz in the chat room made him responsible for her probable murder at Harper's hands.

His investigation had ultimately led him in a very different direction. In the process of learning about Liz, he'd learned a lot about Richard, and about the incredible emotional strength, courage, and determination of his victim.

"Drink up," he urged, nodding at the steaming mug. "It's not Starbucks, but it'll warm you."

"Hmm, thanks. I could use some caffeine right about now. I'm this far from nodding off." She held her thumb and index finger a half inch apart. "What about you? Aren't you having any?"

"Later. First I have to find out if we've got company. You stay here while I go take a look outside. Okay?"

Panic filled her eyes. "Now? Can't it wait?" she asked.

There was a desperate, breathless edge to her voice he hadn't heard before.

"Jack. I—I need you here." Setting the mug down on the hearth, she reached out and grabbed his hand. As they touched, skin to skin, a current crackled between them, almost electrical in its intensity.

Slowly she stood. "Wait a few minutes. Okay? Please, Jack?" she pleaded, searching his handsome face. "I—I was just—just starting to . . . you know, settle down? Get myself together?"

They were facing each other now, their hands linked, their bodies almost touching.

Jack swallowed as his body responded predictably, aroused by her closeness. By his long-standing attraction to her as a woman. There were parts of him that were single-minded. *Blind.* Parts that didn't give a damn whether the timing was right or not. Parts that still wanted. That still got hard.

"Liz, I can't wait. I have to go out there. I need to find out what he's doing. Right now."

She lowered her head. Rested her cheek on his chest. Repeated softly, "I know that. I know, Jack. I . . . don't go. Not just yet. Please? Give me five minutes. That's all I ask. Just—five—minutes."

"Sweetheart. Liz. I wish I could hold off. But I can't." He slid his arms around her, held her protectively, his fingers linked behind her back as if he were holding a child.

But there was nothing childlike about the way she felt in his arms. Or about the way her breasts thrust against him, right through the bulky folds of her clothes. No. There was nothing even remotely childlike about this complex, fascinating woman, who managed to be gutsy, vulnerable, and sexy as hell, all at the same time.

"I know you have to go. But not yet, okay?" she murmured, curling her arms around his neck. "Five minutes. That's all I ask. Just five."

Her slim fingers plunged into his crisp black hair, raising prickly bumps across his arms, neck, and back.

"I just need to get this stupid sh-shaking under control," she murmured, sounding close to tears, yet furious at herself at the same time. "That's all."

"I understand," he murmured softly, not surprised that she was trembling. A year's worth of running, of fear, loneliness, heartache, had all come down to this moment. To this mountain cabin. To the two of them against Harper. His arms tightened around her. "Take some deep breaths, then slowly let 'em out. It'll get rid of that sick, panicky feeling. And try not to think about Harper, okay?"

"I wish I could. But I can't stop thinking about him. About what he's capable of."

Jack told himself he was only comforting her, but his body knew the truth. His body read the signals one hell of a lot better than he could. Who was he kidding? *He wanted her.*

He stroked her back, her hair, forcing himself to think of other things. "Shh. It'll be okay. Promise," he murmured, steeling himself to ignore his

111

arousal. To tamp his feelings down, where they belonged.

"I'm not usually such a wimp," she explained, her voice muffled against his chest. She tilted her head back to look up at him. Her smoky eyes glittered with unshed tears, before she closed them. Moisture leaked from beneath the thick, inky lashes, making trails that glistened on her cheeks in the moonlight. "And I usually don't throw myself at strangers, either! It's just that—oh, Jack, I've been so scared for such a long, long time, and now this! I'm sorry I got you into this mess."

"Hey. Don't beat yourself up. You didn't get me into anything I didn't ask for, okay?" he soothed. "I came looking for you. I wanted to warn you. It was something I had to do. For my *own* peace of mind. My choice."

"You're a nice man, Jack. Hold me. Hold me tight," she urged. "I don't want to think about him. That he's out there. Or what he's doing."

He ducked his head, intending to drop a reassuring kiss on her forehead. But in the brief moment between lowering his head and his lips brushing hesitantly, teasingly over hers, something very different happened. Something fierce, something urgent and unexpected, exploded between them. Burst into flame!

Instead of a brotherly kiss, he hauled her into his arms and crushed his mouth over hers, plundering her lips in a fierce, hungry kiss that was far from sweet. Far more fierce, more *sexual* than the platonic little kiss he'd intended.

Ah, the hell with it, he told himself, surrendering to the moment, dragging her against him with none of the restraint he'd used before. If a few hot and heavy kisses made Harper go away for her, then so be it. He'd banish the son of a bitch clear to Timbuktu, if it helped! Right now, what she needed was a pair of strong arms. The comfort and warmth, the strength of another body. *Another man.*

Holding her fiercely, he feasted on her mouth, on the sexy sweetness of lips that tasted like wine.

What they were feeling was older than time. A primal need to celebrate life in the face of danger or death. He knew that, rationally, but he no longer gave a damn.

Nothing mattered but her—warm, feminine and yes, softly pliant in his arms. The urge to protect her, to make love to her, overrode everything. It trampled logic, destroyed reason. Demolished restraint.

His kiss deepened as he framed her face between his hands. As he devoured her eager lips. As he branded the silky line of her throat. He ran his hands up beneath her jacket's bulky folds, beneath her pale pink sweater, to stroke her sinuous back. To cradle her bottom in both hands and draw her snugly against his hips.

Liz's reactions stunned her. Dear God, she

hardly knew the man, but that didn't seem to matter to her. She *wanted* him. Needed him. Right now! Desired him with a raw, urgent hunger and heat she'd never felt for Richard, not even at the start, when she thought she loved him.

Jack was an attractive man. His lean, muscular body, pressed to hers, the powerful arms around her, the rasp of his rough cheek, were so male, and so arousing, she shivered with longing.

"Oh, Jack," she whispered, breathing hard when he finally came up for air and drew his lips from hers. One of his hands still cupped her head, those long, powerful fingers tangled in her hair. The other still cradled her face. "This is crazy!"

"You're telling me! Just say the word, and I'll stop." His voice was thick with lust.

"I can't." Her lips brushed his, parted and eager. "I don't want you to stop!" Her breathing was shallow and unsteady as they hungrily kissed again.

This close, their bodies touching, she could feel the hard ridge of him pressed against her hip. It made her crazy. She was tempted to slither out of her jeans. To fall back across the leather sofa and pull him down on top of her, inside her. So very tempted . . .

Raw sex would give her the oblivion she sought. A moment's respite, a release from the fear that had shadowed her for so long. Logic told her it would change very little else. Once it was over, Richard would still be out there somewhere. Still stalking her . . . them . . . still wanting her dead. But that didn't seem to matter.

She whispered Jack's name again and again, like a mantra. Her fingers tightened feverishly in his hair. Her nipples were taut, painfully sensitive to the friction of his chest. Her pulse raced. The body she'd believed numbed and dead was now humming with desire, purring with lust and excitement. Between her thighs was a vibration like the quivering string of a classic guitar, exquisitely tuned, that betrayed her need.

When his hand found her, pressed, she moaned with pleasure—a raw sound that ebbed to a low murmur. The sound unleashed a storm.

Reason, restraint spun out of control. They hurtled toward some dark, forbidden ledge on which they teetered, just a hairbreadth from plunging into the yawning abyss.

With a husky murmur, a groan that began deep in his throat, Jack lowered her to the leather sofa and followed her down, his mouth hot, hungry, his hands skilled, knowing as he began to strip away her clothing.

His senses were full of her. Of her scent, the feel of her body, soft with surrender, warm with desire, as she lay beneath him, those surprisingly long, jeans-clad legs now tangled with his.

He was still looming over her, looking down at her, his hand on her belt buckle, when reason returned, dousing him like a bucket of ice water.

What the hell was he doing? What was he thinking? This was crazy!

He wanted to make love to her more than he wanted to breathe! Wanted to hold her in his arms forever. To promise her no one would ever hurt her again, because he, Jack McQuinn, wouldn't let them. He wanted to drive out her terror in a meltdown of desire that would hurl them both to the stars. But that wouldn't be right, he reminded himself. Not here. Not now. It would only be the frantic coupling of two strangers, thrown together by danger. By fear. By circumstance, rather than their own free will. Or love.

He shook his head.

Danger. The threat of destruction. They were powerful aphrodisiacs. The sizzling heat of desire built in direct proportion to the desperation of a given situation. He knew that. The greater the fear, the hotter passion burned, and the bigger the turn-on.

Knowing that, could he let this happen? Could he lead a woman he'd begun to care about over that precipice? Take advantage of her emotional state, her terror—and still live with himself afterwards? Could he make love to her, knowing she might hate him in the morning? Knowing a killer stalked them both, and that every moment was precious?

The answer was no.

He wanted her—had, if truth were known, wanted her long before he'd met her in the flesh.

But taking what he wanted here, now, went against everything he believed in. She deserved better. He would no sooner take advantage of her fear, her vulnerability, than he would abandon her to Harper.

It was one of the hardest things he'd ever done, but he forced himself to do it. He lifted himself off her, breathing as if he'd run a minute mile as he gently released her.

Immediately she struggled to sit, fussing with her hair, her clothes, her embarrassment a living thing between them.

"Jack. I'm so sorry," she whispered, instantly stricken. This was her fault, she told herself. Not his. She'd led him on. Asked him to stay. To hold her. She'd known exactly what she was doing. She swallowed. Despite everything, despite what Richard had done to her, she was still his wife.

What would Jack think of her now? He was practically a stranger, someone she hardly knew, who'd been kind enough to help her. And she'd thrown herself at him like a—a cat in heat. She didn't blame him for pulling away.

A shudder moved through her. Silent tears slipped down her cheeks. "I don't know what came over me. I—I didn't mean to—to throw myself at you like that. It just—happened. When you said you were going outside, I panicked."

"Hey. It's okay, slugger." He stroked her silky hair. The urge to taste her again, to take her in his arms, to lay her beneath him and explore her soft, sweet curves, was still there, still strong. What had changed was his self-control. His thinking. It was clearer, stronger now, as was his resolve. Ethics he hadn't known he still possessed reasserted themselves. What he felt for her was stronger than lust. Better.

"Don't cry, sweetheart," he murmured, stroking her hair. "We'll get through this, okay? And when this is over, if you still feel the same—baby, watch out! Wild horses won't keep me away from you then." He made a silly growling sound.

His teasing broke the heavy, unbearable tension that had risen like a wall between them.

She blinked back tears, managed a little smile. "Really?"

He grinned, raised his hand. "Scout's honor."

"Ditto, McQuinn," she admitted shyly.

"We'll be okay." He kissed the corner of her mouth, tasting her tears. He kissed her eyelids. Her nose. "Promise."

"I believe you. Okay—you can let go of me now." Knuckling the moisture from her eyes, she pulled free of his arms. "It was just too much, all of a sudden. Overwhelming."

"Sssh. I know. Does your family know you're okay?" he asked at length as they sat there. Maybe talking about her family would take her mind off Harper. "That you're alive?"

"Not yet. They have no idea. Why?"

He shrugged. "I was just curious. The Scotts are

nice people. Telling them we'd called off the search for you was one of the hardest things I've ever had to do." *Second only to telling Sarah's parents that their oldest daughter was dead.*

"You met them?" She sounded surprised. "You actually spoke to them?

He nodded. "They flew into Honolulu when they heard you'd disappeared. They were devastated. Your dad and brothers went out with the search parties. Were you planning on telling them someday?" He hadn't intended to sound accusing, but it came out that way.

"Of course! I wanted to tell them from the start, but I was afraid Richard would find out I was alive, somehow, and come looking for me. He would have hurt them if he thought they were hiding me. You have no idea what he's capable of."

"Maybe not. But I can make a pretty good guess," he said with feeling, remembering the charred and blackened remains of Richard's second victim, scattered across the cold steel table of the autopsy suite. No vehicle fire burned that fiercely, not without an accelerant of some kind. What had Harper used? he wondered. Gasoline? "Last week, when you thought he'd been killed, you didn't call your family then?"

She drew a shuddering breath. Shook her head. "No. Maybe I should have, but I didn't. I planned on waiting one more week. It's a good thing I did, as it turned out."

He nodded. "Laura Scott told me how they adopted you. You were the little girl she'd always wanted."

She nodded, blinking back tears. Her voice was husky when she spoke again. "That's right. I was thirteen when they took me in. I'd been bounced around from one foster family to the next since I was six. That was the year my birth mother died."

"You still remember her?"

"A little, yes. With the Scotts, I was happy for the first time since she died. I wanted to stay with them more than anything in the world. But I was afraid, too."

"Of what?"

"That after a while, they wouldn't want me anymore, like the other families. I had nightmares I'd be taken away from them."

"But you weren't?"

"No. The Scotts legally adopted me. It was the happiest day of my life. I—I've hated doing this to them!" Her voice broke. "Letting them think I was—you know, dead."

"Hey. You'll make it up to them," Jack said, hugging her. "They'll be so damned happy to hear you're alive, they'll forgive you anything," he assured her, his voice husky. "Just focus on us getting out of here. Okay?"

She sighed. "Okay. I hope you're right."

He grinned. "Hey. I'm always right."

She smiled through her tears. "You've been so nice about all this. I'm sorry I hit you."

"Lucky for you, we McQuinns have hard heads, slugger!" He paused. "Liz? Can I ask you something?"

"Of course."

"What was it that finally made you leave Harper? You and I had been chatting online off and on for—what? Six months?"

"About that."

"Then all of a sudden—bam! You're ready to pack up and go."

"I guess I was."

"Why? Was it because you weren't alone anymore? Because your new—friend—gave you the courage to leave Richard?" Jack couldn't bring himself to voice his second question: *Where is the jerk now, when you need him most?* Was he jealous? Damn right.

"Something like that," she said vaguely, her smile distant and mysterious. A Mona Lisa smile. "It wasn't that sudden, not really. I just—I wanted my life back, Jack. I'd had enough of . . . of being hurt. Of being a prisoner in my own home."

Jack nodded, but he didn't entirely believe her. He'd questioned his fair share of suspects. By his reckoning, she'd answered a bit too quickly for honesty. All the signs said she was lying through her teeth—or at the very least, had a secret. Was holding something back. But why? Why lie to him about that? What wasn't she telling him? And why did he have the nagging feeling that she'd left out something that could make all the difference to the outcome of the situation they were in?

Lies or no lies, he still ached to hold her. To keep her safe forever from the Richards of the world. From the violent monsters who called themselves men, but were cowards and bullies of the lowest kind.

"You're one hell of a woman, Liz," he said softly. "It took guts to leave Harper, after what he put you through."

"Guts? Guts had nothing to do with it. I was more terrified of staying than I was of going." She jammed her hands into her pockets, hunched her shoulders, and sighed. "Not brave at all. Just . . . desperate."

"But you did it anyway. *You got out.* That's the difference. Doing what has to be done when you're terrified—that takes real courage. That's why I want you to take this. No, no, take it! Hang on to it until I get back."

She looked down at the gleaming 9-mm Glock Jack placed in her hands. "Jack, no. Please. I can't. Don't even ask."

"Shh. You can," he insisted firmly, going to the door and opening it. She trailed after him. "You can do anything you set your mind to doing. If Harper gets in, shoot him. Don't ask questions. Shoot."

"But—I've never fired a gun before!"

"It's not rocket science. You take off the safety—right here—then you aim at the biggest target—that's Harper's chest. Try to keep your arm steady, then squeeze back on the trigger. There'll be a recoil that jerks your arm up, so aim low. You've got nineteen rounds in the clip. Should be more than enough."

She wetted her lips. "You really think he's out there, don't you? That he found the turn-off?"

"Oh, yeah," he admitted, thinking about the dead phone lines. The lost power. His dark eyes were very serious now. "He's facing a double homicide rap if he's caught, sweetheart. The man's got nothing to lose anymore. *Nothing.* Use the gun if it comes to it. Promise me?"

Her jaw tightened. "All right." She sighed. "You know, it's funny. For the longest time, my fear of being killed kept me from leaving him. But in the end, it was that same fear that made me get the hell out. Jack?"

"Yes?"

"I wouldn't have got away from Los Piñons without you."

He shot her a rueful grin. "Are you kidding? I have this lump on my skull that says you'd have done just fine, slugger!"

"Perhaps. But thank you anyway."

"You can thank me when I get back. Go inside. Bolt the door behind me, okay?" he urged her with a quick look around. Harper could be watching them even now.

She nodded.

"And don't open it until I give the password."

"Which is?"

"What else? J.F.K."

She smiled again. "Got it."

He nodded. "Before I forget—this belongs to you." He fished in the pocket of his cords, withdrawing the silver-and-turquoise earring that had drawn him southwest to Santa Fe—and her—like an ancient lodestone drawing metal. "Your friend Kokopelli, right?"

She smiled with pleasure. "Yes!" Taking it from him, she held the earring up. Moonlight winked off the tiny hunchbacked flute player.

"He's a storyteller, right?" He'd looked the symbol up on the Internet.

She nodded. "And a fertility god." She sighed heavily. "Richard thinks Southwestern art is tacky. It didn't matter to him that I love it. He tossed out all the Southwestern jewelry my mom and dad gave me, but I managed to save this little guy. Since I couldn't wear just one earring, I hid him, kept him as a good luck charm."

"Then he must have been working overtime."

"Why's that?"

"Because he led me straight to you." Ducking his head, he planted a kiss on her lips. "I'll be back, sweetheart. Bolt the door, okay?"

As he slipped through the open doorway, she noticed how cold it was outside. The wilderness surrounding the building was blanketed in glistening white, above which the full moon floated like an ivory crystal ball.

There was an enchanted wintry hush. One in which she could hear her own frightened heart beating, beating frantically, like a little bird beating its wings against an iron cage, desperate for freedom.

Like me, she thought, tucking the earring in her pocket. When she closed and bolted the door, Jack had already vanished into the night.

She was alone.

Long after Jack left the Visitors' Center, his kisses, his words, stayed with her, comforted her. God, he'd done so much to help her, right from the first, giving her good advice as Keoki in the chat room. Coming to New Mexico to find her. He claimed he'd even quit his job because of her. She'd kissed him. Had come close to having sex with him. So why—*why?*—hadn't she trusted him with the truth? Why hadn't she told him *everything?*

She swallowed. She didn't know why, but she couldn't tell him. Not yet. She just couldn't.

SEVEN

Jack stayed close to the log walls of the Visitors' Center, where the shadows were deepest.

He circled the log cabin and the two outbuildings, but there was no sign of Harper that he could see.

Choosing a moment when the moon's light was hidden by scudding clouds, he sprinted across the small clearing, ducking back into the cover of the shadowy pines and junipers alongside the trailhead that he and Liz had followed up to the Visitors' Center.

He kept to the side of the track, steering clear of the unmarked snow. If he walked through it, he would leave footprints as clear as signposts for Harper to follow—if he hadn't already followed the footprints they'd left the first time.

The first order of business was to make sure Harper was really out there somewhere. That they weren't flinching at shadows. It was unlikely, but there was a slim chance Harper might have missed the turn-off they'd made, and was back in Santa Fe by now. Theoretically at least, the power could have gone out on its own.

It was much more likely that Harper, armed and dangerous, was prowling around, trying to get into the Visitors' Center—or looking for a way to pry them out.

If he were Harper, and desperate, what would he do?

An icy chill sluiced down his spine.

Frowning, he halted, and turned, looked back the way he'd come. The Visitors' Center was an inky silhouette against the night.

What he saw froze him in his tracks.

With Jack gone, Liz prowled the shadowed lodge like a caged animal, gingerly cradling the Glock in her hands, desperately hoping she wouldn't need to use it.

As she paced, she considered Jack's parting question. When had she decided to leave Richard? And why had she left when she did? What had sent her into headlong flight after two long years of being trapped in a brutal marriage?

She'd told him the truth—but not the whole truth. As much as she trusted Jack, there were still things she wasn't ready to share with him. Soon, but not yet.

Remembering brought back such painful, terrible memories, such fear and negative emotions, that even now—or perhaps especially now—she couldn't bear to confront them, let alone talk about them.

Richard had beaten her the evening he caught her using his computer, always where the bruises wouldn't show, and always after making sure that every window and door in the house was shut tight. He'd screened a DVD in the master bedroom, the volume set at High to drown out her cries.

That night, one of his vicious blows had knocked her backward to the tiled floor of the bathroom. When she'd fallen, she slammed her head against the marble tub surround, and had lost consciousness for seconds—minutes, maybe even hours.

It was only then that Richard—probably frightened by her utter stillness, the spreading puddle of blood beneath her head—had stopped beating her and left the house. He was afraid he'd gone too far and killed her.

Unconscious, she had dreamed she was hiking in the Kahana Valley with the Outdoors Hawaii Club. Instead of cold tile beneath her, she'd been cradled by the warm red earth of the mountain range.

Springy ferns had cushioned her battered body. More ferns made a leafy canopy over her battered head. Sunbeams lanced through the branches of the trees, turning the scarlet blossoms of the *ohia lehua* tree to fuzzy pompoms of fire. Unseen birds called in the lovely hush, filling the dewy air with their liquid song. Along with the birdsong, the sound of several waterfalls calmed her troubled spirit. It was all so beautiful. So tranquil. A place to heal, just as Jack had said. She hadn't wanted that tranquillity to end. *Ever.*

I'm dead, she'd decided, curiously glad and unafraid. *And this is Heaven. How strange. It looks just as I imagined it!*

As she'd lain there, she'd prayed she'd died and gone to Heaven. That at last she was free of Richard, free of his rape, his violence. She prayed that the tranquillity she felt now would never leave her.

"Beam me up, Scotty!" she'd murmured. "I'm ready to go."

But no, even as she lay, hurt and bleeding, on the marble bathroom floor, drifting in and out of consciousness, she'd known she couldn't give up and die. There was something more important than her own life, something that gave her the strength to make good on her plans for escape.

EIGHT

Jack had been gone about twenty minutes when she heard furtive scratching and muffled bumps at the door they'd barricaded with the chair.

At first, she thought Jack had come back. She hurried to open the door, but was only halfway there when the blood drained from her face.

Dear God! Flames were lapping at the bottom of the weighty plank door! More flames ran up the door to flicker between the wooden rungs of the chair. Still more danced over its leather cushions. She heard a sudden loud "whoomph!" and the heavy door burst into flames.

For an instant, she was frozen in place by shock. For vital wasted seconds, her stunned mind struggled to make sense of what she was seeing. Gut instinct told her to run outside. To escape through the other door, but what would she encounter out there? A frantic Jack, and safety—or Richard, and a bullet with her name on it? He could pick her off like a duck in a shooting gallery.

A sudden urgent pounding at the other door yanked her back to her senses. She hurried to let Jack in, hesitating only long enough to ask the password.

"JFK! Open up! Hurry!" came his urgent voice from the other side.

She slid the bolt. In almost the same moment, Jack thrust past her, slamming the door behind him as he hurried through to the lunchroom. His grim expression frightened her more than the burning door.

"What happened? What's going on out there?" She hurried after him, her face stark white as he grabbed a bunch of keys from a key rack in the office. "Jack? Talk to me! What is it?"

"Harper. He's trying to burn us out!" he told her grimly, stowing the keys he'd retrieved in his pants pocket. "Come on!"

Taking the Glock from her, he grabbed her hand and pulled her after him toward the door he'd entered only moments before. "Come on! We can still get out this way! He's out there, but we don't have a choice. We'll have to keep our heads down, take our—*whoa!*"

She would never know what he'd intended to say, for in that moment, the door before them burst into flames with yet another loud "whoomph!" A sudden tremendous blast of heat surged toward them. It scorched her eyebrows, singed her bangs. She and Jack reeled away, shielding their faces with their arms.

Flames licked at both the back and front doors now! Acrid smoke, the stench of burning wood, the reek of gasoline, filled her nose and made her eyes water. Both doors were fully engulfed, as was their makeshift barricade. Its leather seat and back cushions were smoldering, melting, giving off a choking black smoke.

They were trapped between the two fires—and the Center was rapidly filling with deadly smoke and toxic fumes.

"Oh, my God! We're trapped!" She could hear the rising panic in her voice.

"No, we're not! We can get out through the skylight! Come on! Help me turn this puppy over."

"This puppy" was the wood-framed sofa. Together, both of them coughing from the thick smoke, they wrestled the eight-foot wooden sofa across the room, until it was directly below the skylight.

There, they flipped it over onto its arms so that the sofa stood straight up on its side. Its sturdy wooden crosspieces formed a serviceable ladder. She bit her lip. If Jack's plan failed, there was no other way out. They would be burned alive. The smoke made her eyes sting and tear. Her nose was running.

"Jack! Hurry!" she screamed. What was he doing? Where had he gone?

When she saw the pole in his hands, she understood immediately. They needed the hook to crank the skylight.

"Start climbing. I'll be right behind you. *Go!*" he shouted, urgently. It seemed an eternity until the skylight was opened wide enough. Cold air and oxygen rushed through the gap, making the flames leap hungrily toward them. "Hurry up!"

He held the sofa steady while she climbed up it. Crouched on its rustic wooden side, she slowly uncurled until she was standing on tiptoe, her arms outstretched for balance.

Now if she could only curl her fingers over the edge of the rafter, she could pull herself up onto it. From there, she could squirm out through the narrow skylight, to freedom.

"Get on with it, dammit!" Jack ground out. "Do it! Now!"

The commanding edge to his voice galvanized her into action. Gingerly standing, she reached up, clawed desperately for the rafter several feet above her.

Thick black smoke was already gathering in the pitch of the gable roof.

It took all of her upper-body strength to drag herself up, so that she was first sitting, then standing, on the broad wooden beam. Balanced precariously there, she took a careful sideways step, then another, like a tightrope walker, then reached above her, grasping the icy metal of the skylight's steel frame.

Jack was coming up fast below her. He reached for the rafter on which she was now standing. She risked a quick downward glance that almost proved disastrous.

Below them, the fire was rapidly spreading. Flames licked and danced over the Center's log walls. More flames flowed in liquid golden sheets up the doors and along the walls, greedily cackling and popping with witchy laughter. The thick black smoke made her eyes stream. It choked her lungs, turned her nose and throat scratchy and raw.

Shaken, she tottered, grabbing desperately for a handhold. She had to get out of here. She couldn't die, not now—not when she had so much to live for. Richard hadn't been able to kill her. Neither would his damned fire.

Anger swept away her fear. With supreme effort, she managed to hoist herself up, shoulder and arm muscles screaming, grunting with the sheer effort it took, forever grateful for a boost from Jack, crouched on the rafter below her.

"Pull up!" he urged. "Harder, dammit! You can do it!"

"I can't! It's too hard!

"You can!" he urged. "Don't let that son of a bitch win! *Pull!*"

She managed—only God knew how—to pull herself up and, finally, poked her head out through the skylight's narrow opening, greedily sucking in crisp, cold air.

With yet another supreme effort, another boost

from Jack, she squirmed through the narrow gap, and out onto the roof.

Slipping and sliding, she crawled a few feet down the pitch of the roof, then sprawled there, exhausted, her chest heaving as she tried to catch her breath.

Moments later, she began edging her way down the steep roof, which was slick with melting snow, crawling like a crab, sucking great gulps of icy air into her raw throat and lungs as she went.

Jack, much bigger and heavier than she, had a harder time getting out through the skylight. But finally he managed to squeeze his head and broad shoulders through the gap. He crawled out onto the sloping rooftop alongside her.

They were inching their way down the steep incline when a shot rang out. It clattered around the foothills. Beside her, Jack grunted. He immediately flung one arm out, flattening her against the roof.

"Keep down!" he ground out. "Stay low."

Slowly they slithered down to the eaves. A second shot tore apart the night. The sound echoed around the hills like a peal of thunder. This time, Liz felt the bullet pass between them, only inches from her cheek, then gouge a bite out of the roof.

She had never known such terror.

"Here! Take these keys. Open the sheds. The rangers' snowmobiles are in there. Go to Pecos. Get help!"

She didn't ask where he was going. She didn't have to. He had the Glock drawn even before he landed, catlike, on the ground. He was going after Richard.

Once she'd dropped safely into his arms, he jerked his head toward the sheds. "Stay low, but keep moving. Go for it!"

He gave her a sharp shove between the shoulder blades to get her going in the right direction, but she needed no second urging. Head down, she raced toward the outbuildings.

When she reached the sheds, she looked back over her shoulder. But Jack was already gone, swallowed up by the deep shadows of the pines. Using the trees as cover, he was heading toward the trailhead, in the direction from which the shots had been fired. Would she ever see him again?

She'd opened the first padlock when something on the ground caught her eye, just a few feet away. Shaking her head in disbelief, she bent and picked it up off the snowy ground, her hand trembling uncontrollably.

Knees buckling, she sank slowly to the snow as if she were praying, holding the small object crushed to her breast. An agonized wail wrenched its way up from deep inside her. A desperate sob that was carried away on the wind.

Jack would never catch up with Richard. She knew that now, just as surely as she knew where he'd gone. Knew why he'd left the Center without making sure they were both dead: He was planning the ultimate revenge on her . . .

"Nooo!" she sobbed, overwhelmed with dread,

sick to her stomach as she knelt there in the snow. "You bastard! You sick, twisted bastard! *Noooo!*"

Jack was fifteen yards from the two parked cars when he saw the SUV's headlights go on, briefly lighting several yards of the turn-off in front of it. Then the vehicle reversed, turned and peeled out onto I-25, engine roaring, tires spinning, gravel spraying. The SUV picked up speed and headed northwest, back the way they'd come.

Shit!

Jack squeezed off a shot, and knew a moment's elation as the SUV swerved violently to one side, tires screaming on the glistening icy blacktop.

He was pretty sure he'd taken out the back right tire, but he couldn't be sure. If nothing else, maybe the blown tire would slow Harper down. Give the San Miguel County police a chance to apprehend him.

Turning, he started back toward the Center, and Liz.

She was unlocking the padlock that secured the shed door when he reached her.

In the gloom, he could see nothing in the windowless shed but the gleam of metal here and there, where moonlight and the light from the burning Center struck the vehicles.

"Will you look at these little beauties!" Jack crowed. "Pecos is only two, maybe three miles from here. We can call the cops from there, let them track down Harper."

138

"He got away," she said in a wooden tone that was more statement than question.

Frowning, he turned to look at her. Where was her elation that they'd escaped death and Harper? "He did. That's right. Sorry."

Her haunted eyes searched his face. Demanded an answer. *"Where's he gone, Jack?"*

"Who cares where the hell he's gone, as long as it's miles from here."

"I care. I care very much—" Her voice broke, trailed away. Her features crumpled.

His smile faded. Concerned, he slid an arm around her shoulders. "C'mon, sweetheart. Lighten up! We'll be fine now," he reassured her. "Hey. Look at this. The key's already in the ignition! Fifteen minutes, we'll be in Pecos."

"No, Jack. I have to get back to Los Piñons," she whispered. Her voice was dead, like the scratchy rustle of fallen leaves. *"Now."*

His gut lurched. He didn't like the way she sounded. Was it shock, a reaction to their escape—or something else? "Pecos is closer, sweetheart," he insisted gently. "Los Piñons is miles from here!"

"I don't care. That's where I'm going!" she shot back. She set her jaw and marched away from him, straddling one of the snowmobiles.

"Liz? What's wrong? C'mon, sweetheart. Talk to me!"

She didn't hear him. Or if she had, she gave no response.

139

As Jack had said, the key was already in the ignition. She turned it, startled by the sudden loud growl of the two-stroke engine as it shredded the wintry night.

Over Jack's shoulder, she saw the burning Visitors' Center. It was fully engulfed now, like a huge Olympic torch that flared against the night. The fire's heat gave off so much warmth, the snow on the white-robed pines that guarded the clearing was melting, she noted absently.

"Sorry, Jack," she said huskily. "But I can't go to Pecos."

With that, she shot past him, the snowmobile's runners shushing as they skimmed the snow beneath them.

In a matter of seconds, Liz and the snowmobile were a dark blur against the shadowed mountain. One that quickly vanished between the white-robed pines.

"What the hell's your fucking problem, lady?" Jack demanded angrily. He stared after Liz, confused, the blazing Visitors' Center in the periphery of his vision, before he shrugged and threw his leg over a second snowmobile.

Dammit, he'd come almost three thousand miles to find her. She wasn't ditching him—not without a damned good explanation!

NINE

"What the hell's wrong with you?" Jack shouted over the growl of the engine as he overtook her, deliberately swerving his snowmobile across her path. She either had to stop or slam into him. In her present mood, he wouldn't want to bet on which she'd do.

Her snowmobile abruptly halted, missing him by inches.

"Get out of my way, McQuinn!"

"The hell I will! For crying out loud, what's gotten into you?"

"He's gone after her! He'll hurt her. I know him! Hurting people is what turns him on!"

"Who? Who's Harper after?"

"Kennedy," she whispered. "My baby!"

"What!"

"Yes. And Richard is paranoid! He'll think she's yours. He'll try to get at me by hurting her! She's only six months old, Jack!" she sobbed. "I've got to stop him!"

The missing piece of the puzzle dropped into place with an almost audible click.

Liz had been pregnant when she left the islands. That was what she'd meant when she said she wasn't alone anymore. There was no loser boyfriend who'd run out on her when she needed him most. But there *was* a baby, a little girl she'd named Kennedy.

"You're sure he knows?" He'd tailed Liz before breaking into her apartment, but hadn't caught on. He'd assumed the baby on her shoulder at the ice-cream parlor was her friend Trini's child.

Tears streaming down her cheeks, she nodded. "Yes! I found this back there, by the sheds. He must have dropped it when he was setting the fires. It was in K-Kennedy's c-car seat." Words and tears spilled from her.

"It" was a small pink terrycloth rabbit. One of its floppy ears was lovingly chewed and worn.

A baby. That explained the elusive fragrance in her apartment. *Baby powder!* How had he let that get by him? he wondered, wanting to kick himself.

His gut tightened into a cold, hard knot as the reality of what she was telling him slammed home. "So Harper didn't know about the baby when you left?"

"No! I hardly knew myself! I was three months pregnant before it hit me that my periods had stopped. I thought something was wrong with me—you know, because of all the—because of the beatings." A shudder ran through her. "When the pregnancy test came up positive, I was frantic! Richard didn't want children. He said if I got pregnant, he'd make me get rid of it. Besides, he was hardly father material. It wasn't only my life at stake anymore, so I did what I had to do. I left him!" Her expression tortured, she threw up her hands in frustration. "I don't have time for this! Let me through."

"Wait! Where's your baby now? Not in your apartment?"

She shook her head. "With Trini in 6A. Get out of my way, McQuinn! Let me go!"

"How much does Trini know about Richard?"

"Nothing!" Her voice broke. "*Nothing.* I was trying to get away from *you,* remember? I just told Trini that something came up. She promised to watch Kennedy until I got things sorted out."

"Okay. Here's what we do. Pecos is less than two miles from here. Your place is over twenty. If we can get to Pecos, we can stop him. He can't get far with that blow-out. Let's roll!"

She shook her head. "Wait. Pecos is in the wrong direction. No way I'm going there!"

"The direction isn't important. We can call the cops from there. Dispatch will get a couple of cruisers out to Los Piñons faster than a New York min—"

"What if they can't, Jack? What if they don't get there in time? What then? No. I can't take that chance!" she snapped. "If you won't go with me, get out of my way!" She tried to shrug his heavy hand off her shoulder. Her eyes were wild with terror.

"No," he gritted, his hand still clamped on her shoulder, his expression grim. "You need to listen up, sweetheart, and listen good. You're scared and you're not thinking straight. If you were, you'd know Pecos is your best—your *only!*—chance to head Harper off in time! Trust me, Liz. Let me help y—"

"*Trust* you? I don't even *know* you! Take your hands off me, McQuinn, I'm out of here!" She spat the words out.

When he didn't budge, she took a wild swing at him. He flicked his head aside, trapping her slender wrist in one powerful hand in the same move. "I can't let you do it, Liz. It's too far."

"It's not! Let me go!" She struggled, trying to pull free, but couldn't.

He knew he wasn't hurting her, but he also knew he couldn't let her escape him.

"Let me go, damn you!" she screamed, still trying to pull away.

"I will. Just as soon as you calm down and listen to me. Get a grip, Liz! Getting pissed off won't help Kennedy!"

She reacted as if a bucket of ice water had been dumped over her head. Immediately she stopped straining, stopped trying to break his hold. Her muscles went slack.

"There. That's better."

But the very second he released her, she snapped to life, then steered her snowmobile around his, her expression furious, her features set and hard.

"Thanks for nothing, Jack!" she yelled over her shoulder as she roared past him, the snowmobile's runners skimming over the marked trail.

She vanished into the dark line of trees without a backward glance.

"Christ!" He couldn't fault her maternal instincts, but her logic? He snorted in disgust. Her logic was seriously screwed. Given her way, she and the baby would both wind up dead.

The guts, the sheer obstinacy, the willpower that had enabled her to withstand seven years as a foster kid, then two years of abuse at Harper's hands, were rapidly crumbling in the face of sustained stress, terror, exhaustion, fear for herself and her child.

Her extreme pallor, the look in her eyes, had sent chills down his spine. She reminded him of a cornered feral cat, desperate to defend its young. A woman on the brink of complete physical and emotional breakdown.

He wanted to pull her back from the edge. To wrap his arms around her. To keep her from falling into the abyss. But first, he had to overtake her.

Swearing under his breath, he wheeled the snowmobile around, snow flying with the skidding 180° turn.

Running the snowmobile full-out, he roared after her. Like it or not, Liz was going to Pecos, even if he had to throw her over his shoulder and carry her there himself.

As he rode, he offered up a fervent prayer that they could get someone to Los Piñons in time to save her baby.

The alternative was unthinkable.

Eyes swollen almost shut, Liz rode through the shadows of the pines, junipers, and aspens, her heart aching and heavy, her stomach in knots from fear.

As she rode, her mind screened a horror show in her head. One in which her baby starred as Richard's helpless victim.

Dear God, Kennedy was so small, so precious, so helpless. And she loved her so much!

The trail before her was lit by patchy moonlight that filtered down through the tops of the snow-laden trees. Full and round, the moon patterned the pristine snow with lacy black shadows.

Here and there, slanted golden eyes shone from the dark brush like baleful lanterns. Those demon eyes were the eyes of wild creatures; of bobcats, coyotes—perhaps even wolves. Were there still timber wolves in New Mexico? she wondered, gooseflesh prickling.

Despite the hungry predators that watched her pass through their wintry domain, she gave little thought to the dangers she might encounter as a lone woman riding unarmed through the foothills, stalked by the gibbous moon. Her thoughts were too distracted, too centered on the human predator stalking her child, to consider dangers to herself, either real or imagined.

She feared her baby's father more than anything or anyone else. He was a monster that walked on two legs. Pure evil calling itself human.

Kokopelli will protect me, she told herself, fingering the silver-and-turquoise earring tucked in her pocket for comfort. *For luck.*

The flute player would watch over her. He'd keep her safe, as he'd always done. She was in his world now. A vast, unfamiliar world.

For the first time, her courage faltered. She slowed the snowmobile, uncertain whether to go on, or turn back and head for Pecos, as Jack had urged.

Turn back, a small voice niggled. *He was right! It's your only chance!*

God, what was wrong with her? Why was she so indecisive?

Her fears for Kennedy had affected her ability to think straight, had undermined her confidence. But was that nagging little voice right? Had she set herself an impossible task in choosing Los Piñons over Pecos? Was she jeopardizing her baby's life?

Oh, God, was she?

Traveling twenty miles across this treacherous terrain at night was next to impossible, she admitted belatedly, swallowing over the agony in her throat.

147

A cliff edge seen too late—a fork in the trail that led nowhere—a detour around a mountain lake—and all hope of saving Kennedy would be lost. How long would it take Richard to get back to her apartment? Forty-five minutes? Thirty? Less?

Less, surely!

She prayed the tire Jack had shot out would slow Richard down, because if not . . . She swallowed over the painful lump in her throat. If not, she didn't have a hope of getting there in time.

The full impact of her choice hit her then with the force of a battering ram, driving the breath from her lungs in an agonized wail. Her hands were icy, her stomach knotted with anxiety, terror.

Stupid! Stupid stupid stupid!

She had less than thirty minutes to warn Trini to get out. Thirty—maybe fewer—minutes to get her friend and their two kids out of the apartment, and she'd already wasted precious minutes she couldn't regain.

Oh, God, what had she done? What had she been thinking?

She'd allowed fear to get the better of common sense, of judgment. And in the process, she'd put her precious baby—as well as Trini and her baby—in harm's way! If they were killed—! Oh, God, if he killed them, their blood would be on her hands. Their deaths would be her fault.

Hers!

And Kennedy . . . oh, God, Kennedy.

Jack had been right, she thought despairingly,

sick to her stomach with guilt, heartsick with dread. He'd warned her. He'd tried to make her see that there was no way she could make it to Los Piñons before Richard did. She should have listened to him. Should have gone to Pecos!

Distracted by her dark thoughts, blinded by tears, she never saw the boulder that lay directly in her path, an inky shadow against the darkness beyond.

Heavy winter rainfalls had dislodged the massive boulder from its ancient aerie in Truchas Peak; part of a December mud- and rockslide that now littered the trails far below.

The snowmobile's runners slammed into the huge obstacle, crumpling metal. The force of the crash sent Liz over the handlebars, as if she'd been thrown from a bucking bronco.

She landed heavily on her left shoulder, grunting with pain as her collarbone took the brunt of the landing.

The momentum hurled her over the steep slope that ran alongside the heavily forested trail, spinning her end over end, like a rolling log.

She came to an abrupt halt forty feet below, her fall broken by a sapling that jarred her bones.

She huddled facedown in the snow, unconscious and unmoving. Damp and cold seeped through her jacket as she lay there, chilling her to the bone.

When she came to, her teeth were chattering. She tried to move, then discovered she hurt everywhere. Every breath she drew brought a stabbing pain in her side. *A busted rib,* part of her mind registered. Several scratches scored her face and bare hands. Warm blood trickled from them.

How long had she been unconscious? she wondered. Seconds? Minutes? Longer?

Get up, Liz! You have to get up—do it for Kennedy! a voice in her head urged.

"I can't. I can't get up. I can't do it. Not anymore. I hurt all over. And I'm so tired."

Another smaller voice whimpered, *Mommy! Help me! I need you, Mommy!*

"Kennedy? *Kennedy!*"

That tiny desperate cry in her head was her salvation.

She *had* to get up. Had to answer her daughter's plea! With every passing second, Richard was getting closer to her baby—a flesh-and-blood bogeyman! She had to stop him!

"I'm coming, baby," she sobbed, groaning with the sheer effort it took to push herself up, off her stomach, onto her palms. "Mommy's c-coming, kitten!"

Her painful shoulder, her bruised collarbone, refused to bear her weight. Gritting her teeth, almost fainting from the pain, she rolled over onto her knees, then awkwardly uncurled to stand—no easy feat on the steeply sloping hillside.

Her left arm dangled. Swollen. Useless. Throbbing. Every breath she drew was agony. She set her jaw, forced herself to toughen up. What was she? A wuss? A cry-baby? A coward?

150

Richard had done worse than this, she reminded herself sharply. She was used to pain. Immune to it. She would survive this! Do what had to be done. For Kennedy.

Oh, yes, she would, she told herself, awkwardly clambering and crawling back up the steep slope, breathing hard from the sheer effort it took to put one foot in front of the other. Inch by precious inch, she hauled and dragged her aching body back up the slope.

She would not only survive, she would get to Kennedy in time. She had to, or die trying. She didn't want to live, not without her baby.

Far below, the blacktop snaked away into the distance, a slick ebony ribbon that glistened in the moonlight.

The sight stirred embers of hope.

The snowmobile was wrecked. It lay on its side, runners in the air, its growl silenced. But her legs were unhurt, and she was a seasoned hiker. She could still climb down the steep slope to the road that followed the old Santa Fe Trail. From there, surely, she could hitch a ride to Los Piñons in a passing car. True, there weren't any headlights approaching in either direction right now, but that didn't mean there wouldn't be.

She was about to begin the long, steep climb down to the road when she heard the growl of a snowmobile coming up fast behind her.

She spun awkwardly about, and saw Jack riding toward her. Man and machine cut a sharp, black silhouette against the snow beyond: an errant knight in scarred brown leather, riding a metal charger.

Relief flooded through her. Such enormous relief, such tremendous joy, she trembled in reaction.

He'd come after her! He hadn't abandoned her. *Oh, thank God! Thank God!*

"Jack!"

He didn't lecture her. Never said "I told you so." Didn't raise his voice, or lash out with his fist in anger. He simply brought the snowmobile to a stop, and looked at her, his handsome face concerned, caring, his dark eyes intense.

Her closed heart opened, went out to him in enormous gratitude—and perhaps the first fragile stirrings of something more. Something soft and tender. A warmth and yearning she'd never expected to feel again, for any man.

"You okay?" He gently stroked a thumb across her scratched and bloodied cheek.

"I am now." Her voice was low, barely above a whisper. She wanted to say so much more, but the words wouldn't come. Later, she promised herself. Later. If she could still find the courage . . . "Why? Don't I look okay, McQuinn?" she shot back with a toss of her head. Her chin came up.

"You want an honest answer? No. You look like sh—like hell, lady!"

"Oh, yeah? Then let's get the heck out of Dodge!"

"Where are we headed? To Pecos?"

"To Pecos."

"Hop on."

She quickly swung her leg over the snowmobile, slid her good arm around Jack's waist, and pressed her cheek against the damp leather of his bomber jacket. Oh, God, he felt so solid. So strong. So—*so unshakable*. Anything seemed possible, with Jack's help. Even saving Kennedy. She wanted to stay there, safe, secure, snuggled against his back, for the rest of her life.

"Hang on!" he shouted over his shoulder, and then they were off, skimming over the snow. Fifteen, twenty, thirty, thirty-five miles an hour.

They roared north through the darkened foothills, toward the sleeping village of Pecos, two miles up the valley.

We're coming, kitten! We're coming! she sang silently. The words became a litany, a fight song she repeated over and over as the wilderness fell away beneath the snowmobile's runners.

Time passed with exquisite slowness. In an odd, almost surreal contrast, the Pecos wilderness streamed past them in a dizzying blur. In what seemed only minutes, trees and snowy foothills gave way to white pastures corralled by split-rail fences. To darkened ranches, mission ruins—even a monastery.

Finally they came to an adobe ranch house. A single lamp was burning on the porch. Like a lighthouse lantern, its golden beam shone a beacon of hope through the darkness.

Jack turned down the long rutted gravel driveway that led to the ranch house, passing beneath an arched wooden sign that read *Rancho Encantado*.

Please God, let someone be home! she prayed as Jack dismounted. He strode to the big oak Spanish door and beat on it with his fist.

Heart racing, she dismounted and hurried after him, glancing down at her watch as she went. It was 11:58. Two minutes to midnight.

Could they make it in time? Or were they already too late?

If she lived to be a hundred, Liz would never forget that wild ride through the Glorieta Pass. Nor Edouardo, the gruff rancher who answered the door in his pajamas, in response to Jack's shouts and pounding fists, his hunting rifle at the ready. Nor would she forget plump Anna, kind Anna, his Anglo wife. Anna had convinced her husband to give Jack their cell phone, so that they could call 911, then talked him into driving them to Los Piñons.

"There's a baby, Eddie," Anna urged him softly. "Do it for the baby."

Their bone-shaking journey in the bed of Ed's rusty pickup seemed to last an eternity on the snaking black road that wound through the foothills, but it was really less than twenty minutes.

Tires screamed, rubber squealed as they turned into the Los Piñons parking lot.

The first thing Liz noticed was that her car was

gone—towed, probably, by the tow truck that had passed them on their way out. The second thing was that there were several patrol cars in the lot, obviously dispatched to the scene in response to Jack's call to report a possible child kidnapping/hostage situation.

Their telltale blue lights off, the vehicles were parked some distance from Trini's darkened apartment.

Behind a barrier of yellow crime-scene tape, a crowd of Los Piñon's residents waited, wearing jackets and coats over their nightclothes. They had clearly been evacuated from their apartments in the event shots were fired. Their faces were pale and anxious in the glaring floodlights that lit the scene. Anxious, yet ghoulishly curious.

Liz's stomach clenched. She felt close to throwing up. Were Kennedy and the others inside the Alvarez's ground-floor apartment? Was Richard holding Trini and the two children hostage?

Liz tensed, ready to jump out of the truck and run through the barrier, past the cops, to 6A. Every instinct she possessed screamed at her to get her baby out of there.

"Don't even think about it," Jack growled, reading her body language correctly. He clamped a hand over her shoulder to keep her inside the moving truck. "Let the cops handle it. You try to get past them, they'll be on you like white on rice."

Two uniformed police officers, weapons drawn, legs spread, had taken up positions on either side of Trini's front door. Weapons angled skyward, they appeared to be waiting for a signal.

A third armed police officer approached Edouardo's vehicle, flagging him down as the truck barreled into the parking lot. Abruptly the rancher braked.

In the bed of the truck, Jack immediately raised his hands. He motioned Liz to do likewise.

Identifying himself as the 911 caller, he advised the officer that he was armed. His I.D. was in his right back pants pocket. He carried no sharp objects.

The officer motioned him out of the vehicle at gunpoint.

While Jack braced himself against the side of the truck, hands behind his head, legs spread apart, the cop patted him down, examined and removed the clip from his weapon, inspected his driver's license.

Afterwards, they spoke softly, casting occasional glances in Liz's direction.

"Doesn't appear anyone's inside," Jack told Liz at length, pocketing his wallet as he came over to the truck again. "But they've sent two officers around back to make sure. If Harper's holed up in there, they'll call in a SWAT team."

"He's here, all right. *Somewhere*. I can *feel* him!" She rubbed the back of her neck. God, her skin was crawling!

Hunching her shoulders, she jammed her fists deep into her pockets and looked surreptitiously around her, toward the treeline, unable to shake the disturbing sensation that Richard was nearby. That his pale eyes were tracking every move she made. Biding his time. Patiently, relentlessly waiting, watching. A spider waiting for an unsuspecting butterfly to stray into its sticky web, so that it could move in for the kill.

"He's up there. Watching us. Laughing." She jerked her head toward the treeline. "Somewhere nearby."

Jack nodded. "You're probably right. The police may have arrived about the same time he did. Hopefully, they scared him off."

"What makes you think that?"

"Officer Delgado says a San Miguel County patrol officer found a rented black SUV on the side of the road a couple of miles from here."

"When?"

"About fifteen minutes ago. The vehicle fits the description I called in, right down to the blown rear tire. They ran the plates. The vehicle was rented to a Jerome Cohen from a rental agency down in Albuquerque. No sign of the driver. Jerome is Harper's middle name, right?"

She nodded mutely, sick with fear. "Could he have come and gone, do you think?" she asked in a voice barely above a whisper. "Or could he have taken them somewhere else? Oh, God, Jack! Where is she? Where's my baby?" There was dread in the gray eyes that searched his face. Terror that they were too late.

Jack hauled her into a fierce bear hug, held her in a crushing embrace. Her body was rigid with terror in his arms. "It's okay, sweetheart. *They're okay.* Delgado says no one's been home since early this evening. A neighbor saw your friend Trini and the kids leaving right after you totaled your car. *Alone.* He spoke to them. He says Mrs. Alvarez's car is still gone."

"Really?" Dare she hope? She looked around. Trini's car wasn't in its stall. Hope began to dawn.

"The officers checked your apartment first. They found the front door closed but unlocked."

"Because I left by the balcony, remember?" she reminded him, her words muffled against his chest.

"That's right. There's a message from Trini on your answering machine."

"What message?"

"She's taken the kids to her mother's. She didn't leave any address, or any information that Harper could use to find them. So you see, they're safe. Kennedy's safe! She's with Trini's mom. You know where Trini's mom lives, right?"

Trini's mom, Mrs. Josefina Santos, had been like a mother to her, and a grandmother to Kennedy. "Yes! Oh, thank God!" Her knees buckled. She felt dizzy, so overwhelmed by relief, she would have fallen if Jack hadn't caught her.

But as his arms tightened around her, she yelped in pain.

Immediately he loosened his grip. "Hey! Are you hurt? Jeez, you weren't shot?"

"No!" She winced. "But my arm's dislocated, I think. Maybe some bruised ribs, too. No biggie."

"No biggie?" He shook his dark head. "You're going to the hospital, lady. *Right now.*"

"If you say so." She smiled wanly, too exhausted to argue with him. She didn't care where she went, or what she had to do, just as long as Kennedy was safe. Nothing mattered but Kennedy. Relief, joy sang inside her. *Kennedy was safe. Thank God! Oh, thank God! They'd made it!*

His brows lifted. "No arguing this time?"

"No arguing. I'll go anywhere you say. But first—"

"I knew it!" He grinned.

"First, I need to see her. Okay?"

His features softened. "You've got it."

"Promise?"

"Cross my heart," he swore, crossing it.

On the fringe of the jagged line of piñons and cottonwoods that climbed into the dark foothills of the Sangre de Cristos, Richard Jerome Harper was breathing heavily as he watched patrol cars maneuver around the Los Piñons parking lot like cumbersome beetles.

Those dickhead cops hadn't seen him when they showed up. He'd made damn sure of that. Just minutes after the black-and-whites arrived, a battered Ford pickup had come screeching into the parking lot.

He'd watched, recognizing the man who jumped down from the truck bed. So. She and her detective lover-boy had survived the fire. Too goddamned bad! He'd been hoping they'd be cinders by now. Cinders and ashes.

He watched McQuinn walk over to talk to one of the Santa Fe cops, his hands raised like a fucking Boy Scout. Harper snorted in disgust. Frigging cops! Everyone knew how it was with cops. Didn't matter where they came from, they stuck together.

Two other cops had taken up positions on either side of the door, weapons raised. Two more had disappeared—gone around back, he guessed, looking for him. He was laughing now.

They were assholes, all of 'em! Staking the place out, as if he'd be freaking stupid enough to walk into their trap.

Didn't they get it? He'd been chief of cardiothoracic surgery, for chrissakes! A skilled physician. A brilliant surgeon. Not some stupid dick with a big shiny badge and nothing between his ears.

His talent, his vast knowledge, his education and skill with a scalpel, had saved countless lives across the U.S. Who did they think they were looking for? A Neanderthal with the IQ of a pinto bean?

Well, the cops had bought themselves a good long wait. By the time they crawled back under the rocks they'd come out from under, he'd be across the border in Ciudad Juárez, deep in old Mexico, drinking tequila and riding some pretty little whore. . . .

Raising the hunting rifle to his eye, he looked down the infrared scope at the detective.

One by one, he trained the scope on the three cops. On his two-timing wife. On the cop who'd had his hands all over her. The cop who'd planted a friggin' baby in his woman!

All four targets were in his line of fire. He smiled to himself. He could pick 'em off, one by one, as easy as shooting tin cans at a carnival.

Pow!

Pow!

Pow pow, you two-timing whore!

But, hell! Where was the fun in that? Where was the rush? The thrill of the kill? The challenge?

Killing was only fun when you were close enough to watch it happen. To witness even the smallest detail. To see tiny beads of sweat pop from skin pores . . .

. . . pupils shrink to pinpricks from sheer terror . . .

. . . when you were close enough to savor the tears. The begging. The pleading.

To smell the stench when they lost control.

To hear hearts slow, watch eyes grow dim, as the life force drained out of them in a crimson tide.

And afterwards . . .

Aaah, afterwards there was utter silence. An uncanny silence unlike any other. Absolute. Infinite.

Nooo, without the thrill of the hunt, the stink of

fear, the desperate screams of the soon-to-be-dead, it was no fun at all. And Ricky Boy Harper was all about fun. In fact, fun was pretty much all he had left now, thanks to his cheating bitch-wife!

By running off and playing possum, Elizabeth had destroyed him.

Because of her, he was now a shadow man. Forced to lie low, like a hunted animal. An animal on the run.

The hunter had become the hunted—and that wasn't right. No, sir.

Because of her, his lofty position as chief of cardiothoracic surgery at the Kamehameha III Hospital was gone. A position he'd *earned*, goddamn her. He'd lost the bowing and scraping, the reverential looks of lesser mortals, the awe in which he'd been held. The esteem. It had vanished in the blink of an eye, all of it, just like his pretty Porsche. His prime Hawaiian real estate. His stocks and bonds. His nonliquid assets.

All he had left now was the cash he'd managed to stash in the weeks leading up to his fiery "death"—and it was all her fault. All of it! Elizabeth's—and her nosy lover's.

Did they laugh at him as they lay in bed together? Poke fun at the ease with which they'd ruined him? Brought him down? Destroyed his brilliant career, his marriage, his life?

They would pay, he swore. Maybe not today . . . maybe not tomorrow . . . but they *would* pay.

She would pay.

With her life.

Day by day. Inch by inch. One step at a time.

Slowly. Painfully.

He would play with her like a cat toying with a mouse before it became bored and bit off the head of its prey.

Drawing a cell phone from his pocket, he flipped open the cover and dialed his wife's home number with angry, stabbing fingers.

From where he hid amongst the trees, he was close enough to hear its muffled ringing in the adobe apartment building just below his hiding place.

His hand shook with fury as the robot voice of her answering machine told him to leave a message after the beep.

Oh, he'd leave a goddamned message, all right. One she'd never forget. One guaranteed to make Ms. Eliza-beth piss her pretty little drawers in terror.

Neither she, her bastard, nor her lover would ever feel safe again, he swore. No matter where they ran, or how deep they tried to bury themselves, he'd find them. And when he did, he would kill them all.

"Next time, sweet thing."

He rasped the words into the cell phone, his voice the anonymous whisper of an obscene caller.

"Catch ya'll next time, y'hear?"

TEN

Casa Paloma Hotel
Santa Fe, New Mexico
Three days later

"Do you have to leave tomorrow?"

"I do if I want to get my job back."

"Do you? Want it back, I mean?"

"No," he admitted after a moment's hesitation. "To be honest, I've been thinking about moving closer to my family."

She nodded. "Me, too." She paused, uncertain how to continue. The simplest way was to just come out and say it. "Jack, I want to thank you. We'd be dead if not for you."

"I doubt that. You're a survivor, Liz. You would have come through."

"I don't think so. Not this time." She shuddered. It had been so close. She could still taste the fear in her mouth. "Thank you, Jack. Thank you from the bottom of my heart. And thanks for dinner tonight, too." Laughing, she rolled her eyes. "It was great—even if it wasn't the Four Seasons."

"Hey. Don't go knocking our first dinner together, okay? I liked your choice of restaurants." He grinned. "Not only did we enjoy the finest cuisine Los Niños Allegros had to offer, I also had the company of two very hot young ladies," he teased, "and the best burgers and ice-cream sodas I've tasted this side of Brooklyn. In my personal opinion, that's what fine dining is all about. Fine food, great atmosphere, the best company. Am I right, sweetheart?" He tickled Kennedy under the chin. "You tell Mommy I'm right."

"Mummm," Kennedy gurgled in his arms, drooling over his shirt. "Mumm ba ba." She stuffed a handful of Jack's shirt into her mouth and gummed it, smacking her lips.

Liz laughed. "She's teething. Here. Let me take her. She gets wriggly when she's tired. Besides, you can't hold her comfortably with only one arm." Was she a little jealous at the ease with which Jack had won over her daughter? Yeah. Maybe a little.

She wasn't the only one who'd been hurt during their escape from the Visitors' Center, she'd discovered when they reached Santa Fe General's ER that night. Jack had been injured, too. He'd taken what trauma workers called a GSW—a gunshot wound—from Richard's rifle as they slithered down the roof of the Center.

The bullet had plowed into the flesh of his outer right shoulder, then exited cleanly in back without damaging so much as a muscle or a nerve, although he'd lost quite a bit of blood. She'd been so wrapped up in her own problems, she hadn't even noticed, she thought with a hefty twinge of guilt.

Her own dislocated shoulder had been treated, her collarbone and ribs taped, her scratches cleaned. They'd left the ER sporting matching his-and-her blue slings. Hers on her left arm, his on his right. *Très chic!*

But with only two good arms between them, carrying a squirming baby was a major undertaking.

"By the way, there's drool on your shirt."

"Ah. Now do you believe me?"

"About what?"

His brown eyes twinkled. "That I'm irresistible! Women drool all over me."

The corners of her mouth tilted up in a smile. "You wish! Hand over my child, McQuinn."

"No way. She's fine where she is, aren't you, sweetheart? Besides, we Kennedy namesakes gotta stick together, yeah, kitten? Right? Who's a clever girl?" He jiggled the giggling baby up and down in his good arm.

Wearing a fuzzy, pale yellow terry sleeper, complete with footsies, Liz's baby was as cute and cuddly as a teddy bear. With her inky curls, flushed pink cheeks, long-lashed gray eyes, and rosebud mouth, he'd been smitten the moment he set eyes on her.

He believed the feeling was mutual.

"Brrllhh!" Kennedy squealed. She flirted those knockout eyes at him in the coy way only six-month-old heartbreakers can. Burying her face against his chest, she kicked her little legs excitedly.

"*J.F.K.* McQuinn and *Kennedy* Harper. That's right! I didn't even think about that. Jack, if you really don't mind holding her for a bit longer, I'll call the airline and confirm the reservations my mom made."

"Go ahead. She's almost asleep anyway. She'll be out by the time you're done, won't you, kitten?" It was the nickname her mommy had given her, but it suited her.

With the drowsy baby cradled on his broad chest, Jack lowered himself to the king-size hotel bed, which was covered with a quilt in Southwestern colors. The rusty reds, pinks, oranges, and grays matched the bedside lamp bases, big Pueblo clay pots with parchment shades.

While Liz made her call, Jack patted Kennedy's bottom and crooned a lullaby, making up lyrics he'd long since forgotten while he considered the last two days.

With Richard Harper's whereabouts unknown, his farewell threats caught on tape for the authorities by Liz's answering machine, Jack had serious misgivings about leaving her and Kennedy alone or unprotected. But what choice did he have? He couldn't guard them 24/7. Life spun on, and as he'd reminded Liz, he had a life on hold in Honolulu.

Still, the odds of Richard coming back to make

good on his threats, once the manhunt went cold, were huge.

Jack had been able to convince Liz it was too risky to return to her Los Piñons apartment, or resume the life she'd been living in Santa Fe. Relocating was a step in the right direction, and better than nothing. At least in Florida, she'd have family looking out for her.

He'd checked Liz and her daughter into his hotel, then gone back to the apartment with her to help her pack.

Kennedy's clothes and diapers and Liz's belongings were now stashed in the two large zip-up bags across the room, by the window. Ditto Kennedy's stroller, carrier and new car seat. Liz's few pieces of furniture had been trucked to the local Goodwill. Since she'd owned very little, it hadn't taken long to move her out.

Yesterday, Liz had given notice to her landlord, resigned from her job in Santa Fe General's ER, forwarded her mail, then moved everything she was keeping into the Casa Paloma Hotel, fronting the central plaza, here in Santa Fe, where Jack had a room—largely unused—down the hall from hers.

Dinner tonight had been on him, but the choice of restaurant had been all hers, he recalled, smiling to himself. They had been celebrating their escape, and the long-overdue call she'd finally placed to her family in Florida.

For the past year, the Scotts had believed that the adopted daughter they loved was dead, a victim of Hawaii's lovely yet treacherous Kahana Valley.

Needless to say, Laura, Jim, and their three grown sons had been overjoyed, and totally overwhelmed, to hear that their daughter, and the infant granddaughter they had not known existed, were both very much alive and well.

After a lengthy phone call—complete with much laughter, tears, and countless explanations—further calls to the airlines had been made, and flights to Florida booked.

Liz and Kennedy would fly to Tampa in the morning. They would not be coming back to New Mexico, nor returning to Hawaii. Liz planned to raise her daughter close to the family she loved and had missed so desperately. She wanted to give Kennedy the kind of childhood she'd never had.

And while she flew to Tampa, Jack would be flying in the opposite direction, back to the islands. Back to paradise.

Right now, Jack thought, staring up at the ceiling, with the exception of seeing Kona again, the prospect of returning to Hawaii—beautiful as it was—was less appealing than having his teeth pulled.

Maybe things would have been different if they'd caught Harper and put him behind bars. As it was, he was still very much at large.

Yesterday, they'd gone to the Santa Fe Police Department to make statements about Harper's murder attempts, and explain the razed Visitors' Center.

From one of the detectives there, they'd learned that a car had been stolen from the Los Piñons parking lot moments after the police finished searching the foothills for Harper. The police believed Harper was the thief.

He had probably been somewhere close, hiding, watching from a safe distance, while the police searched the apartments. Just as Liz said.

Not normally a man given to violence—unless you counted his enjoyment of ice hockey—Jack itched to plow his fists into Harper's face. To feel bone and flesh give way beneath his knuckles. To watch him bleed. He ached to give Liz's husband a taste of his own medicine. And he would do it some day, he swore. Oh, yeah, he would teach Harper, up close and personal, how it felt to be someone's punching bag.

The vehicle stolen from the Los Piñons parking lot had been recovered the following morning, abandoned not far from the Mexican border.

Jack figured Harper was probably a fugitive down in Mexico right now—but he could just as easily have made a U-turn at the border and gone north—gone anywhere in the U.S. Money was no object for that son of a bitch.

Jack scowled. Dammit, he couldn't settle as long as Harper remained at large, a continued threat to Liz and Kennedy, despite the APBs the

Santa Fe Police Department had sent all over the country.

There was, too, the jolt of electricity that had sizzled between them at the Visitors' Center. Remembering that kiss would keep him awake nights, pondering the might-have-beens. The lost prospect of great sex—maybe more—with a beautiful woman he'd been attracted to since the first time he saw her Missing Person poster.

Had it been lust, pure and simple, jump-started by danger? he wondered. Or the start of something deeper? Something bigger than lust? Bigger, perhaps, than both of them, as the old cliché went?

Jack appeared deeply asleep when Liz hung up the phone. So did Kennedy. She clung to Jack's chest like a baby monkey, one small, pink thumb tucked into her mouth.

A wave of tenderness swept over Liz as she looked down at the sleeping pair. Tenderness for Kennedy. Tenderness for Jack, too, who looked even sexier asleep. No man should have long, thick eyelashes like his, she thought, wanting to touch them. To touch *him. Anywhere. Everywhere!*

For the umpteenth time in the past few days, heat flashed through her belly like summer lightning as she looked down at him. At the hard planes of a ruggedly handsome face, now softened by sleep.

God help her, she wanted him.

Richard was on the run. She was no longer in danger. So what else could cause those hot twists of pure lust—of desire—whenever Jack turned those sleepy bedroom eyes on her? Whenever he touched her, however innocently or indirectly.

She actually envied her daughter, safe in the circle of his strong arms.

"Done?" the sleeping man asked without opening his eyes.

Not asleep after all, the rat.

"Done," she agreed. "Our flight leaves at ten, so we should be at the Albuquerque airport around eight-thirty to clear security. We have electronic tickets waiting."

"You'll need to be up and running by six, then." He glanced at his watch. "It's almost eleven now. I should get going. Let you two get some sleep."

He'd go down to his room by way of the bar and have that stiff drink he'd promised himself. A nightcap. A double Scotch to numb the dull ache in his shoulder—and drown his sorrows.

"Will you girls have breakfast with me before you fly out?"

"We'd love to. What time is your flight?" Leaning down, Liz gently lifted Kennedy off his chest. She kissed her daughter's flushed cheek, then held her close for a good-night cuddle.

"Ten-forty-five." Jack sat up, swung his legs over the side of the bed, and ran a hand through his dark hair as Liz carried the baby over to the portable crib the hotel had supplied. "Room Service okay?"

"Sounds good to me."

"Why don't I drive you to Albuquerque afterwards? Since I'm headed that way myself."

"Thanks, Jack. That would be great." She shot him a smile that made his toes curl.

She changed Kennedy's diaper, settled her in the crib, then drew a fleecy blanket up over her. Bless her, she didn't so much as stir, even when a tiny pink thumb popped out of her mouth like a cork.

When Liz turned back to Jack, he was standing by the door. Although he was freshly shaved, and his shaggy black hair had been neatly trimmed at a local barber's, he still managed to look deliciously dark and dangerous somehow. His good hand rested on the doorknob. Clearly, he was ready to go.

Her stomach lurched at the thought of him leaving. Of never seeing him again.

Why?

Was it because Richard was still out there somewhere, armed and dangerous, and she desperately needed someone—anyone!—to watch her back? Or because she couldn't bear to say good-bye to him? To Jack, the man? Because what she felt for Jack—even if they had only known each other for a few days—went deeper than gratitude?

"I guess I'll be going," he was saying. "Anything you need before I leave?" He sounded equally reluctant to depart.

"No, nothing. You thought of everything. You've been wonderful." Just saying "Thank you" seemed so inadequate. He'd saved her life. Her daughter's life. How could words ever repay him for that?

"Before I forget, I—er—got a little something for you." He reached into his jacket and withdrew a small package wrapped in tissue.

"Oh! What is it?" She accepted the small box from him as if it were fragile crystal.

"A little farewell gift." He shrugged it off. "No big deal. Go ahead. Open it."

"You didn't have to do this, Jack. You've done so much for me already. You can't imagine." Slowly, with undisguised pleasure, she untied the ribbon, taking her time unwrapping the gift, as she always did.

The anticipation, the care she took to unwrap even the smallest package, to savor the way something was presented, were as precious to her as the gift itself. She'd been that way since she was in foster care, when getting a gift that had been chosen just for her, instead of one labeled "Girl, Age 6-8" was a rare treat. To her, the wrapping was an important part of a gift.

When she lifted the lid, a pair of silver earrings set with tiny turquoise stones winked back at her in the light. They were petroglyph earrings, almost identical to the single Kokopelli earring still tucked in her jacket pocket.

Richard had tried to destroy the originals—a gift from her father—simply because she loved them.

The single earring she'd managed to save had become a symbol of her defiance. Of her unspoken refusal to surrender to Richard's abuse. Of her independence.

In a way, the new pair was a symbol, too. One that showed she'd gone full circle from light to dark and back to light again.

She gasped in pleasure, and immediately put the earrings on, securing the posts, then turning her head from side to side so that the silver wires caught the light.

"Thank you! They're lovely, Jack! How do they look?" She tilted her head.

"Beautiful. When I saw them, I knew you had to have them. For luck," he murmured. "Have a happy life, slugger." He touched the tip of her nose. "And stay out of trouble, okay?"

He grinned, but the smile didn't quite reach his eyes, nor erase the sadness in their dark depths. He looked, she realized suddenly, the way she felt. As if there were something missing. A step still left for them to take. Words left unsaid . . .

"I'll try," she murmured, despite the tears that stung her eyes. She'd known Jack for only a short time. But somehow she felt as if she were losing an old and dear friend. Someone who would have stood beside her through thick and thin.

Her heart ached.

Was that what happened when two people spent even a brief time together under the worst circumstances?

Did danger forge a bond between them? One so

strong it wasn't easily broken? Or was it all in her head? Wishful thinking, maybe?

Let him go! a small voice urged her. *Break with the past. Start over. Start fresh.*

Tomorrow, she would begin her life all over again. She would build a new life, a good life, with Kennedy. She'd be reunited with her family. She'd find another position doing the nursing she loved. She would make new friends. And she would do it all without having to worry about what Richard said, or thought, or did, ever again. Without stressing out about whether he would be angry with her, or whether he would hurt—or even kill— her and Kennedy.

After tomorrow, Richard would have no part in her new life. Her marriage to him would be like a terrible nightmare, one only half-remembered come morning.

And once she got on that plane, Jack—like Richard—would also belong to her past. Was that what she wanted?

No! a part of her cried.

Yes! another insisted. It was too soon for a man—any man—to hold a place in her future, she argued with herself. She wasn't ready. Didn't know if she'd ever be ready.

She told herself she would wear the earrings, and every time she did, she'd remember Jack. With fondness. With gratitude. Perhaps even with daydreams about what might have been. He would be a brief but important part of her past—nothing more.

But that was easier said than done.

Reaching up, she cupped his face in her good hand. Looked up into his sexy brown eyes. Bedroom eyes.

His jaw felt like hi-grade sandpaper to her touch. So rugged, so masculine, against her own smooth skin. She gave an inward shiver. Goose bumps prickled down her spine. They could have had mind-blowing sex together . . .

"Thank you, Jack," she murmured. "For caring enough to quit your job to warn me. And for getting me out of that fire. *Everything!*" she murmured.

She went up on tiptoe, intending to kiss his cheek in final—platonic—farewell.

But as her lips hovered a hairbreadth from his, that now all-too-familiar heat sizzled through her belly. Her imagination went into overdrive.

And so, angling her head, she brushed her lips across his generous mouth instead of his cheek. Experimentally. Tentatively. Tasted lips that were firm. *Wonderful.* Boldly teased his tongue with her own.

"Mmm," she murmured on a sigh, kissing him again. "Jack? Stay here tonight. Don't go."

Her mouth uttered the words, but it was her heart that formed them.

"What?"

"Stay with me, Jack. Stay the night . . ."

Instead of letting him walk out of her life, she

took her courage in both hands, followed her instincts, and leaned toward him.

Reaching up, she curled her good hand behind his neck. Drew his dark head down to hers. Inhaled.

He smelled of soap and shampoo. Of surf and spindrift and citrus-spice aftershave. Clean, sexy, masculine smells. She clung to him, hungrily, fiercely. Tomorrow, he could leave. Go where he must. But tonight—for this single, special night— he would be hers. *Only hers.*

"I should go," he murmured, his mouth almost touching hers, his hot breath fanning her cheek. But one hand—his free hand—settled lightly on her hip. "I . . . have . . . somebody . . . waiting for me back home."

Her heart caught, faltered. But then, what had she expected? They'd known each other for such a short time, and most of that time had been spent in a chat room. What did she really know about him? He could be married. Involved. Have a half-dozen kids!

"Waiting here, you mean? In this hotel? Or back in Hawaii?" She asked the questions lightly, pretending she didn't care what he told her.

"Hawaii," he murmured, blowing very gently on her neck. She shivered. "Her name's Kona."

Kona. A Hawaiian name. Her heart plummeted. "Is she your girlfriend?" She almost choked on the word.

"What she is," he murmured, nuzzling her earlobes, her silky throat, "is blond. Blond and gorgeous."

Jealousy reared its ugly green head. "Your wife?"

His lips twitched. With his mouth just a half inch from her ear, he whispered, "My golden retriever. She's the only female in my life right now. We've been together two, almost three wonderful ye—*hey! What? What's up?*"

"Jack!" She punched his chest lightly, her laughter quickly fading as he caught her to him again.

"Come here, you," he taunted softly. He wasn't smiling. Not anymore. He was looking down at her with a dark sensual intensity that sucked all the oxygen out of the room. She swayed, feeling light-headed, breathless, and more than a little dizzy.

One night together. That was all she asked. All she wanted. One mind-blowing, steamy, sweaty night.

"So, Jack? What are you saying? Will you stay?" she asked, arching her brows, her fingers crossed.

He looked over his shoulder. Over *her* shoulders. Around the room. "You see any wild horses?" he challenged softly, those dark eyes now lit by a wicked sparkle. One eyebrow went up.

"Wild horses?" What on earth was he talking about?

"When we were at the Visitors' Center?" he prompted. "Remember?"

She laughed. Now she remembered.

"No, McQuinn, there's not a wild horse in sight," she said softly. "Nothing to k—keep you away from me." Her voice broke as she said the words.

Grabbing the front of his bomber jacket, she led him over to the king-size bed.

"Be gentle with me, okay?" he begged. "Don't hurt me."

"You idiot!" She giggled like a sixteen-year-old, too aroused, too excited to make a funny comeback.

When he sat, she pushed him over onto his back, then followed him down, laughing at his expression as she landed flat on top of him.

Didn't expect that, did you, McQuinn!

Truth was, she hadn't expected it herself. She actually felt a little tipsy, but that was unlikely on two cherry Cokes.

As seductions went, hers was clumsy, but effective.

Leaning up, off Jack's chest, she reached over and turned off the bedside lamp.

The room was immediately plunged into shadow, broken only by the amber glow of the nightlight that spilled from the adjoining bathroom.

Ducking her head, she kissed him again, longer and harder this time. Kissed him until they were both breathless and forced to come up for air.

"You didn't answer me. What about it? Will you stay, McQuinn?" she demanded finally. She searched his face.

In answer, his arms—both the good and the bad—snaked around her. In one fluid move, he swept her beneath him, so that she was now on the bottom, he on top.

He looked down at her, his voice husky as he asked, "What do *you* think, slugger? Do I look like I'm going anywhere?"

"What I think is that you cheated, McQuinn. You took off your sling!" she accused, pouting. "No fair."

"So sue me," he taunted, grinning as he ducked his head to nibble on her earlobe.

"I've got a better idea," she murmured, peeling off his bomber jacket, then tugging the shirt from his belt, single-handedly. "I'm going in, Jim . . ."

With soft laughter, her hand slid beneath layers of sweater, of cotton, to glide over his flat belly, ripped with a six-pack of muscle.

Hmm. The boy worked out!

Her hand surged up and over the smooth, warm flesh of his abs, bisected by a sparse T of hair, then across his broad chest.

His nipples were tight and hard as stones. But then, so was the ridge that rode against her belly. . . .

"Mmm-hmmm. Very nice," she whispered.

"I live to please," he murmured, grinning. "Liz, honey? Have you thought about this? Really thought, I mean?" His eyes searched her face. He wasn't smiling anymore. "If you're doing this to . . . you know, to thank me or something, there are other ways. A greeting card, maybe. Or flowers. Or how about a nice phone ca—"

"Shut up, McQuinn. Just shut up and kiss me. We don't have all night."

He rolled to her side, leaned up on one elbow, and looked down at her. In the half-light that spilled from the bathroom, she saw his grin widen as, one by one, he slowly began freeing the row of tiny diamante buttons that closed the front of her lavender silk shirt, tugging the tails from her belt.

"Always the tough cookie, huh, slugger?" he murmured as her shirt fell away, revealing the new lacy black Victoria's Secret bra beneath. Thank God she'd worn matching panties!

"Not always. I do have a . . . soft side, too, you know," she whispered throatily, talking to the top of his head as he pulled up her bra to nuzzle her bare breasts.

She moaned as his mouth closed over a nipple.

He sucked. Swirled his tongue over the nubbin of exquisitely sensitive flesh until she wanted to howl like a coyote with pleasure.

She felt the caress sizzle through her bloodstream. Become a tickly pulse between her thighs.

"You do, huh?" he murmured.

His grin did crazy things to her breathing. So did his mouth—*oh, God, that mouth!* She couldn't stand it—but at the same time, didn't want it to end.

Taking his hand in hers, she lifted it to her lips.

Kissed the well of his palm. "Oh, I do," she whispered, shivering.

He ran a fingertip down her cheek. Traced the fullness of her lips. Gently fondled one breast, then the other, circling both aureoles with his fingertip, then with his tongue, before his hand swept lower.

It came to rest at the very base of her belly. He unzipped her snug black pants, peeling them off as easily as peeling a banana.

"Show me, baby," he murmured as his hand swept down her body. Heat followed wherever he touched her. Pleasure poured through the black lace triangle like warmed honey.

He hooked two fingers beneath the narrow lacy waistband of her panties and slid them down, over her silky legs.

"Show me . . ."

She awoke in the gray hours before dawn, completely naked, enfolded by Jack's arms. Her head was on his wounded shoulder, his chin on her head.

Her body felt sleek, content, sated by the steamy pleasure they'd shared. But in the harsh light of the new day, her conscience had resurfaced. She felt torn by doubts this morning. Wracked by misgivings. Uncertainty. Second thoughts. Although, oddly, she had no regrets.

Lifting Jack's heavy arm off her chest, she squirmed out of bed and padded across the room to check on her daughter.

Still fast asleep, bless her. Liz stroked Kennedy's soft dark curls, careful not to wake her.

Going into the bathroom, she stepped into the shower and turned the faucets to FULL, determined to wash Jack out of her system. She'd had the one night she wanted. The mind-blowing sex. Today was another day. She hoped that after she'd removed from her body every trace of him, of the night they'd shared, she would be able to move on. Start over. Imagine a future in which he had no part.

But neither roaring torrents of steamy water nor scented foaming body soap could wash away a single caress, nor erase a solitary kiss.

She could remember each one, fondly recalled exactly where and how he had placed it on her body, as if each kiss, every touch, had been seared into her skin. Imprinted on her memory.

Arms above her head, she stood there, thoughts idly drifting, enjoying the pounding hot water as it sluiced down over her breasts, her abdomen and belly.

Had Jack noticed her scars as they made love? she wondered as she turned to rinse her back. He must have. The light that spilled over the bed from the adjoining bathroom had revealed almost as much as it hid.

Richard had always been very careful to hit her only where her clothing would hide the proof of his abuse. The scars from those beatings showed now as paler marks across her body, light against skin that was still faintly golden from long Florida summers.

Although she knew the scars were not her fault, and nothing to be ashamed of, it made no difference. She was ashamed of them anyway. To her, the marks symbolized her defeat at Richard's hands, her subjection.

When she'd been pregnant with Kennedy, she'd chosen a woman, Selena Garcia, as her OB-GYN. She'd cringed at the questioning looks, the empathy in Dr. Garcia's eyes when she first examined her, sensing that the physician knew exactly how she had come by her scars.

"You're about sixteen weeks pregnant," Dr. Garcia had said, stripping off her gloves when she finished examining her. "Everything looks just fine." She glanced down at the clipboard in her hand. "It says here you don't remember the date of your LMP?"

Her Last Menstrual Period. "No. I don't."

"Then let's see. You should deliver your baby around the middle of June. Is the father still in the picture?"

Their eyes had met, woman to woman. *She knows. She's been there*, Liz had thought. *She's walked in my shoes.*

"No. He's . . . dead." No lie, where she was concerned. He *was* dead to her.

"Aah." Dr. Garcia had nodded, but she'd asked no further questions nor made any further comments. "So be it."

Jack was nothing like Richard, Liz thought as she soaped her legs and feet. Signs of Richard's controlling nature had been there from the very first, although at the time, she hadn't recognized them for what they really were. Naively, she'd assumed that his possessiveness, his jealousy, were signs that he cared deeply for her.

How wrong she'd been!

As a young operating-room nurse on Dr. Harper's surgical team at Oceanside Medical Center, she'd been overwhelmed that a surgeon of his caliber had even noticed she existed.

Giddy with excitement when he asked her out, she'd ignored the warning bells that went off in her head. The alarms that said if something seemed too good to be true, it probably was. When love came in the door, common sense flew out the window, her mom was fond of saying.

Liz was flattered, and Richard had known it. She accepted his first invitation, then another and another.

"I've never met anyone like you before!" he had exclaimed a few months later over dinner at Cockatoo, a well-known and popular Miami restaurant favored by jet-setters. "I'll have to make very sure you don't get away!"

"Oh? And what exactly do you mean by that?" she asked, laughing, and delighted. Coming from Richard, such a compliment was high praise indeed. She'd been over the moon, although she'd tried to act casually.

In response, he'd drawn a small black velvet box from his pocket. Reaching across the table, he took her hand in his. "Elizabeth, will you marry me?"

There had been no mention of love, although she hadn't noticed it at the time.

She covered her mouth with her hands. "Oh, my God, Richard! Yes, I'll marry you! Yes, yes, yes!" she whispered through happy tears as he slipped the sparkling diamond solitaire onto her finger.

Her family hadn't shared her happiness. That weekend, when she told her parents that she and Richard were engaged, Laura Scott had burst into tears. Her dad quickly left the room, his Adam's apple bobbing as it did when he was upset. If Richard had had any doubts about her parents' feelings toward him, he had none after that evening.

When she recovered from her disappointment, Laura Scott had apologized. She'd explained she had nothing against Richard personally; it was just that she didn't think he and Liz were right for each other. There was the age difference, for one thing. Richard responded with tight-lipped stony silence.

Lower-keyed than his wife, Jim Scott had suggested only that the couple wait a while, to see if their feelings for each other changed. They could have a long engagement, surely? Even live together, if that was what they wanted. What was the big hurry?

But Liz wouldn't hear of a delay. Starry-eyed and eager to become Richard's bride, she'd been deaf to their pleas. Her parents would come around when they saw what a wonderful husband Richard was, how happy he made her, she just knew it! Besides, she didn't want to risk losing him. Richard had warned her more than once that he wouldn't wait forever.

Besides, why should they postpone their wedding when they loved each other so very much? Richard was everything she'd ever dreamed of in a husband. He was successful. Dedicated. Attentive. Sophisticated. A brilliant surgeon who saved countless lives every year with his knowledge and skill. She found him physically attractive, too. An Eric Roberts lookalike, he had prominent cheekbones, a square jaw, and steely, ice-blue eyes. But unlike the dark-haired actor, Richard had white-blond hair, worn cropped short, and gold-framed glasses.

His fair coloring, strict operating-room discipline, brusque manner, and lack of small talk had earned him the nickname "The Nazi" among the hospital staff. But when she was with him, Liz felt sophisticated, worldly—and oddly safe.

Was that the key to his appeal? she'd often wondered since then. Deep down inside, was she still the insecure foster kid she'd always been? Still needy little Liz, still desperately seeking security, still desperately craving a father figure? Did Richard—older, financially secure, respected by his peers—represent that security to her?

She hadn't recognized his possessiveness for what it had been: cruel attempts to alienate her from the people and places she loved. Concentrated efforts to break her will, to control her, to demolish her spirit and self-respect. Her courage and belief in herself. Her independence.

The difference between Richard and Jack was vast. Where Richard said, "You can't do this or that," Jack said, "You can do it! Go for it!"

What if Jack wanted to be with her after tonight? What if he was everything Richard had never been—what then? What if he loved her?

He had followed her, come all this way to find her, after all. Had he done it because he felt responsible for the advice he'd given her, as he claimed? Or had he been driven by something else?

And if he loved her, could she love him back as he deserved to be loved? Could she make a new relationship—any relationship—work?

She arched her head back, letting the hot water stream over her face, telling herself she had to try. Life was all about trying. About taking risks, making choices, learning from the wrong ones, building on the right ones.

Then again, perhaps a one-night stand was all Jack wanted.

She'd toweled dry before she realized she'd left her underwear and clean clothes in the other room.

Belting the white terrycloth robe the hotel had supplied, she emerged from the bathroom, wet hair in a towel turban, to find Jack on the phone with Room Service.

He hung up as she entered, a grin lighting his

handsome face. "Yo, gorgeous. I've ordered breakfast. Anything in particular you wanted?"

"Juice. Coffee. Eggs. Bacon. Hash browns. Toast—a horse—everything! I'm starving." She couldn't help the big smile that sneaked up on her, mirroring his, catching her by surprise. Blushing, she looked away, unable to meet his knowing eyes.

He grinned back. "Why am I not surprised to hear you're hungry, O insatiable one?" He frowned as if seriously considering the question, then shot her a wicked, knowing look as he stood and drew her into his arms. "Ah. Right. Now I remember. Come here, slugger." He kissed her softly on the lips. "Hmm. Good morning, beautiful. Did you sleep well?"

Is the Pope Catholic?

She lightly punched his chest. "Like a log. Hmm. 'Morning, McQuinn."

"Applesauce and rice cereal okay for Kennedy?"

"Perfect. They're her favorites."

"Hey. They don't call me Super Uncle for nothing. I asked for a high-chair, too."

"Great."

Kennedy had pulled herself up. She was now standing at the side of the crib, holding on to the bars, bouncing her little bottom as she watched them. "Mumm!"

"I think someone's hungry. Okay, Uncle Jack. Let's get this show on the road!" She turned to Kennedy, picked her up and kissed her good morn-

191

ing, then laid her down to change her diaper. "Are you hungry, kitten? Is Mommy's girl hungry?"

"'Uncle Jack,' huh?" Jack echoed, wearing a quizzical expression as he came to stand behind her.

He slid the collar of her robe down, baring one shoulder, and kissed it.

"Mmm. I could get used to that. And to this, too. To the two of us. How's about it? Interested?" He was no longer smiling, but deadly serious as his eyes locked with hers.

"In a long-distance relationship?"

"It doesn't have to be long distance. What do you say?"

She laughed softly as she lifted Kennedy into her arms. Still holding her daughter, she leaned back against Jack's chest.

His arms encircled them both.

"Talk me into it."

ELEVEN

Near Tampa, Florida
Six months later

And talk her into it he had, Liz thought as she stood on the weathered wooden boat dock that jutted into the water, watching a comical flock of pelicans as they dived for fish. Dozens of phone calls, letters, and e-mails had flown back and forth between Hawaii and Florida over the past few months.

One-year-old Kennedy rode on Liz's hip, cute as a button in a ruffled red sundress. She showed several teeth when she smiled, which was often.

"Bud! Bud!" she said, waving a chubby hand toward the pelicans.

"Yes, my clever girl. Those are birds. B-i-g birds. Can you say 'pelicans'?"

After a moment's hesitation, Kennedy shook her head from side to side, soft dark curls bouncing.

Liz laughed. Kennedy had recently discovered the attention she got from saying no.

"She said no, bless her! Will you look at her! Ohh, Grandma's girl is just as smart as a whip, isn't she?" Laura Scott exclaimed, laughing as she held out her arms to take her granddaughter. "Come to Grandma, sweetheart!"

A petite, sandy-haired woman in her late fifties who radiated energy and vitality, Laura buried her face in Kennedy's neck, kissing her noisily. The little girl squealed in delight, grabbing fistfuls of her grandmother's short hair.

"Where's Jack, honey? I thought he was off this afternoon." Laura asked Liz as she laughingly untangled herself. In her crisp white capri pants, pale pink polo shirt, and sporty white deck shoes, she looked relaxed, cool, and comfortable; an active young grandmother who bore little resemblance to the high-powered realtor she turned into each morning, dressed to the nines.

"He'll be here. He had to stop off at the company warehouse for something."

"What is it about men? They always manage to show up when either the work's done or the food's ready." Laura rolled her eyes. "How does he like his new job?"

"He says he likes it just fine. But I think he misses being a cop."

"Really? Did he put his application in?"

"Yes. But there aren't any openings for detectives in Tampa right now, so he's on a wait list."

Jack and his golden retriever had relocated to Tampa just six weeks ago. He was renting a pet-friendly condo on the beach, close to a bark-park, dividing his time between playing tourist and consulting for a major security company that operated out of Tampa. The company handled both private and commercial alarms and security surveillance systems in the area. Jack's experience as a police officer and a detective had made him a prime candidate for the job. He'd applied over the Internet, interviewed the day he arrived in Tampa, and been hired following a second interview one week later.

Liz had decided to accept the offer of her parents' rental, a beach house, for her and Kennedy to live in, on condition they let her pay rent, since they would be out a tenant. They agreed, and the new living arrangements suited both parties.

The beach house gave Liz the independence and privacy she needed, and would not have had if she'd moved back into her parents' rambling ranch house. The rent was affordable, thanks to her new job at a women's hospital nearby, and to her generous landlords. The Scotts didn't have to find a tenant, and she didn't have to go house-hunting. It was a win-win situation.

Another plus was that Richard didn't know the Scotts owned a beach house, let alone its location. That made it feel safe to her.

Living in the beach house was a dream come true for Liz. She'd always loved the weathered old place with its silvery-gray boat dock that jutted out into the gulf, a barely rippling bolt of turquoise silk this afternoon.

Small fishing boats bobbed on the water like corks. Gulls wheeled and screamed above them, hoping for a free meal. Long-legged oystercatchers waded in the tide pools.

In her teens, the beach house had been Liz's favorite summer hangout. She and her three brothers had spent endless summers fishing off the dock, boating, building bonfires at night, toasting marshmallows, doing all the things teenage kids love to do at the beach.

Now she and Kennedy came down to the dock several times a day to swim or sun themselves, or watch the antics of the comical pelicans that shared their little part of the world, along with the manatees, the sea turtles, and the inevitable tourists in search of sun and fun.

Jack joined them on weekends. He also came by several evenings a week to check on them, and, she suspected, to eat dinner. She smiled at the thought.

"Thinking about Jack?" her mother asked with a knowing look.

"Maybe," she hedged, shooting Laura a grin that said she was right.

"I thought so. You always get that look on your face. Can't say I blame you, though. Your Jack's quite a guy." She patted Liz's arm. "Good for you, honey. It's about time your luck changed for the better."

"You do like him, then?"

"Of course! What's not to like? He's a wonderful man. A good-looking one, too. And I especially like the way he lets you be you and doesn't try to change you. Not like . . ." She didn't finish her comment, but they both knew whom she was going to name.

Her mother had never made a secret of her feelings about Richard. She'd cried throughout their wedding, and the wedding supper at a gourmet restaurant that followed. By contrast, Liz had been oblivious, deliriously happy, as the white stretch limousine swept them away to the airport on their honeymoon in Barbados.

Richard made her feel like Cinderella, swept away by her handsome Prince Charming. Her euphoria had been short-lived, however. The honeymoon had soon been over, in every sense of the word.

"When I think of what you went through with him . . . And having this precious baby all alone!" Laura shook her head, her eyes filling with tears. "Sorry. It's the hormones," she excused herself.

"How about Daddy and the boys? Do they like Jack?" It was important to her that the other four men in her life liked him. To date, they'd proven themselves pretty good judges of character.

"Oh, yes! They liked him from the first time we met him in Hawaii. He was so busy then, but he still took the time to keep us informed, and really seemed to care about us and what happened. You weren't just a case number to him, God bless him. For that, if nothing else, I think we'll always love Jack."

They walked back to the house together in companionable silence.

Inside, the beach house was a cool and shady refuge from the brilliant afternoon sunshine outdoors. Out there, the dazzling light reflected off the water as if it were a mirror. In here, that same light was diffused, muted, and softened by long, gauzy white sheers that hung alongside the windows and French doors.

The filmy curtains billowed in the light breeze that blew off the gulf, or fluttered in the current of the ceiling fans. They reminded Liz of sailing ships, their full sails bellied by the wind. A ship like the model sailing vessel on the mantel above the fieldstone fireplace. Dad's handiwork, she remembered with a smile. He'd spent hours building it, and she'd helped him.

Every room in the small house echoed the beach/nautical theme, with floors and furnishings of bleached or pickled wood, and walls painted either white or gray-blue. Splashes of navy blue, lemon-yellow, or sand were in the pillows and other accessories. The darker accent colors added punch to the color scheme.

The coffee table also contributed to the nautical theme. Made of bleached pine, the piece had rope glued to its surface in swirling patterns. The fanciful knotted designs were protected by a thick layer of beveled glass. The table reminded Liz of the "Sailors' Valentines" of shells and scrimshaw that she'd seen at the whaling museum in Hawaii.

In the center of the coffee table was a large pelican of light-colored wood. The piece, originally a doorstop, had been carved by a local woodcarver from a heavy block of driftwood. "Pelican Pete," she'd named the bird when she first saw it. The name had stuck.

The only room she'd changed since she and Kennedy moved in was Kennedy's room, which Liz and her mom had painted and redecorated together. Kennedy's nursery was their first project since her return to the Scott fold.

They had painted and stenciled an ocean mural on the walls: underwater scenes in wonderful watery greens and a rainbow of blues that featured colorful tropical fish, giant seashells, bubbles, sea creatures, and seaweed. All of the mermaids had long, flowing black hair, like Kennedy. Liz had gone back to her original black hair coloring, too, since leaving New Mexico, figuring a fresh start and a fresh identity went hand in hand.

While her mom sat cross-legged on the braided oval rug she'd spread over the bleached pine floors, and played baby games with Kennedy, Liz went into the spacious kitchen to start dinner.

Choosing vegetables from the refrigerator bin, she began scraping or chopping red and green peppers, carrots, onions, broccoli florets, mushrooms, and Chinese pea pods. As she worked, she thought about Jack.

Thinking about him was becoming something of a habit, but a good one, she decided, smiling to herself.

She loved what was happening between them. The way their relationship was deepening, growing. The fun they had together, both in bed and out of it. Her smile deepened. She'd never dreamed that sex could be so steamy, yet both fun and funny, until she met Jack. She also loved the way he was with Kennedy. His patience, his gentleness.

In the months since she'd left New Mexico, she'd had plenty of time to think about things. She'd come to realize just what caliber of man Jack was. A man's man, yes, but a *real* man in every sense of the word. Kind. Dependable. Strong in ways that had nothing to do with muscle and everything to do with intelligence and inner strength.

He was someone she could both look up to and consider her equal. Someone, if truth were known, she could share her life with. Have more children with. Grow old with.

He'd held back the first time they slept together in Santa Fe, hiding his desire for her, concealing his true feelings in laughter and gentle teasing. She knew that now. She also knew why.

He hadn't wanted to pressure or rush her into having sex with him, not after the sexual and physical abuse she'd endured at Richard's hands. Nor had he wanted to take advantage of her gratitude, or the relief that followed her escape.

And so he'd let her take the initiative—all of it, she recalled, blushing as she remembered that night. Remembered the way she'd led him to the bed, like a lamb to the slaughter. The way she'd pounced on him.

She sighed. She certainly hadn't needed much encouragement! The chemistry between them had been pretty powerful, hot and heavy right from the start.

Oh, he'd wanted her—there was no doubt in her mind about that, not after the night of steamy lovemaking they'd shared—but he'd been prepared to wait. To have her on *her* terms rather than his, and for that, she was grateful.

By not putting the moves on her until she'd made it very clear she was interested, he'd allowed her the freedom to decide just how far and how fast their relationship would proceed. She'd taken control of the situation, and of her body, something Richard had never permitted.

Controlling her, using her, had been everything to her soon-to-be ex-husband, she recalled bitterly. He'd never considered her pleasure important, or even necessary, although he'd forced her to pretend she enjoyed his lovemaking.

With Jack, she'd been comfortable with her body for the first time in her life, discovering a level of sexuality buried inside her that she'd been unaware of before, and a man with whom she was not afraid to be deeply sensual.

Jack could turn her on with a look, a loaded glance, a wicked gleam from those sleepy bedroom eyes. She could tell him her deepest desires, what gave her pleasure and what didn't, knowing he would never condemn or judge her for it. Giving her pleasure seemed to heighten and sharpen his own—

"Lord! Look at the time! I really should be going," Laura declared, breaking into Liz's thoughts as she came into the kitchen. She carried her coffee cup over to the sink and rinsed it under the faucet.

"I told myself I wouldn't stay here all afternoon, but here I am again! I just can't seem to stay away from you two. You and Jack are still having the barbecue this weekend, right?"

"Of course. I missed meeting Jimmy's wife by being away when they got married. No way I'm missing the chance to meet Rob's latest! What's she like?"

"Sweet. Quiet. I've only met her twice, but I like the girl. I think Maria's been good for Rob. You know how crazy he can be! She balances his wild side. By the way, I'm bringing potato salad and fried chicken." She gathered up her purse and car keys from the coffee table. "Anything else you'll need, honey?"

"I don't think so. If there is, I'll call you. I can't

wait!" She grinned. "Why the hurry, anyway? Don't tell me Dad has you on a curfew?"

"Not him! You know your father better than that. No, we're having dinner with some friends tonight. We have reservations at The Terraces, so I wanted to get my hair trimmed on the way home. That's all."

"The Terraces?" Liz rolled her eyes. "La de da! That sounds like fun—and expensive. Which friends?"

"Peggy and Mike Weber. You remember them? Mike works with your father. Peggy's a schoolteacher."

"Oh, those two. Right."

"They just came back from an Alaskan cruise. After dinner, they'll bring out their vacation photos, just like last year. But this time, Dad and I are ready for 'em!" There was a mischievous gleam in her green eyes.

"Oh?"

"Yes. We have loads of pictures of you and Kennedy to show off! Those poor things won't know what hit them." She laughed in delight. "They don't have any grandkids yet."

She said it in such pityingly smug tones, Liz had to smile. Her mom and dad had been ecstatic to learn they had a granddaughter. Their only regret was that they hadn't been there for Liz's pregnancy or Kennedy's birth.

"Say bye-bye, sugar. Give Grandma a big kiss.

Mmm. I love you, love bug. 'Bye, honey. Love you, too." She cupped Liz's face and kissed her cheek, brushing a strand of dark hair back.

"Oh, it's so wonderful to have you back!" Her eyes filled with tears. "I can't tell you how awful it was when you disappeared. How much I missed you. I just couldn't believe you were gone. That I'd never see you again. I have to keep pinching myself to prove you're really here."

"It's good to be back, Mom. You have no idea how great it feels—or how much I missed you guys. I love you, too. Wave bye-bye to Grandma, kitten. Say bye-bye!"

From the doorway, Liz watched as her mother reversed down the short drive in her gold Camry, both of them waving as she left.

"Ba ba?" Kennedy asked, gray eyes shining as she peered up into Liz's face. She opened and closed her chubby little fist—her way of waving. "Ba ba?"

"That's right, honey. Grandma's gone bye-bye."

Liz had just added the shrimp to the stir-fried vegetables when a dark figure filled the screen door, blocking out the light.

As a shadow fell across her, Liz glanced up. She cried out, dropping the knife with a clatter. Her hand flew to her pounding heart.

The brilliant light outside silhouetted a tall, broad-shouldered man, yet threw his features into inky blackness.

Without taking her eyes off the screen door, Liz palmed her chopping knife in one hand, and pulled Kennedy closer to her legs with the other. Thank God, the height of the pass-through hid her little daughter from the person at the door.

"Jack? There's someone at the door!" she called loudly, startled by the quaver in her voice.

She hoped the man would think someone else was at home. That she wasn't alone.

"Yeah. *Me!*" came a familiar voice from the doorway. "Were you expecting someone else?"

"Oh, my God, Jack! You scared me! Next time, say something. Don't just—*stand* there," she scolded, badly rattled. "You came this close to being . . . to being . . ."

Speechless, shaking her head, she held up the small knife.

"Peeled? Julienned?" He winced. "Ouch!"

"That's not funny, Jack!" she snapped.

"Sorry, slugger. Didn't mean to scare you. But from now on, keep this screen door locked. Okay?" Jack urged as he came inside.

Kona padded at his heels, her tongue lolling, her furry tail waving to and fro. She swiped her long pink tongue over Kennedy's face by way of greeting.

The baby squealed and grabbed for a fistful of red-blond fur. "Dog! Dog!"

Jack wrapped his arms around Liz's shoulders and kissed her. "How's my girl? Hey, are you okay? I didn't mean to scare you, baby. Sorry."

"Everything's great—now." She punched his chest. "How about you?"

"Pretty good. Except that I missed you," he murmured, kissing her again. "And I missed you, too, little slugger," he added, bending down to kiss Kennedy.

She had pulled herself up and was now clinging to his pants legs. She'd be walking soon, he thought as he picked her up.

"Something smells good. What is it?" With his free hand, he grabbed a spoon and tried to steal a mouthful of stir-fry from the wok.

She swatted him away. "What do you mean, what is it? It's a shrimp stir-fry, And no, it's not ready yet. I'm waiting for the rice. Go get a cold one from the fridge and kick back."

"Ouch! You're twisting my arm. C'mon, kitten. Your mom's trying to get rid of us. If she doesn't feed us soon, Uncle Jack won't give her the present he bought her." He carried Kennedy outside, headed toward the boat dock.

"What present?" Liz called after him, curious. "Jack? What present?"

They ate dinner seated opposite each other at a weathered table on the small screened-in patio, a fat candle flickering between them as they enjoyed the sunset and the tasty shrimp stir-fry she'd cooked.

Lightly seasoned with fresh ginger, garlic, and soy sauce, it was an island recipe she served with fluffy rice and a good California Chardonnay.

The "present" Jack had brought her, Liz discovered after dinner, was a set of motion-activated floodlights—security lights that Jack intended to install for her at the rear of the beach house. They would illuminate the patio, and the shrubbery and bushes in the small garden behind the house, as well as the sandy area that led down to the boat dock. Places where, she suspected, Jack thought potential intruders might hide.

He talked at some length about those possible intruders, giving her a sales pitch that sounded as if it came straight from one of his security consultations. But she knew that at the heart of all the talking was his very real concern about Richard finding her, and she loved him for it.

"Gee, you really know how to impress a gal, Jack," she joked, eyeing the bulky light kit. "Wine, candlelight, a breathtaking sunset—and to top it all off, these lovely—um—huge security lights! So romantic!"

She fluttered her lashes.

"What can I say? Size is everything," he said with a wicked grin.

"But I have bad news, I'm afraid. You can't install these lights in back of the house. Not this house anyway. There's a city ordinance against it."

He stared at her in frank disbelief. "Yeah, right."

"No, really. There is. Lights that are visible from the beach at night aren't allowed in this area from May through October. That's hatchling season. You know—turtle hatchlings?"

"*Turtles?* This is a bad joke, right?" He looked at her as if he were waiting for a punch line.

"No, it's not. Apparently, when baby turtles hatch from their eggs, the first thing they do is head toward the brightest light they can see.

"Before electric lighting came along, that would have been the full moon, shining on the ocean at night. The hatchlings scurried into the sea, toward it, and were safe. Those that didn't get eaten by something bigger than they, survived to become grown-up turtles who bred and had their own hatchlings." She laughed at his bemused expression.

"But nowadays, turtle hatchlings are more attracted to security lights in the homes along the beaches, apparently, than to moonlight shining on water. So it's illegal to put lights back here that may confuse them."

"My ass! You're making this up!"

"No, city boy. I'm not. You can check, if you don't believe me."

"Are you serious? You *are* serious, aren't you?" Jack looked incredulous. And annoyed.

"Very. Each year, thousands of turtle hatchlings follow security lights inland, and end up getting run over, or eaten by dogs, or whatever. Turtles—especially the loggerheads—are on the list of endangered animals, you know. So no lights allowed." She shrugged. "Sorry."

He thought for a moment. "Okay. I'll tell you what. I'll install the lights, and you can turn them on from . . . what's left? November to April," he insisted. "Deal?"

She looked at the stern set of his mouth, at the stubborn granite of his jaw, and knew there would be no arguing with him, not on this subject.

His closed look said the floodlights would go in whether she liked it or not, turtles or no turtles. And, if she were completely honest with herself, despite her concern for the endangered species, it was reassuring to hear he was looking out for her safety.

"Deal. Thanks, Jack." She planted a smacking kiss on his cheek. "I must say, security lights are the most . . . unusual present I've ever had. Very sexy."

Jack grinned. "Tell me about it! Do I know how to romance a girl, or what, huh? Huh? So, beautiful? You wanna go to bed and fool around?"

Liz shot him a sexy smile. "Maybe." Kennedy had already been fed, bathed, and put to bed for the night. She would sleep like a log until six tomorrow morning. They had hours to themselves.

"You can . . . you know . . . show me how grateful you are for the lights." He waggled his dark brows at her, looking suitably lecherous. "Maybe I'll let you have your way with me. You know— commit unspeakable acts on my body?"

"Unspeakable, huh? Pervert! I thought you'd never ask," Liz said with a giggle, dropping onto his lap and curling both arms around his neck.

Both of them burst out laughing as Kona shoved a cold, wet nose between them.

"Down, Kona," Jack commanded. "That *was* Kona and not you, right?"

"Right. My nose was the warm, dry one."

"Ah! Thought I recognized it."

The dog retreated to the welcome mat by the screen door, looking crushed.

The retriever was protective of Kennedy. She didn't mind Liz, but could be sulky when she and Jack hugged or cuddled each other.

"Poor Kona," Liz said sympathetically. "It must be so hard on her, having to share you with me. She's used to having you all to herself."

"She'll learn. Lucky for both of you, there's enough of me to go around! Care to join me in the shower? I'm a certified black-belt in naked back-scrubbing."

"A black belt, huh? I'm impressed. Okay! Last one in cleans the shower!" She was already stripping as she leaped off his lap and made a mad dash for the bathroom, flinging her yellow tank top over her shoulder. Her bra followed.

They staggered out of the stinging shower twenty minutes later, scrubbing bathroom tiles the last thing on their minds.

Jack strode across the master bedroom, naked. Liz—equally naked—was straddling his flanks, her bare legs locked around him, his arms supporting her weight.

They were still kissing, tongues touching, as they tumbled to the bed.

She fell back, pulling him down after her, her hair a skein of damp silk across the pillow, her eyes closed.

Long lashes trembled on her cheeks like dark butterflies as he kissed her. Kissed lips that were cherry red, swollen, moist. Her nipples were flushed a deep rosy pink, cresting her high, firm breasts as he fed on them. And her thighs . . .

He groaned and slipped his hand between them. Slid one finger deep inside her. Felt her heat.

"You're so tight, baby. So wet. You drive me wild," he growled, his eyes dark and intense with desire as he looked down at her. "Out of my mind."

"Hurry," she whispered thickly, rocking her head from side to side. Her breath caught on a sob. "Oh, God! I need you, Jack! I want you so much! Hurry!"

Leaning up, Jack reached for a foil packet on the wicker nightstand, praying he would last long enough to roll on a condom. To deliver what she needed.

Moments later, he was buried inside her, her legs spread high and wide, kissing her deep and hard as he drove into her silky heat. "Oh, baby. Ohh, baby!"

Her hips lifted to meet his powerful thrusts, rising and falling in a dance as old as time. Both of them moving to the same urgent beat.

Every thrust brought them closer to that mind-blowing explosion. To that moment of pure sensation. To a climax that was almost too fierce, too intense, for pleasure.

The sound of their heavy breathing, the slap of flesh against flesh, filled the room. Erotic, intimate sounds that only added to their pleasure.

When the dam burst, it flooded her senses with scalding white light.

She dug her nails into his back and cried out, holding on to him for dear life as the orgasm rippled through her, wave upon wave of pleasure. Her body tightened around him, her muscles like fingers, stroking, squeezing, drawing him deeper, past the point of no return.

"Aaaah, baby!" he growled as the unbearable tension broke. Pleasure jolted through him like lightning.

She cried out, her body arching beneath his, his name torn from her like a prayer. An exultation. "Aah! Yes! Oh, Jack! *Jack!*"

In the calm that followed the storm, he rolled to her side and hauled her into his arms. Both of them were breathing heavily.

They lay there, bodies touching, her damp head cradled on his broad chest. Their fingers were laced, their legs tangled in the rumpled sheets.

As the moments passed, their heavy breathing slowed to normal.

"Jack?" she asked at length, her voice sounding too loud, too husky in the shadowed silence. A silence underscored by the rhythmic splash of the ocean as it lapped against the shore beyond their bedroom window. "Are you sleeping?"

"No. I think I'm dead. You killed me."

For once, she didn't laugh.

"I just wanted you to know something."

"What?"

"I love you, Jack."

He rolled toward her, drew her closer. Leaning up on one elbow, he kissed the tip of her nose. "I love you, too, sweetheart. Never ever doubt it. *I love you, too.*"

TWELVE

Life is good, Laura Scott thought with anticipation as she locked her car with the remote and walked across the parking lot, her navy heels clicking smartly.

A warm breeze ruffled her short, sandy hair and played with the trailing ends of her long, navy-and-white silk scarf as she headed toward the Gulf Shores Realty offices at the corner of the shopping center.

Her noon showing had gone well. Her clients, a retired British couple, had loved the place she'd shown them. They'd asked her to write up an offer immediately. It was a good offer, too—one which she was optimistic would immediately be snapped up by the sellers, who were highly motivated.

If the sale went ahead as planned, the commission would once again make her the year's top realtor for Gulf Shores Realty. Not a bad record, considering that a career in real estate had been her second choice.

Ten years ago, when Steve, the youngest of her three sons, left home for college, she'd found herself an empty-nester with too much time on her hands, her enjoyment of being a mom no longer satisfied with her three boys grown and gone. None of them needed her anymore—or at least, none of them needed her constant attention.

She and Jim had been considering becoming foster parents ever since the boys were in high school. It was time, they'd decided, to apply in earnest, before they were considered too old.

They'd filled out the necessary applications, been interviewed by social workers, and had attended the required classes in child care.

But after a year went by without their being assigned a child to foster, Laura had come to think it was not meant to be. She decided to go back to school herself.

She'd enrolled in a real-estate class, and been surprised by how much she enjoyed it. Within the year, she'd passed her licensing exam and was getting ready to rejoin the workforce—this time as a brand-new realtor with Gulf Shores Realty. She could hardly wait for her first day with the company.

With three kids now attending college, her commissions would help pay the boys' tuition bills, and stretch the college fund she and Jim had set aside for their education.

Having a job would also give her some independence, and the opportunity to meet people. She wouldn't sell houses, she told herself; she'd sell *homes*. It was a personal creed she would live by.

But the very same week that she was scheduled to start her new job, they'd received a long-awaited letter from the Florida Foster Care System.

Their application to become foster parents to an older child had been approved. She and Jim would be meeting their foster daughter, thirteen-year-old Elizabeth Anne Emmerson within the week.

Laura had been faced with a difficult choice. Should she pursue her new career and forget being a foster mother? Quit her job to become a full-time mother again? Or try her hand at doing both?

Since Elizabeth was an older child, and would be in school during her working hours, Laura had opted to do both.

To her relief, everything had worked out perfectly.

Despite her work schedule, she'd had ample time to lavish on the shy, awkward, but often defiant thirteen-year-old Elizabeth. Time to give her the love and attention she so desperately needed. To work with her, help her overcome her problems. To introduce her, little by little, to her new family—one that had quickly come to love her.

Adopting Liz the following year had been the icing on the cake.

At last, she and Jim had the daughter they'd always wanted! A daughter they'd grown to love and cherish as deeply as they loved their three boys.

Laura bit her lip, blinked back tears. Believing

their precious daughter missing, presumed dead, had been the darkest moment of her—their—lives. Just thinking about it now, after the fact, still upset her terribly.

Could she have prevented it from happening? Was there something more she could have—should have—done, that would have increased Liz's self-esteem, her self-confidence, both of which would have protected her against an abusive, egotistical jerk like Dr. Richard Harper? Could she and Jim have done more to keep her from marrying him in the first place?

When the letters and phone calls stopped coming from Liz in the months leading up to her disappearance, Laura had known something was very wrong. Liz would never have stopped writing or calling her family, not of her own free will. Call it mother's intuition, but Laura had been convinced that something terrible was happening to her daughter—and that her son-in-law was probably responsible.

To her surprise, Jim had agreed one hundred percent.

They'd been making preparations to fly out to Hawaii to see Liz, to find out what was going on, and why she hadn't responded to their letters or calls, when they received the call from the Honolulu Police Department, telling them that their daughter was missing.

That call had turned their lives into a living hell. . . .

* * *

"Oh, Laura, good! You're back early. Please hold, sir. Mrs. Scott is back in the office." Maggie, the receptionist, covered the receiver to speak privately to Laura. "There's a Robert Shaw for you on line two."

Laura nodded. "Thank you, Maggie."

"Good afternoon, Mr. Shaw. This is Laura Scott," she began, taking a seat at her desk. She opened her appointment calendar. "How may I help you?"

The well-spoken caller gave her the MLS number of the property he was interested in, and asked if it was still available.

When she hung up the phone minutes later, Laura had the pleasant tingle of anticipation and excitement that she felt before a prospective sale.

The only thing she wasn't too happy about was that this client had requested a seven-o'clock showing. She glanced at her watch. It was three now. She'd give Jim a call. Let him know she would be home late, so he wouldn't worry. There was plenty of paperwork to keep her busy until the showing.

The sun was already going down as Laura, looking smart in her lightweight French navy suit and navy heels, slid behind the wheel of her sporty gold Camry.

She quickly drove away from the real-estate office in the small mall, winding her way through the side streets as she headed for the luxurious beach house where she was scheduled to meet her prospective client, Robert Shaw, and his wife.

The long, lonely road she finally turned onto was practically deserted, but familiar to her. She'd sold several expensive older homes in the same general area. The house she was showing was a beautiful place, but it needed a little work. The previous owner had died over a year before, and the house had stood empty since then, waiting for the right buyer. Perhaps Robert Shaw was the one.

Swampland and thick vegetation grew along either side of the road. Deep drainage ditches full of dirty water also flanked it.

She hummed along with the radio as she drove, listening to the "oldies" and thinking about dinner the evening before at the Terraces.

It had been such fun. After a delicious gourmet meal, featuring the seafood for which the Terraces' chef was famous, Peggy and Mike Weber had produced their vacation pics as they lingered over their after-dinner coffee. They had been green with envy when she'd shown them their darling granddaughter's photos.

It was as if the nightmare of Liz's disappearance had happened to someone else, in another lifetime, instead of to her, Jim, and the boys.

Sitting there, sipping wine, watching Jim's face, so happy and relaxed in the candlelight, she'd felt as if they'd finally woken up after a long and terrifying nightmare, except that the nightmare had not been completely forgotten. It never would be.

If she closed her eyes, she could still remember the loud whirring sound made by the search helicopters' blades as they hovered over the densely vegetated valley. The way the bushes and shrubs had bent low to the ground, as if blown sideways by a hurricane.

The way the eyes of the firemen, police officers, and civilian search parties had slid away from her questioning when they emerged from the valley without her daughter.

Such agony had filled her chest when, after ten long, heartbreaking days, the search had been called off, and she'd believed Liz lost forever.

She had not been able to protect her.

She had failed her dear sweet girl, the streetwise daughter she'd fostered and come to love with all her heart.

When they'd confronted Richard at the Honolulu Police Department later that day, his eyes had been pure ice, his expression cold, closed, unreadable.

A shiver had run down her spine. Not for the first time, an unspeakable thought had entered her head. *Was Richard capable of killing their daughter?*

Her son-in-law hadn't even bothered to be at the command center in the valley's small dirt parking lot each day, waiting for news, with the rest of the family. Nor had he pitched in to help the search parties find his beautiful missing wife, that heartless son of a bitch.

By way of explanation, he'd said he preferred to leave the job of searching to the professionals, who presumably knew what they were doing, whereas he didn't.

Later that same night, she remembered voicing her deepest, darkest fear. She'd cried and asked Jim as they tossed sleeplessly in their beds at a Honolulu hotel if he thought Richard was capable of murdering Liz.

Her own fear, horror, and dread had been reflected in Jim's eyes as he nodded that he did.

After hearing Liz's account of what had transpired in Hawaii, then in New Mexico, and Jack's terse descriptions of the heinous crimes the authorities believed Harper had committed, she'd understood all too well what kind of hell her daughter had endured. What kind of man she'd married.

Not a man at all, but an evil unfeeling monster.

While ruminating on all this, Laura happened to glance up in her rearview mirror.

Her eyes widened in surprise.

There was another car following her on the empty road. A heavy, dark-colored luxury car. A Lincoln, perhaps? The prospective buyer of the house she was going to show, probably. Since she'd never met the man, and didn't know what model car he drove, she couldn't be sure.

Her lips pursed. Buyer or not, he was a lousy driver. He followed way too close for her comfort.

Laura stepped on the gas and the Camry shot forward in a streak of gold. Sixty. Seventy miles an hour. Far too fast, really, for such a narrow road, but what choice did she have? If she went any slower, the car behind would slam into her.

When had that other car begun following her, anyway? she wondered. She'd been so deep in thought, she hadn't even noticed.

Her unease deepened as the car behind her sped up, again dogging her tail.

She wished now that she'd taken Jim's advice and refused to give such a late showing. But the client, an Orlando businessman, he said, had said he was relocating to the area and desperately needed to find a suitable home for his family before the month's end.

He'd begged her to show him the property tonight, claiming he'd seen it featured on the Gulf Shores Realty site, and believed it was the fixerupper he was looking for. He didn't want to wait. There was a chance somebody else would make an acceptable offer, or snap it up at the asking price before he saw it.

He could drive down from Orlando as soon as he finished work that afternoon, but wouldn't be able to meet her any earlier than seven. He'd been so apologetic, and had sounded so very nice, she'd shelved her misgivings and agreed to make an exception just this once. She'd hoped he would take a quick look at the house, then lea—

Dammit! What in the world was the car behind her doing now?

Was he trying to run her off the road?

Annoyance—unease—became true fear as the heavier car suddenly pulled around her. It shot forward. At first, she thought he intended to overtake her, and heaved a sigh of relief.

But he didn't overtake. He slowed down, stayed right alongside her—the side of his vehicle so close to hers, it was a miracle he didn't scrape her Camry's sides.

More furious than frightened now, Laura hit the horn with the heel of her hand, looking sideways at the other driver and yelling as the horn blared.

"Pull over, you damned idiot!" she screamed. She couldn't see the driver through his heavily tinted windows. "You almost ran me off the road! Are you crazy?"

Despite her shouts, the other car kept pace with hers.

A dangerous curve lay ahead. She swallowed, her mouth suddenly dry. She had to block out the other car. To concentrate on her driving, on keeping the Camry squarely on the road, or she'd end up in the muddy drainage ditch.

The other car continued to dog her.

She tried falling back, tried speeding up, but nothing worked.

"Goddammit!" she muttered. There was no doubt whatsoever left in her mind now. This was not a case of reckless driving. Nor was it accidental.

The other driver was trying to force her off the road!

A chill swept down her spine.

He was trying to kill her!

Her heart pounded like a jackhammer as they roared, neck and neck, toward the mean curve, like dragsters locked in a deadly race for a prize.

Then suddenly the other driver yanked his steering wheel hard to the right. His car veered sharply in her direction, crowding her over, onto the ragged right shoulder, where tarmac gave way to weeds and dirt, and a deep drainage ditch.

She fought to control her vehicle, but the other driver did it again, this time giving the far lighter Camry a hefty nudge.

The maneuver sent her skidding toward the drainage ditch, out of control.

Laura screamed.

Metal shrieked as it ground against metal. Sparks showered. Tires squealed, rubber burned as the heavier car bulldozed into her Camry's side, hurling her headfirst against the window, pushing her off the road.

Her outside wheels lost the shoulder, spun on air, then abruptly dropped. The rest of the car followed.

The sudden violent drop of the entire right side tipped the Camry over, onto the passenger's side door.

The vehicle made another half roll, then slipped sideways down the ditch's muddy banks.

It settled, hood down, in the drainage ditch, window-deep in swamp water.

Upside down, awkwardly suspended by her safety harness, Laura scrambled desperately to unlock her seat belt.

It would not release.

Screaming, she clawed at the window, her perfectly manicured nails breaking as she stabbed at buttons, desperately tried to roll down power windows. To open the door. The electrical system didn't respond. Nothing worked. *Nothing.*

Water was trickling into the car, but she couldn't unfasten her seat belt, couldn't crawl out! Would it fill the car? Was there enough water in the ditch to do that? she wondered. Her head hurt. It felt fuzzy, as if her skull were stuffed with cotton. Her nose hurt, too.

How would she breathe if the car filled with water?

The answer was, she wouldn't—*couldn't*—breathe, not without air!

If the car filled, she would drown.

Oh, dear Lord, her life couldn't end here! She just couldn't die. Not like this. She had to stay calm, mustn't panic—that's what Jim always said. She had to get out!

The Lincoln that had nudged Laura Scott into the ditch slowed to a halt at the side of the road.

DOUBLE PLAY

The driver drew a cell phone from his pocket. He flipped the cover and dialed 911 to report the accident, giving directions to the dispatcher.

". . . it looked to me as if the driver had been drinking prior to rolling over. Yes, the car was weaving. Yes, that's correct. It's upside down in the drainage ditch about two miles down the old beach road. And please, tell them to hurry!" he finished.

Closing his phone, he made a lazy U-turn and drove back the way he'd come.

Speeding up as he passed the overturned car, he was laughing as he drove away. He had seen a pale hand clawing at a mud-splashed window inside the vehicle.

It was only a matter of time now.

A half mile down the road, he turned onto a side road, killed the engine, and waited.

In the distance, he could hear the banshee wail of an ambulance approaching. The rumble of a fire truck.

The first-responders would soon be here.

Show time.

THIRTEEN

"Mrs. Rojas's call light is flashing."

"I'll get it," Liz offered.

"Thanks. Would you tell her Mark from anesthesiology is on his way with the epidural? She's really uncomfortable," Sandy said.

"Will do." Hooking her stethoscope around her neck, Liz left the nurses' station and headed for room 312 at the end of a long, pale green corridor, its walls hung with delicate pastel watercolors.

Mrs. Rojas, a handsome red-haired Hispanic woman in her early forties, was obviously in active labor. Her stomach peaked with yet another powerful contraction as Liz entered her room.

She waited until the contraction had subsided before introducing herself to her patient.

"Hi, Mrs. Rojas. My name's Liz. I'll be helping Sandy take care of you tonight. She said for you to hang in there, okay? Mark is on his way with your epidural."

"*Gracias a Díos!*" the woman said fervently,

mopping perspiration from her forehead and neck with a huge white handkerchief.

"Would you like me to rub your back?" Liz offered, remembering her own lonely twelve-hour labor with Kennedy.

"Please. That would be wonderful! My husband, he is working tonight. He wanted to be here, to help me with the birth, but . . ." She shrugged her shoulders philosophically. "It cannot be helped."

Liz glanced at her watch. Almost nine. "What time does he get off? He might still make it in time for the delivery. This baby is . . . what? Your second? Third?"

"Fourth. A son, at last! He will have three older sisters, this little one."

Liz laughed as the woman rolled her eyes. "Fourth! Then you're probably right. His daddy may not be here in time for the delivery. If you'll turn onto your left side, I'll rub your back for you."

"Oh, thank you!"

Liz poured lotion into her palm and began massaging the woman's back with smooth circular motions, asking questions about Mrs. Rojas's three daughters and the baby boy she would soon deliver.

"With three big sisters to help take care of him, that little guy will be spoiled rotten. There. Is that any better?" she asked several minutes later.

"Much better. Your hands, they are so cool and soothing."

"I'm glad I could help. Is there anything else I can do for you?"

"*Sí*. You can make this baby come out right now!" Mrs. Rojas said with feeling. She rolled her eyes.

Liz laughed. "I wish I could. Would you turn over onto your back now, please? That's great. Scoot up, just a little, so I can get this b.p. cuff on your arm. There. That's perfect. After I take your vitals, we'll see how the contractions are coming along. Did Sandy say how many centimeters you're dilated?"

"Six, the last time she checked."

"That's great. You're over halfway. It won't be—"

"Aaah!"

"Another contraction?"

"Yes!" the woman gasped.

"Okay. We'll wait to take your b.p. Don't forget your breathing. Good. That's great. Keep it up. You're doing so well, Mrs. Rojas."

"Please! Call me Theresa," the woman panted.

"Okay, Theresa it is."

Liz waited until the contraction had ended before continuing her exam.

"Finished?" The woman nodded. "Okay. Let's get your blood pressure now. Don't talk for just a moment, okay?" Liz asked, pumping up the cuff.

She stayed with Theresa Rojas until Mark Danson, the anesthesiologist, had given her the epidural. They exchanged a few words; then she headed back down the hallway to the OB nurses' station. She was smiling as she went.

Mark was tall, dark-haired, lean, and good-looking, in a lanky kind of way, with warm brown eyes that lit up whenever his path crossed with Liz, which wasn't very often, since Mark routinely worked the swing shift.

"Hey, Liz. How's it going? I didn't know you were working tonight. You caught the swing shift this week, huh?"

"I wish! No, I'm on relief. Two days, two nights, and one swing shift."

"Ouch! Too bad."

Nobody liked working the relief shift, but the hospital was short of nurses, and—as the "newbie"—she didn't have much say about her shifts as yet.

"How do you like working at St. Ann's Women's and Children's so far?"

"I love it here," she said simply, flashing him a smile.

He smiled back. "Good! See you around, okay, Liz?"

"Sure," she agreed, smiling.

The other nurses claimed Mark was getting up the nerve to ask Liz out. They enjoyed razzing her about it, although she'd made it very clear that she was only interested in Jack.

As she passed the elevator, the doors opened. She glanced up, surprised to see Jack step out of the elevator as if her thoughts had conjured him up.

He wore a blue-and-white Hawaiian shirt over blue Levi's and sneakers—what her mom called his *Miami Vice/Magnum P.I.* look. Old TV programs aside, he looked very dark and handsome against the ultrafeminine pastel decor.

"Hi! What are you doing here?" she greeted him.

"Just the lady I was looking for," he said, pointing at her. "I need to talk to you, gorgeous. Got a minute?"

"Maybe." She eyed him suspiciously. Was it her imagination, or did he sound a little *too* breezy? "Why? What's up?"

He had never come up to Labor and Delivery before. She suspected he stayed away because he was a little embarrassed by all the female OB patients in various stages of labor and undress. So what was he doing here now, unless—

"Oh, my God! *Kennedy!* Something's happened to Kennedy!"

Her hand flew to her mouth.

She'd dropped Kennedy off at her sitter's before starting the swing shift. Marilyn Kane was an OB nurse who worked the day shift, and an old friend of hers. They'd hung out together, lived just a few streets apart throughout high school, finally going their separate ways to different nursing colleges.

Jack put his hands on her shoulders. "Whoa. Slow down. Don't even go there. Kennedy's fine," he reassured her. "But . . . there was a car accident tonight on Old Bayside Drive. Sweetheart, your mom rolled her car."

"Rolled her car—? Oh, my God!"

"They took her to Bayview ER."

"She's not—?"

"No, baby. No! But—she was injured." His arms went around her, hugged her tightly.

"H—how bad is it?" she asked anxiously, her frightened eyes searching his face.

"They're not sure yet—and that's the truth. The ER docs were doing a CT scan when your dad called me to come get you. He wanted to stay with your mom. He figured you'd understand."

"Of course," Liz murmured, distracted by the thoughts teeming in her head. "I have to see her, Jack." She anxiously wetted her lips, afraid to voice the questions clamoring to be asked, not at all convinced she wanted to hear the answers.

In an instant, her old fear of being abandoned, of losing yet another mother—a fear never very deeply buried—had resurfaced, springing up like a monstrous weed. At stressful times like this, she reverted to the frightened foster kid she'd once been, and it infuriated her.

She was a professional, for Pete's sake. An adult. A parent! Yet right now, she felt about six years old all over again, anxious and helpless.

By far the strongest memory she had of her childhood was of sitting all alone in the battered waiting room of a huge Catholic charity hospital, surrounded by the smell of illness and disinfectant. Down the hall, her mother lay dying, her ailing heart growing weaker and weaker, until it stopped altogether.

She closed her eyes, images of MVA victims she'd nursed—their bodies crushed, broken, bloody, burned—filling her mind. Those memories were pitiless in their clarity.

Please, God, not again! Let Mom be okay, she prayed fervently, her fists balled, her jaw clamped tight. *Don't take her away from me.*

"They'll have to call in another nurse before I can leave the floor. Hold on while I contact the night nursing supervisor," she told Jack crisply, keeping her emotions carefully under control as she hurried back to the nurses' station.

She dialed the extension, her fingers stabbing the numbers. "Five minutes, and we're out of here," she promised Jack, her hand over the receiver. "Hello? Pattie? This is Liz Scott in Labor and Delivery . . ."

By the time she and Jack arrived at Bayview, Laura Scott had been moved from a bay in Trauma to a bed in Intensive Care. Although connected to several beeping monitors, she was comatose.

Her mother had several injuries, Liz learned from her father—a broken wrist, a broken nose, a cracked orbit, a head contusion, several minor lacerations, and a concussion.

"What the hell's an orbit, anyway?" Jim Scott wondered aloud.

"The bony eye socket, Dad. Right here," Liz supplied, pointing to her own face.

"Yeah? Then why don't they call it that?" he grumbled.

Her mom's injuries had knocked her father for a loop, temporarily turning the mellow, good-humored man she knew and loved into a short-tempered, irritable stranger.

"Sorry, honey," he added quickly, slipping his arm around her shoulders and squeezing. "Didn't mean to snap at you."

"I know, Dad. It's okay. Try not to worry. Mom will be okay," she promised, rubbing her father's back.

She hoped she sounded convincing, but deep down inside, she was not so sure of the outcome.

Laura had been conscious and reasonably coherent when she was extricated from her overturned vehicle at the scene. But while being loaded onto the ambulance for the seven-minute ride to Bayview ER, she had lapsed into a coma—a result, her doctor believed, of her head striking the windshield.

The violent whiplash effect of such accidents often caused injuries like her mom's, Liz knew. The victim's brain shifted, hitting the opposite wall of the skull, which caused it to swell. The condition, known as contra-coup, was not unlike shaken baby syndrome.

When the brain swelling subsided, Dr. Patel was confident her mother would come out of the coma.

236

However, it could be a matter of hours, days—even weeks—before that happened.

In the interim, a plastic surgeon had cleaned and sutured her mom's bloody facial lacerations, straightened and taped her broken nose, and inserted an i.v. to supply needed fluids and electrolytes. An X-ray had determined that she would probably not need surgery to repair the orbit. They could do no more for her. Her recovery would ultimately depend on her body's own restorative powers; on rest, and time.

Looking down at her mom, her face bruised and swollen beyond recognition, her normally active body immobile, Liz's heart ached. This couldn't be happening! Not again. She'd been reunited with her mom for such a short time. Her lips quivered. Her eyes stung with tears. *Life could be so cruel.*

"I love you, Mom," she whispered in her mother's ear, her voice choked, her throat constricting as she stroked Laura's sandy hair.

Leaning down, she kissed her mother's cheek, squeezed her free hand. "We all love you. Dad and I are right here, waiting for you to wake up, so you hang in there, okay? Get well. The boys are on their way. They'll be here soon. You're going to be okay, Mom. You have to be. We have that big barbecue coming up, remember? I won't let you miss that! I need your help . . ."

They said comatose patients could hear the voices of their loved ones and caregivers. It was believed that talking to such patients helped to bring them out of the coma. If that was true, she'd talk the hind legs off a donkey, Liz promised herself.

"I've decided to make Hawaiian-style BBQ ribs," she began in a conversational tone. "I have this great marinade recipe that I got from one of the members of a hiking club I belonged to. It calls for pineapple juice and soy sauce, among other things. It's so good, and you won't believe how easy . . ."

"Was Mrs. Scott able to tell you what caused the accident?" Jack asked Jim Scott in the ICU family waiting room, two doors down the hall from Laura Scott's room.

Since Intensive Care patients were allowed only one visitor at a time, Liz had stayed in the room with her mother, leaving her father to wait—and worry—outside.

Jack was glad of the opportunity to talk to Jim alone. The news of Laura's accident had set warning bells jangling in his head.

Liz's mother hadn't struck him as a reckless driver, nor a speeder. There had been no rain that might have caused her to skid off the road, either. So what the hell had happened?

He had his suspicions but hadn't voiced them to anyone yet. There was no sense in frightening Liz or her family until he had proof.

A deeply tanned, tall man in his fifties, his dark brown hair now silver at the temples, Jim Scott folded his lean frame into a green vinyl-upholstered chair. Stretching his long legs out before him, he ran a troubled hand through his hair.

"Damned if I know what happened, Jack. I got to the ER before the ambulance arrived. The police were all over Laura as soon as the EMT's rolled the gurney into Trauma. They wanted blood alcohol tests done, they said."

"Did they say why? Was alcohol found at the scene?"

He shook his head. "No. But apparently, whoever called 911 claimed my wife's car was weaving before it rolled into the ditch. Those damned fools suspected Laura of drunk driving, for crying out loud! *Drunk driving!* My wife's never had so much as a speeding ticket in thirty years of driving! I told those s.o.b.s her blood alcohol would be zero, and I was right," he finished with angry satisfaction.

Jack nodded. "I hear you, sir. But the police have to check these things out. To *dis*prove them, as much as anything else," he said gently in an effort to defuse the man's anger. "Like it or not, it's their job. Can I bring you some coffee from the machine?"

"Sure. Thanks, son," Scott said gratefully. "Black, no sugar— Hey, Jimmy!" he exclaimed suddenly, looking past Jack to the doorway. "And there's Sharon, too. Glad you could make it, kids!" he exclaimed, jumping to his feet as the oldest of his three sons and his only daughter-in-law joined them, both looking anxious.

239

Jim greeted them by hugging them both. "It'll make all the difference to your mother, having you kids here. You've both met Jack, Liz's friend?"

"Sure. Hey, Jack. How's it going?"

James Scott was a younger version of his father, tall, lean, and dark. He ushered his pregnant wife into a comfortable chair, but remained standing himself. "How's Mom doing?" he asked, turning to his father.

"She's unconscious, Jimmy," his father began, looking bleak and older than his years. He quickly filled James in on everything that had happened.

James frowned. "A coma! I don't like the sound of that. Rob and Maria were just driving into the parking lot when we came up. They'll be here in a few minutes. Where's Liz?"

"She's in with your mom. She's taking the accident real hard, Jimmy." Tears welled in his eyes. He dashed them angrily away.

"I'll talk to her, Dad. Can we go in?"

"I should pick up Kennedy," Liz said as she and Jack left the parking-lot elevator several hours later. With her mom in a coma, she needed to hold Kennedy. To wrap her arms around her daughter and reassure herself that she was all right.

She wearily arched her aching back as they crossed the second floor of the parking building to Jack's Explorer, their footsteps echoing. It had been a long day.

The almost-deserted cavernous concrete structure was as gloomy, grimy, and poorly lit as a bat cave. Several of the overhead lights were broken, too, Liz noticed with a shudder. The old parking building smelled of gasoline, mildew, and urine. The place gave her the creeps.

"Now? It's almost two a.m.! Trust me, your sitter won't appreciate the early wake-up call. Leave Kennedy with Marilyn for tonight, baby, like you planned. Let everyone get some sleep. We'll go get the Kitten first thing in the morning. Promise."

"I guess you're right," Liz agreed with a reluctant sigh. Jack was right. Besides, she felt too emotionally drained by the evening's events to argue the point.

She'd called Marilyn earlier from Bayview to tell her what had happened. Her friend had insisted Kennedy stay with her overnight, freeing Liz to be at her mom's bedside with the rest of her family.

Marilyn and Jack were both right, Liz told herself firmly. Kennedy was fine where she was for the night. The tot had taken to Marilyn and her kids like a little duck to water, probably because she loved being fussed over and played with by Marilyn's daughters, Kate and Alexis, who adored her and treated her like their own baby sister.

"I'll drive you home. We'll pick up your car tomorrow. Okay?"

"Okay. Um—would that be your home or mine?"

"Mine. We'll have a sleepover." He shot her a wicked grin and winked. "Toasted marshmallows. Scary stories. Wild, hot sex. Tempted?"

241

She cast him a serious look. "Doesn't sound like any Girl Scout sleepover I ever went to. You almost had me at the toasted marshmallows, but—nooo. I think I'll pass tonight."

The grin fled. "You will?" He looked crushed.

"Yes. Why? Disappointed?" she demanded, a little miffed. How could the man think about sex at a time like this?

But then, she wasn't much better, she thought with a guilty sigh. The subject *had* crossed her mind as they were leaving the ICU. She'd thought how nice it would be to simply fall asleep in Jack's arms tonight, her anxieties, her fears driven out by some world-class lovemaking.

"Sorry, slugger. I thought the . . . um . . . toasted marshmallows might take your mind off things. You know—melted marshmallows are sooo hot. And sweet. Not to mention *gooey*." He raised his eyebrows several times.

Unexpectedly, she felt herself blushing.

"Yeah, right. Marshmallows, my ass! What a letch!" she shot back, managing a grin despite her despondent mood as she fastened her seat belt. "Drive, cowboy. Your place. But keep that nasty mind on the road—and out of the gutter."

"Hey. I was just doing my best to take your mind off things. Can I help it if it's the only way I know how?"

He reached across and took her hand in his, interlacing his fingers with hers. Drawing her hand to his lips, he kissed it, his expression serious now.

242

"Your mom will come through this, sweetheart," he told her huskily. "I know she will. She's a tough cookie. A fighter, just like her daughter."

She nodded, but said nothing, too choked up to speak. Another second and she'd be in his arms, bawling like a baby.

Despite what she'd told Jack, she welcomed the intimacy, the comfort of his lovemaking when they reached his home that night. She went into his arms like a ship into safe harbor, with a murmur of pleasure that was almost a sigh.

And when he held her close, it was as if that ship had finally reached home port after a long and difficult journey.

Pure bliss!

He began by kissing her lips, tasting them, raking his teeth across her lower lip, then slowly worked his way down her body, inch by inch, caressing each hollow, each silky curve, until she hummed like a wire, every nerve ending alive. Aware.

His lips, his tongue, his hands were everywhere, kissing, caressing, until arousal, warmth, pleasure fused in a single sizzling sensation. He nuzzled her stomach, showered the curve of her hips, the tiny well of her navel, with butterfly kisses that quickly fanned the sparks of her passion into sizzling wildfire.

He didn't let up until she was squirming with pleasure and begging for more, his kisses no longer enough. Not nearly enough.

She wanted him inside her, she thought as she pulled him down, across her body, her touch urgent. She needed him. Needed him *now*. Needed his closeness.

That night their loving had none of the mind-blowing urgency of their previous encounters. They came together slowly, sweetly, like melted honey drizzled from a spoon. And at the end, when the shadows were filled with the sounds of their lovemaking, the climax was oh, so very tender!

Afterwards, freshly showered, briskly toweled dry, both physically and emotionally spent, she slipped one of Jack's too-big gray NYPD T-shirts over her head and promptly fell into his arms, and bed.

She was fast asleep the moment her head touched his bare chest, too exhausted for dreams, either good or bad.

In her emotional state, she'd desperately needed to be held, to feel protected and cherished. Jack, bless him, had delivered on all three counts—and more.

Across the street from Jack's beachfront condo, an older-model gray sedan with damage along its right side was parked beneath a ragged Phoenix palm tree, the driver slouched in his seat.

The man had watched as the black Explorer he'd followed from the Bayview Hospital drove into the Gulf Villa condominium parking lot.

He'd seen Elizabeth get out of the passenger

side, and sling a straw tote bag over her shoulder.
She'd looked sexy in light-blue nursing scrubs. Her
hair—now black and long again, the way he liked
it—was drawn up into a curly ponytail that was
both provocative and innocent.

The two of them had been holding hands and
laughing—laughing!—as she looked up into that
son of a bitch's face, smiling at something Mc-
Quinn had said.

Were they talking about him? Mocking him?
Was that why they were laughing?

He'd almost gagged on his fury.

That cheating whore!

Hatred burned the back of his throat like bile.
His powerful hands tightened around the steering
wheel, knuckles white, as if they were barbed wire,
garroting her slender throat.

True to form, like a frightened rabbit, the stupid
bitch had bolted back home to her momma when
she left New Mexico, hightailing it back to the
holier-than-thou Scotts with her brat and her
lover, just as he'd expected.

It was disappointing that he'd found her so
damn easily. It robbed him of the challenge, the
thrill of the hunt. Because—now that he knew
where they were shacked up—it was as good as
over, he realized with regret. Only a matter of time
now before he had her to himself. Had her in every
sense of the word, he thought with relish. And in
every way.

He would make her pay for her cheating, her

two-timing, for destroying his life, before he ended hers.

It had all begun to crumble when she staged her little vanishing trick in Hawaii. Her disappearance had brought the police sniffing around, asking questions, digging into things that were none of their goddamned business, like his past. He'd known then that it was only a matter of time before they started asking questions about Ellen.

Then down in New Mexico, he'd been forced to flee across the border like a wetback. To lay low in that cesspit, Ciudad Juárez, like a whipped hound, and all because of her. Because of what she'd started.

Ever since then, he'd been planning what he would do when he caught up with her. What he should have done before she ran off and left him. Exactly how he would take his revenge.

He had come up with the perfect plan: He would use his treasured scalpels, his surgical skills, to carve up her beautiful face and body. After all, she had used that face to attract other men. Used her body to cheat on him. There was a kind of justice in that, he thought, grinning a wolfish grin.

Reaching into the glove compartment, he withdrew a soft leather pouch that, when unrolled, contained several narrow pockets. Each pocket held a scalpel, part of a matched set. The instruments he was holding were some of the finest surgical tools in the world, made in Vienna close to one hundred years ago.

The exquisite set had been a gift from Ellen, his first wife, the night before their society wedding. Long before the well-educated, cultured facade he'd created for himself began to crumble, exposing the real Ricky Boy. The red-necked good old boy who lay within.

He would use these fine instruments to slice Elizabeth's face into bloody ribbons like venison jerky, he thought with a chuckle, caressing one of the beautifully crafted steel scalpels.

He lightly ran the ball of his thumb over a blade. A line of tiny red beads welled up instantly. That would teach her to cheat on him, to disobey him. To run off, so that the police came nosing around, poking into his life, digging up old matters that were none of their fucking business.

He licked the line of red drops, relishing the taste of his own blood, salty and metallic. The steel blades winked slyly back, at him, reflecting the light from the streetlamp. Those pretty scalpels were more intimate, more fitting, than using a gun on her. They would allow him to get up close and *real real* personal, as the saying went.

He would use them to strip the smile from her mouth. To gouge the light from her eyes. To cut the heart from her chest. To carve his monogram into her silky flesh. "Property of R.J.H., M.D."

When he was finished with her, she would be hideous. A monster. Blind. Helpless. Grotesque. No man would want her—not even a blind man. Certainly not that dog, McQuinn!

Then, when she crawled to him on her belly, begging for her life, for the life of her illegitimate child, he would kill them both. Kill them *all*.

He was a wanted man. There were APBs and warrants for his arrest across the country from Hawaii to Arizona to New Mexico, and probably to Florida. He had nothing left to lose. Not anymore. And if he couldn't have her, hell, he'd make damned sure nobody would.

That's the way things went, right, Miz Ellen? When a wife stepped out of line, two-timed her man, it was her husband's duty to punish her. To bring her to heel.

Still toying with the glittering scalpels, he stared up at the red-tile roofs of the Gulf Villa condo building where he'd watched the lights come on in a corner apartment, then go off again all too quickly.

The timing was right. That must be where she lived. With *him*.

A slow grin spread across his face as, starting the car, he drove away from the condo building, headed eastward, to where the sky was lightening with the coming dawn.

He had a few hours to kill until the couple left again. A woman. That was what he needed now. A whore . . .

248

FOURTEEN

Jack glanced down at his watch as he slid the key into the lock of his spacious end-unit the following evening.

He'd worked late, fine-tuning a proposal for a very expensive security system to be installed at the mansion of a rock star who was relocating to the Tampa area.

It was now almost six. He still had enough time to take Kona for a run, followed by a quick shower, he thought as he tried once again to turn the key. Afterwards, he'd head out to Bayview to meet Liz, and—

What the hell was going on here? he wondered, scowling down at the key in his hand. The damn lock was broken.

He pushed the door, surprised when it swung inward on well-oiled hinges.

Stunned by the sight that met his eyes, he stood there, gaping at the mirrored wall of the foyer directly in front of him, not comprehending at first what he was seeing.

Three words had been daubed on the mirror in red paint, as if written in blood.

You're dead, bitch!

Jack's features were immobile, betraying no response to the lurid graffiti. The pulse that throbbed in his temple was the only outward sign of his emotions.

A graceful fronded palm in a black ceramic planter had stood in front of the mirror when he'd left the condo that morning. It had since been thrown aside. Rocks and muddy potting medium littered the marble-tiled entryway and the glowing hardwood floors beyond. Black ceramic shards were scattered everywhere.

Drawing the Glock from his belt holster, he swiftly moved away from the doorway. Stepping soundlessly over the debris that littered the short hall, he made his way into the living room, silent as a shadow.

The overstuffed pillows of the sleek gray sectional had been savagely slashed. White stuffing exploded from the wounds.

The weighty beveled-glass top of the Wyland dolphin coffee table, the end tables, the lamps, had all been shattered. The bookcase had been over-turned, as had the entertainment center. His new flat-screen TV, the stereo, the DVD player, the computer had been similarly demolished.

So be it. None of that mattered, not to him. Things were just *things*, after all. Inanimate objects that could be replaced with money and time. No amount of either could replace the people, the living creatures he cared about.

His weapon raised, he slipped silently down the hall, working his way through the apartment. His back to the wall, he systematically searched the kitchen, both bathrooms, the den.

Opening closets, large cupboards, he visually swept the second bedroom, checking one demolished room after another. His body was taut, his nerves and muscles wound like springs, ready to respond if the intruder lay in wait for him.

It wasn't until he entered the last room—the master bedroom—that he finally heard the telltale whine he'd been praying for.

He found Kona under the bed, where she'd crawled to escape her attacker. Although badly wounded, she was alive, thank God.

"Good girl, Kona," he praised as he knelt to gently draw her out from under the bed. He lifted her heavy body into his arms. The dog whimpered in pain.

His throat dry, he swallowed. Her long golden fur was caked with blood. So much blood.

"Hey, there, puppy. Who's my good girl?" he asked hoarsely.

Unbelievably, she wagged her tail.

The lump in his throat almost choked him.

Eyes burning, he carried Kona from the condo, into the elevator, and rode it down to his car.

Dialing 911 on his cell phone, he gunned the

engine and sped from the parking lot, tires screaming.

"Anything unusual happen since I saw you this morning?" Jack casually asked Liz in the Bayview hospital cafeteria later that evening.

"No, not really. Why?"

His dark eyes met hers. His expression was deadly serious. Frightening.

A quiver of fear lanced through her belly.

"Jack? Why?" she repeated, reaching across the table to brush his hand with her fingertips. "Did something happen to you?"

"Yeah." He hesitated. There was no way to sugarcoat it. "I think he's here."

She looked as if he'd slammed her over the head with a two-by-four. She closed her eyes. Opened them. They were dark with pain and a kind of weary, heavy acceptance.

"Richard," she said, and exhaled noisily. She didn't need to ask, not really. Who else could he mean?

"Yeah."

"What happened?"

He set his fork down. Leaned back in his chair with a long, drawn-out sigh. Took a sip of water—anything to delay telling her. To delay the fear he would see fill her lovely eyes.

"My place was trashed while I was at work," he said simply. He didn't mention the obscenity scrawled on the mirrored wall in the entryway. What was the point in frightening her any further?

As he'd expected, the color drained from her face, leaving it white as chalk. Her hold on Kennedy tightened.

She gasped. "Oh, my God! Do you think he was the one who forced Mom off the road, too?"

"Probably, yeah. Yeah, I do," he repeated with conviction.

Since relocating to the Tampa area, he'd visited the local "cop bars" most nights after work, cultivating a contact or two in the ranks of the police department.

Twelve years with NYPD, followed by three years with HPD, had given him a valuable "in." He spoke the same language as these guys—the universal language of cops everywhere. Cops stuck together, watched each other's backs, stood up for each other. It was an unwritten, yet powerful, creed.

A call to one of those contacts this morning had told him Laura Scott's gold Camry had been towed to a Tampa impound lot last night.

A forensics examination of the vehicle revealed gray auto paint that had transferred to the left side of the Camry, a result of its being repeatedly sideswiped by another vehicle.

The gray paint was being tested in the forensic labs to determine the vehicle's make and model, but preliminary tests indicated a luxury car, American-made. Skid marks on the tarmac surface of the road showed places where the other driver had forced the Camry into the drainage ditch, causing it to roll over. Who else would have wanted Liz's mother dead, if not Harper? She wasn't the kind of woman who made enemies.

"Don't you think so?" he asked at length.

Dry-mouthed, she nodded. An unwanted thought had occurred to her. "Yes. Jack, was Kona home when your place was trashed?"

After a moment's hesitation, he nodded. "Yeah. I think she went for him. Tried to protect her territory. The son of a bitch cut her up pretty bad," he told her heavily. "She's at the animal hospital right now with stab wounds. Internal injuries. The vet doesn't think she'll make it."

"Oh, Jack, no! I'm so sorry." She knew how much he loved the golden retriever. He'd had her since she was a puppy.

Frightened by her mother's tone, and by the tension humming through her body, Kennedy's little mouth quivered, then turned upside down. She started to sob, clinging fiercely to Liz, her face buried against her mother's shoulder.

"Ssshhh, sweetheart. It's okay. There, there, honey. Mommy didn't mean to frighten you." She jiggled Kennedy up and down, hoping to calm her, but the baby sensed her mother's distress and wouldn't be consoled.

"I think Harper followed us home from here last night," Jack continued. "Maybe that's why he forced your mom off the road. You know, to flush us out? He knew if you were anywhere in Florida, you'd come to the hospital if your mom was hurt. I'm thinking when he didn't see you at your parents' house, he caused the accident to force you out of hiding."

They hadn't visited her folks at the ranch house for just that reason.

"That son of a bitch!" Liz said through gritted teeth.

"By now . . ." Jack's voice trailed away, remembering the bleeding graffiti on the mirror.

"Go on."

"By now, there's a damn good chance he knows where you live, baby. He could easily have followed us back to your place this morning."

He was right, Liz realized uneasily, dread spreading through her like a cold fog.

Very early that morning, Jack had driven her to Marilyn's to pick up Kennedy, then taken her home to the beach house on Pelican Point to change clothes before she went to visit her mother and he went on to work. Anyone could have followed them.

Fear filled her eyes, and the sight killed him. He could have kicked himself for being so goddamned stupid. It hadn't even crossed his mind that they could have been followed, until he'd seen the destruction to his apartment. Thank God Liz hadn't been there, alone, or with Kennedy, when Harper went on his rampage!

"So. What are you saying?" she repeated.

He drew a deep breath. "That you can't go home."

"Can't go ho—? The hell I can't!" Liz exploded, eyes smoking, chin jutting obstinately.

Although a tiny woman, she seemed larger, more intimidating, when she was bristling with anger, as she was now—and even more beautiful. Her smoky eyes flashed with fury. High color filled her cheeks. Her lush mouth thinned. Hardened.

"That s.o.b.'s not doing this to me, Jack. Never again. I've had enough! That bastard controlled me. He hurt me! He made my life a living hell for over two years! They were two long, lonely years, Jack. I'm not letting that—that scumbag do that to me or my family ever again! He will *not* drive me out of my home. You hear me? *He will not!*"

Holding Kennedy on her shoulder, she sprang angrily to her feet and stalked away, narrow shoulders rigid as she crossed the cafeteria.

Grabbing the forgotten diaper bag, Jack strode after her, ignoring the curious eyes of doctors, nurses, and visitors.

"No? Then what are you planning on doing?" he demanded when they reached the elevators.

"I'm going to the police, that's what I'm doing. I'm going to tell them everything. And then—"

"Then what?"

"Then I'm going to give Kennedy to her Uncle Jim and Aunt Sharon to take care of until this is over, one way or another." He didn't need to ask

256

what she meant by "over"—her eyes said it all. "She'll be safe in Orlando."

"Okay. That makes sense. I can go with that. But—what will *you* be doing once Kennedy's taken care of?" he demanded. He was pretty sure he knew what her hotheaded answer would be, and the truth was, it scared him shitless. It would be hell talking her out of it, too. Maybe impossible. He'd never seen her look so—so hard, so angry and determined—nor so damned small and vulnerable—as she did right now, he thought as he pressed the elevator button for the second floor.

"I'll do what I've always done," she said in a voice of stone. "I'll be the victim. You know, the bleating goat, staked out to attract the tiger. I'm good at that." Her tone was laced with bitterness, anger, and self-recrimination for what she perceived as her unforgivable weakness.

"Bait, you mean?" Jack growled. He clamped a heavy hand over her shoulder, his fingers punishing as he spun her around so hard, she yelped in surprise. "The *hell* you will, woman!" he growled, shoving his face in hers. "I won't stand by and watch you get yourself killed!"

"No? Do you have a better idea, then?" she shot back. "Well? Do you?"

The hell of it was, he didn't. Yet. And if he couldn't find a way to protect her soon, it would happen all over again, just as it had with Sarah.

It would be too late.

"We need a plan," he suggested softly. "A damned good one. Got any thoughts?"

"I don't know how good they are, but yes, I do," she shot back, her lips compressed in a thin, hard line. "You drive, I'll talk."

FIFTEEN

The oppressive heat and humidity that had begun that Tuesday evening mounted over the next few days, thanks to a storm front building out in the gulf.

The hot, sticky weather lasted well into the wee hours of Saturday—a day that Liz had originally set aside for fun, food, and family, prior to her mom's accident and hospitalization.

The sky was overcast and brooding. There was no wind, not a whisper of it all day long, nor the hint of a cooling breeze to make the humidity bearable. The thick, sultry air draped around her like a wet wool blanket. It sapped her strength and drained her of energy.

She was so frustrated, so wound up, she was ready to explode, Liz thought, blowing her damp bangs.

That morning, she made a halfhearted attempt at cleaning house and catching up on her laundry—chores she'd put off lately. There'd been no time left for chores, between going to work, taking care of Kennedy, and visiting her mom at the hospital. Besides, in this heat, housework was just too much effort.

She ran the vacuum, dusted a little, mopped the kitchen and both bathroom floors, popped a load of laundry into the washer, and called it a day. The air was thick, like syrup. Thank God it was her day off, and she could do as she pleased.

A swim would have been the perfect way to cool off right about now, she thought wistfully as she folded the last of the towels and stacked them in the linen closet. But swimming wasn't a smart option this afternoon, not with lightning flickering in the hazy gray-blue sky that hung low over the gulf like a sagging circus big-top.

Florida, she'd read somewhere, was the lightning capital of the world, with more deaths and injuries from lightning strikes than in any other state. Just days after her return to Florida, a tourist visiting Miami had died when she was struck by lightning while sunbathing on the beach. No, there would be no swimming today, not for her.

After making sure all the doors and windows were closed and locked—which only added to the heat and humidity—she turned the air conditioner to high, switched on every ceiling fan in the house, and went to take a cold shower, her third that day, securely locking the bathroom door behind her.

She showered with the waterproof curtain half

open, unable to get the shower scene from the old Hitchcock movie *Psycho* out of her mind.

When no knife-wielding maniac or madly shrieking violins intruded, she quickly toweled herself dry—something easier said than done, thanks to the humidity—then dressed in shorts and a cool sleeveless, cotton top.

At around seven, she fixed herself a salad with slices of roasted chicken breast, poured a tall glass of tangy lemonade, added several ice cubes, and carried her supper tray into the living room.

She ate while watching reruns of *Sex and the City*, but the heat, coupled with the start of a headache, would not let her fully relax.

Too irritable to concentrate on the TV or to listen to music, Liz prowled the beach house, missing Kennedy.

She missed Jack, too, she thought as she peered through the ghostly sheers at the darkened backyard; at anonymous mounds of shrubbery that took on bulky, menacing shapes in the shadows; at the darker beach and ocean beyond. It didn't matter that Jack was out there somewhere, close by, watching the house. She missed him anyway, she thought, staring into the darkness.

There was no moon tonight, nor any stars. Dark storm clouds hid them from view. There were no crests of bright white surf reflecting off the waves that lapped the shore, either. Only the starless darkness, velvety-black, heavy, and infinite.

She thought longingly of the huge security lights Jack had installed in the patio area, but would not turn them on. Bright lights would drive Richard away if he was out there, stalking her. So the area behind the house remained pitch-black. A frightening no-man's-land between house, boat dock, and ocean.

How would the turtle hatchlings find their way to the water if they hatched on a moonless night like this? she wondered idly as she drifted down the hallway into Kennedy's room, turning off lights behind her as she went.

Knowing she must maintain a semblance of normalcy to any possible observer, she switched on the scallop-shell nightlight.

Its soft golden glow revealed walls that were bright and colorful with the fanciful underwater mural she and her mom had painted. A smiling lavender octopus juggled huge pink pearls in its eight tentacles. A mermaid combed out her long black hair with a pink coral comb while seated daintily inside an open scallop shell. The mermaid held an abalone-shell mirror in her tail, and was being entertained by a chorus line of dancing red starfishes with happy smiling faces.

"Nice life," Liz muttered. "I should be so lucky."

Lifting a life-size baby doll from Kennedy's crib, she sat on the big white rocker and rocked back and forth, her mind restlessly churning.

She missed her mom. Missed talking to her. Laughing with her. Being with her, especially today, Saturday. This was to have been a special day, she recalled. One they'd set aside for a barbecue—a family reunion of sorts.

But in the blink of an eye, everything had changed. Their lives had changed.

Now, Saturday was almost over, her mother remained in a coma, and Richard was out there somewhere, stalking her. Stalking the people she loved.

He was a hunter, a predator, a vicious killer. A ruthless criminal who had her, her precious family, the man she loved, in his gun sights.

The police had been sympathetic about her situation when she and Jack went to them. But sympathetic was about all they'd been.

Police Lieutenant Gary Ishihara had acknowledged that Harper was a wanted man, a murderer twice over, and a fugitive from justice. He'd also agreed that Liz was at serious risk of being harmed by her former husband.

"I'm sorry," he apologized, "but my department is shorthanded and underfunded. There's no way I can supply the 24/7 surveillance team and bodyguard you need. I recommend you leave the area until Harper is apprehended. Get yourself out of harm's way, Mrs. Harper."

Ishihara added that he would contact the F.B.I. to request the agency's help in apprehending Harper. Until the special agents arrived, the police cruiser that patrolled the sparsely populated area of Pelican Point would swing by the beach house at frequent intervals to check on Liz's welfare.

It wasn't what Jack had wanted, but it was better than the alternative, which was nothing. A police cruiser, manned by a couple of officers, plus the plan they'd come up with, would have to do.

Rather than dwell on the fears that were uppermost in her thoughts, Liz forced herself to think of more pleasant things.

As she rocked the doll on her lap, she thought about all the nights she'd rocked her daughter to sleep, both here and in New Mexico.

She'd sung softly until those bright little eyes at last grew heavy and that tiny pink thumb popped out of her daughter's mouth.

"God bless, Kitten," she'd murmured, kissing Kennedy's flushed little cheek. "Sleep tight."

Unlike many babies, who woke the minute they were put down, from the day she was born, Kennedy had been a little angel. She never stirred once she was put down in her crib.

Liz sighed as she rewound the musical mobile that hung on the side of her daughter's crib.

The strains of a German lullaby tinkled on the muggy shadows as she rocked slowly back and forth. Above her head, a half-dozen colorfully striped tropical fish swam in endless circles.

The musical fish mobile had been a shower gift from Trini Alvarez before Kennedy was born, she remembered, missing her friend despite the e-mails they exchanged. It was the mobile that had inspired the underwater theme for Kennedy's room. Liz sighed again.

On Thursday evening, just forty-eight hours ago, she'd handed her precious daughter over to her brother Jimmy and her nervous sister-in-law, Sharon. It was the first time Liz had ever been separated from her baby, and it was killing her.

Was Kennedy already fast asleep tonight—or was she awake and fussy, crying for her mommy? Liz wondered, clutching the doll in her empty arms.

Four months into her own pregnancy, Sharon had been understandably nervous about taking on an active one-year-old who was into everything. But despite her misgivings, both she and Jimmy had agreed to care for their niece.

"It'll be good practice for when our own baby arrives," Sharon had assured Liz, rubbing her growing stomach. "She'll be fine. Don't worry about her, okay? We'll take good care of her."

Easier said than done, Liz thought. Kennedy had been gone for only two days, but those two days already felt like an eternity. She missed her so much. It was like having a big hole where her heart used to be. A physical ache that nothing short of seeing her daughter again could ease.

It amazed her that she could love a child conceived in pain and hatred so very deeply, so unconditionally, while at the same time, she loathed that child's natural father with every fiber of her being.

She'd wondered, at the beginning of her pregnancy, if she would be a good mother to her baby, once it was born. The child would be innocent. Helpless. Dependent on her for its every need.

Would she hold that innocent child responsible for everything its father had done to her? Or love it as it deserved to be loved? Deeply. Unconditionally.

She need not have worried.

She'd begun falling hopelessly in love with her daughter months before her due date, beginning when she felt the first flutter of life in her womb. The last of her fears had burst like soap bubbles the instant a beaming Dr. Garcia placed Kennedy on her chest. From then on, she'd never looked back.

All the risks she'd taken in staging her disappearance in Hawaii, her efforts to escape Richard in New Mexico, and now here in Florida, would all be worthwhile, if only she and Kennedy could be free for the rest of their lives.

She set her jaw. She'd get through this, she vowed. They'd both—all!—get through it, she promised herself. She and Kennedy, and Jack. Dear Jack.

Once Richard was out of the picture, safely under lock and key, they would all have the happy life they so richly deserved. A life without fear.

She must have fallen asleep as she sat there rocking, because the next thing she knew, she could hear an odd muffled drumming sound above her head.

As she struggled up from the depths of sleep, groggily trying to make sense of what she was hearing, she realized the sound was rain. The kind of heavy torrential rainfall she hadn't experienced since leaving Hawaii.

The rain pummeled and drummed on the beach-house roof, the big drops sounding like thousands of pattering feet as they fell.

Going to the window, Liz drew the filmy green "seaweed" curtains aside and peered through the glittering deluge, just as a jagged bolt of lightning flashed, bathing the ocean and shoreline below in bright white light.

The splintering flash was followed seconds later by the noisy clap and rattle of a huge thunderbolt overhead.

She stood there, watching the spectacular storm rage for several minutes, before another brilliant flash lit up the beach like a magnesium flare.

It was then that she saw him.

He was standing on the beach, just a few feet beyond the wall that separated her back yard from the beach, his body motionless, his head turned to look at the ocean.

His features were carved from the night, silhouetted by the brilliance of the raging storm for a fleeting moment. The lightning cast the rest of him in inky shadow, so that he seemed black-robed. Evil. Death personified.

Richard!

With a gasp, she stepped back from the window as if she'd been shot, her pulse hammering, her knees buckling with shock, her mind assaulted by a million memories—all of them bad.

He was out there! Outside her window. Only yards away. The man who had hurt her. Beaten her.

Raped her. Destroyed her self-esteem, her confidence, her life—he was *out there*. So close she could almost touch him. Oh, God—so frighteningly close!

She sank to her knees, trembling uncontrollably. Talk was one thing. Making plans, deciding who would do what, go where, that was the easy part.

This—the reality of it, of *him* being here, hiding in the shadows outside her window—was a thousand times more frightening than she'd ever imagined, even in her worst nightmares.

But there was no going back. Not now, she told herself. She was committed. She had to see this through to the bitter end.

There was no was doubt whatsoever that it was Richard, she thought, her heart racing like a triphammer.

In profile, he was more recognizable now than he'd been back in New Mexico, when she'd glimpsed him, full-face, in her rearview mirror, his coloring dramatically altered.

Back then, his almost-white hair had been dyed brown. Dark contacts had turned the chilling, almost colorless eyes a flat, soulless black. *Empty eyes,* she'd always thought them. *Reptilian.* But neither hair dye nor colored contacts could alter that all-too-familiar profile.

Slowly, as if he could see her, she crawled from the nursery, into the darkened hallway, on her hands and knees.

Crouched there, she slid a trembling hand into

her shorts pocket and withdrew her cell phone. She pressed redial without needing light to see the buttons.

"He's here," she whispered breathlessly when Jack answered on the first ring. "I saw him. By the beach wall. In front of Kennedy's window."

"I'm on it. Breathe, baby. It'll be okay," came Jack's husky reply. "You know what to do. Is everything set?"

"Yes."

"Then get the hell out of there!"

"I will. Be careful, Jack. Be very, very careful!" she pleaded.

"I will. I love you, baby."

"Ditto."

SIXTEEN

Standing on the beach, he watched her through the curtain of rain, through the filmy curtains at the windows, as she moved around the beach house. He enjoyed playing the voyeur. The peeping tom. The watcher in the shadows. Enjoyed knowing he had control over her. Whether she lived or died today would be up to him. His choice.

She wandered aimlessly—or so it seemed to him—for the better part of an hour, drifting from room to room. Kitchen. Living room. Nursery. Lights were turned on and off, seemingly at random.

She was restless—and she was alone.

Now, only the soft amber glow of two night-lights remained lit—one in what he guessed was the kid's room, the other in the bigger master bedroom, where she slept.

He waited a good half hour to give her time to fall asleep, before he made his move.

Show time!

The loud clatter of thunder muffled the noise of shattering glass as he broke a window. As silently as a wraith, he reached through the circle of broken glass to unlock the latch. To slide the window, then the screen, aside.

Dressed all in black, he climbed over the sill.

Inside the master suite, he stood there, looking down at her, loving her, hating her, as she slept, bathed in the nightlight's soft golden glow.

The bitch lay on her belly, her long black hair fanned out across the pillow, her arms and legs flung out, as if in surrender. Her slender body was hidden by the blue toile sheet she'd drawn up over her.

He slicked his tongue over dry lips, like a wolf salivating over its upcoming feast.

He'd insisted she sleep naked after they were married. Her body, after all, was his property. It belonged to her husband, to enjoy in whatever way he saw fit.

He had allowed her no modesty. No privacy. No secrecy. She excited him most when she was naked. Vulnerable. Defenseless. His to command. To control.

Was she naked now, beneath the filmy sheet draped voluptuously over her slender curves? he wondered.

Excited by the image his thoughts conjured up, he wetted his lips again, stroking himself as his groin grew hard with burgeoning lust.

Erotic memories danced like sugarplums in his

head. Smooth pale skin. Lustrous black hair. Lips that were bruised and swollen by his kisses . . .

He would do her first, he decided. *Do her good. Just once more, my darling, for old time's sake.* He'd give her a little taste of what she'd been missing.

But first . . .

He checked his waistband, reassuring himself that the razor-sharp scalpels were still there in the soft leather pouch he'd tucked into his belt, along with the plastic ties he would use to bind her wrists and ankles.

"Ricky Boy's back, sweet thing. Did ya miss me?" he asked, breathing the words softly, his voice no more than a serpentine hiss in the gloom. "I surely missed you, Eliza-beth."

The police cruiser had passed by only minutes ago. He'd been timing it all week. He figured he had the better part of forty-five minutes before it swung by again. Forty-five minutes to do whatever he wanted. To do what he'd come here to do.

Her.

The nearest house was some distance away, but no one was there to hear her screams anyway. The neighbors were traveling in Europe, the newspaper boy had told him. He'd left his own car parked in their driveway, ready for a speedy getaway. Nobody would look twice at a Lincoln Town Car, not in this area, home to "old money" as Ellen would have called it. But just in case . . .

A heavy roll of duct tape in one hand, he loomed

over her. The tape rasped as he unwound it. Fisting his free hand in her silky black hair, he roughly jerked her head back to tape her mouth. To silence her screams. To gag her.

She would be fully aware of what was going to happen, but helpless, silent, unable to utter so much as a squeak.

He recoiled as her scalp peeled off in his hands—

—as her head rolled off the bed, landing on the hardwood floor at his feet with a solid thump!

What the hell—?

The long black scalp in his hands was only a wig!

A wig that had been pinned to the "head" at his feet—a molded wig stand.

With a howl of fury, he flung it from him. Ripped the sheet aside.

Her "body" was nothing but pillows and rolled newspapers.

Rage boiled through him.

Damn her! Damn that bitch! That two-faced, cheating whore! Once again she'd played him for a fool! Made him a laughingstock!

"She's not here, Harper. Disappointed?" a low male voice jeered.

Harper spun around as if jerked by a cord.

McQuinn stood in the bedroom doorway.

The son of a bitch looked bigger, taller than he remembered. Meaner, too. No shuffling Columbo, not tonight. Tonight, the former detective meant business. Harper read it in his eyes.

A trap! The slut had set a trap for him. After all he'd done for her, marrying her, giving her his name, taking an orphan—a foster kid nobody wanted—and making her *somebody:* the wife of a respected surgeon. A brilliant man who'd saved countless lives. An important man who commanded respect. Awe. This was how she repaid him? By setting a trap for him. *Him!*

He leveled the gun at McQuinn and fired.

But instead of a deafening report, there was only a "click."

His weapon had jammed. Worthless piece of shit!

In the distance, he heard the wail of a siren, growing closer. The car would be there within seconds. He wetted his lips. There was only one way out, and that was back through the window, the way he'd come in.

With a shout, he hurled the heavy roll of duct tape at McQuinn's face, turned, and dived headfirst out the window.

"Freeze!" McQuinn roared behind him.

Harper heard the round as it zipped overhead. Stucco sprayed like powder as the bullet dug a deep trough in the wall, but he was gone.

He grunted as he landed heavily on the flagstone patio, but was up and running in a heartbeat.

Running for his life.

Running through the backyard, across the wet beach, with the storm lashing around him, wet sand sucking at his soles, the cop hot on his heels.

Who the hell did McQuinn think he was? Frigging Five-O?

The car! he thought as lightning splintered the darkness, lighting his way. If he could reach the car, he was home free. . . .

That second's hesitation, that sense of déjà vu before he'd fired the Glock, cost him, big time, Jack thought angrily as Harper fled into the stormy night.

If Harper's own weapon hadn't jammed, he—Jack—would be dead now.

Irish luck!

He dived out the window after Harper, flipping on the security lights as he took up pursuit, his long legs eating up the sodden sand.

The patio and the beach beyond were instantly flooded with light. Bright white light that caught the glitter of rain falling from the leaden sky like a glass bead curtain.

There! Off to the right!

He'd glimpsed a flicker of movement up ahead in the shadows.

Jack exploded from the patio, raced down the beach to the neighbors' boat dock.

In another jagged lightning flash, Jack saw the perp tearing up the wooden boardwalk, hammering toward the neighbors' darkened beach house.

Jack thundered after him.

He had only seconds to overtake him before Harper could cut through the neighbors' garden and take off in whatever getaway car he had waiting.

Praying he wouldn't stumble over a gator in the dark, Jack plunged into a dripping jungle of tropical foliage.

Sodden palmetto fronds slapped his face as he moved quickly down the side of the house. Vaulting a tall wrought-iron gate, he splashed down a muddy footpath, feet crunching on wet gravel, bougainvillea thorns scratching his cheeks and forearms.

As he exploded into the front yard, he heard a car door slam nearby.

He swore as the sound was followed by the loud crunch of tires on gravel.

A pair of taillights shot rapidly down the driveway, like a pair of glowing red eyes, then vanished as the car turned onto the street.

The gray sedan—a Lincoln Town Car—slid down the street like a sleek gray ghost. It took the nearest corner with a squeal of tires, then vanished with a parting roar of its engine as it picked up speed.

Jack turned and ran toward his own car.

"Police! Freeze!" came a voice from the shadows behind him.

Jack froze in his tracks. *Shit! Not now!*

"Drop your weapon, pal."

He did so. "Officer, you need to chase down that vehicle! The driver's a fugiti—"

"Yeah, yeah, pal. Put your hands behind your head where I can see 'em."

"Dammit. Listen to me! Harper's getting away!" *"Do it!"*

"You're gonna regret this!" he threatened, following the cop's orders. "What about my perp, huh? While you put me through this crap, he's getting away! Didn't you see that goddamned car peel out just now? What about catching the frigging suspect, huh?"

"Yeah, yeah. Like you care. Turn around, pal. Slowly. Keep your hands up behind your head and keep that mouth shut! Let's take a look at that mug of yours."

Muttering a profanity, Jack turned his head. He found himself pinned by the blinding beam of the patrol cop's flashlight.

He threw up a hand to shield his eyes, flooded with fury and frustration, his mood ugly. "Satisfied?"

"That's McQuinn, you frigging asshole!" the cop's partner growled through the cruiser's window as, with a loud squeal of brakes, he pulled the patrol car alongside them. "Goddammit, Calhoun! That son of a bitch is getting away!"

The cruiser took off in hot pursuit after Harper's car, sirens wailing, engine roaring loud enough to rival the storm. Jack held little hope that he'd overtake him.

"Well, hell, McQuinn, it is you! Richards was right! You looking to get yourself shot, buddy?" Calhoun exclaimed. "I thought for sure I had Harper dead to rights!"

"Yeah. Me, too. Don'tcha hate when that happens?" Jack said caustically, rain streaming down his face. If looks could have killed, Calhoun would have been stone-cold dead. "Shit!"

Even worse than his disappointment and frustration over losing Harper was the prospect of telling Liz that he'd failed, Jack thought heavily. Of seeing her gray eyes darken with fear for herself, her baby, as he admitted that, thanks to a second's hesitation—a fleeting memory from the past—he'd screwed up again, and let a two-time killer escape him.

"I was so worried about you!" she exclaimed with a soft cry when they got back to the beach house much later that night.

After Harper managed to evade the police pursuit, Jack and Liz had gone to the station house and given the detectives their statements. In the interim, a forensics crew had come out to the beach house. They'd lifted fingerprints off the bedroom-window frame and glass, and off the roll of duct tape Harper had thrown at Jack, and they'd made plaster casts of the footprints in the mud outside her bedroom window, gathering evidence to build the case against him for attempted murder, and for breaking and entering.

"Thank God you're okay!" she murmured. "I was so worried when you went after him."

"I'm not okay—I froze. I didn't get him, Liz," he said in clipped, hard tones. "It was a stupid plan. I was crazy to agree to it. He could have killed you before I was able to get inside!"

"Could have, but didn't. The person he almost killed is you! Next time, honey. It doesn't matter. We'll get him the next time around. The most important thing is that—"

"It matters to me!" Jack growled, pulling her into his arms. "It matters to me," he repeated softly. "Don't you get it yet? *You* matter . . . more than anything else in the world."

She could feel his erection, the hardness of him, jutting against her hip as he pulled her into his arms.

His hands were rough with need, with urgency as, still kissing her, he began half walking, half carrying her toward the master bedroom, where the remnants of their failed trap remained, along with a taped broken window and black fingerprint dust on every surface.

"Uh-uh. No. Stop. No, Jack! Not in there," she managed, tearing her mouth from his. "Not until I change the sheets," she whispered breathlessly. *Not until every last trace of Richard is erased.*

He swung her around, pressed her down onto the sofa in the living room.

"Here, then," he said hoarsely as he tugged down her shorts. Her lacy panties followed. "I need you, baby," he murmured thickly, stripping her top off, peeling it over her head.

Beneath it, she was braless, her breasts milky globes in the gloom of the room. He groaned as his hands covered them. "I want you, Liz. I want you now, baby. I need you."

"Yes. Oh, yes," she whispered, raising and parting her legs while he unzipped his pants. He lifted her to the edge of the sofa, and entered her without further ado, groaning as he sheathed himself deep in her heat.

"God, I love you so much, Liz," he said thickly as he began to move, pushing slowly, deeply inside her. "I love you so damn much!"

His mouth took hers in a fierce, urgent kiss as the fire took hold. He thrust into her again and again, riding her with a passion, an urgency, that fanned her own desire into a raging inferno.

His fierce kisses, his wild, urgent lovemaking, betrayed how deeply he loved her, she thought as she moved to meet him, lifting her hips to the rhythm of his thrusts. His mood was also a measure of his anxiety, his fear for her safety—

"Yes! Yes!" she cried, the words torn from her. "Oh, Jack!"

They came together, her nails digging into his shoulders, their raw cries mingling as the storm raged both outside and within.

"I'm gonna find him, baby," he promised her in the calm that followed as they lay curled together on the rug before the fieldstone fireplace, sofa pillows beneath their heads, a worn blue afghan pulled over them. His arms around her, he kissed her throat.

"Sweetheart?"

"Hmmm?" she murmured sleepily.

"I want you to go stay with your brother in Orlando until we find Harper. I'll drive you down in the morning. It's for the best. You said yourself you miss the Kitten."

His tone said it was a done deal. She bristled, fully awake again.

"No, Jack. I'm not going anywhere. And don't you dare use Kennedy to talk me into it!"

"Liz, be reasonable—"

"I am being reasonable. Don't you get it? He won't show himself unless I'm here. Here, and visible. It's me he wants, Jack. I wounded his pride. I left him—the great surgeon! He wants to settle the score with *me!* So I'm not going anywhere," she insisted stubbornly. "I want him out of my life—out of my daughter's life—forever. If that means I have to stay here, take a few more chances, then so be it. He's not running me off, Jack! He's not."

"Doesn't what I want count for anything? Damn it, I'm not letting you take any more chances. I can't. Liz, the next time, we might not be so lucky! C'mon, slugger. Go to Orlando tomorrow. Do it for me, if not for yourself."

"No, Jack. Not even for you."

SEVENTEEN

"Seen this guy around?" Jack asked the statuesque black hooker in the gold lamé hot pants, flashing a Wanted poster of Harper in her face.

Tonight was his third night of cruising the bars, nightclubs, and parking lots frequented by hookers, in search of Harper, who—according to his rap sheet, Jack recalled—had assaulted two prostitutes while a med student in Louisiana. Even if his accusers had subsequently dropped their charges, Pelican Point's seamy side was as good a starting point as any.

So far, none of the working girls he'd met had recognized the man in the Wanted poster he showed them.

Louella was the tenth prostitute he'd talked to that evening, and Pelican Point was fast running out of hookers. Still, if nothing else, trying to uncover Harper's whereabouts had taken his mind off Liz, and their argument, he thought with a scowl.

283

The woman took the flyer from him as if afraid it might explode in her hand. She stared at it for a second or two. "Hmm. 'S hard to say, sugar. Maybe I need a little . . . somethin' t'jog my memory, you know?"

He knew.

A crisp twenty appeared like magic between his fingers. "Still got amnesia?" he asked dryly.

"Yeah, but my memory improvin' some, sugar," she said, laughing as she reached for the bill. Her plump brown hand was faster than a striking rattler.

His was faster.

"Whoa! Not so fast, honey," he bantered, whipping the bill out of reach and grinning back at her. "First you gotta tell me what I get for my hard-earned money."

She pouted. "Okay, sugar. But—I don't talk to no cops, money or no money."

"Is that right? Then you just talk away, baby, cuz I'm not a cop. On my grandmother's grave, I swear it." He raised his hand, as innocent and serious as a choirboy. "So help me God."

The hooker laughed throatily. "Who you think you foolin', sugar? Louella know a cop when she see one, even if he cute like you. You all the same."

"*Was*, honey. Past tense. Like I said, I *was* a cop. A detective with NYPD. But not anymore. I need your help, honey. This guy in the picture—Harper, his name is. Richard Harper—he gets off on hurting women, just for the hell of it. Working girls

284

like you. His wives. His own little old granny, for all I know! The man's not picky. Any of your friends tell you they turned a rough trick lately, Louella?"

"Nooo. Weeell, Juanita, maybe," Louella said at length, snatching the twenty from his hand and tucking it down her impressive cleavage, which swelled through the gaping front of her leopard-print stretch top. "'Nita got herself beat up good the other night, I heard. That poor chile. She ain't no bigger than a little girl-baby, but the john put her in the hospital. Word on the street say the dude was white. Got hisself a fine crib someplace. Don't know if he the one in that picture or some other guy. You know how it is, sugar. Y'all look alike t'us."

"Yeah? I'm crushed. You said I was cute!" he joked. Feeling his cell phone vibrate, he looked down at the small screen. *Liz.* He'd call her back when he was through here, he decided, tucking the phone in his back pants pocket. Right now, he needed answers.

"So. Where can I find this Juanita, 'Ella, honey?" He flashed her a ten this time.

Louella looked down her nose at the bill. Denominations lower than twenty didn't register on her radar screen. "Honey, I may be easy, but I sure ain't cheap! That the best you can do? C'mon, now."

For another ten, Louella gave up Juanita's whereabouts and the make of her john's car. It was a Lincoln.

* * *

Liz slid the cell phone into the pocket of her scrub pants and frowned. No answer. Jack was either too busy to pick up, which she doubted, or he didn't want to talk to her right now. Probably the latter. He'd been a bit moody since their argument, she'd noticed, all scowls and dark looks, and she thought she knew why. He was still blaming himself for Richard's escape. For hesitating instead of shooting him.

She sat back down in the vinyl armchair at her mother's bedside and began reading a magazine article aloud to her. Then describing the things they would do together once her mother was released from the hospital.

Reading and talking helped to take Liz's mind off the argument. It had been their first, and it had upset her more than she cared to admit.

If Jack was prepared to accept her, whatever her faults, despite all her shortcomings, why couldn't he believe that she accepted him on the same terms? Why did he always have to be so damned hard on himself? Had something in his past made him that way? Did he think he had to be perfect— a Robo-Cop?—in order for someone to love him? Was that it?

She'd tried to reason with him, but they'd parted on bad terms the morning after the fight. Jack had gone off to do whatever angry cops did when they were alone, and she'd decided to come here to the hospital.

Although visiting hours were officially over tonight, no one asked her to leave. She supposed she'd become a familiar sight over the past two weeks, sitting quietly at her mother's bedside, either alone or with her dad, one of them reading aloud.

She'd continued the one-way conversations with her mother that she began at her first visit, encouraged by her mother's doctors and the nursing staff, who were very supportive.

Every day they shared with her the small but significant signs that indicated her mom was recovering, slowly but surely. An occasional twitch of her fingers. The bending of an elbow. The flutter of an eyelid. A murmur. A restlessness that had not been present before. All were positive signs that she was coming out of the coma.

It couldn't happen soon enough for her, Liz thought as she read aloud, idly fiddling with her silver-and-turquoise earrings.

She continued her reading until a knock at the door an hour or so later interrupted her.

She set the magazine aside and glanced up at the clock. Almost ten. She was scheduled to work at St. Ann's at eleven.

"Come in!"

She glanced up as a male medical tech dressed in pale green scrubs entered the room.

With a nod of greeting to her, he closed the door behind him and crossed the room, placing a phlebotomy tray of rubber-stoppered tubes on the metal table beside her mother's bed.

Tall and lean, he reminded her a little of Mark Danson, the anesthesiologist she worked with at St. Ann's.

Above the blue surgical mask, his eyes were very dark as they met hers. He acknowledged her with a nod, then quickly looked away.

He was shy, like Mark, she decided. The name on his tag read Randy Moorehouse.

"Hi, Randy. I'm Liz Scott, Mrs. Scott's daughter," she introduced herself as he prepared to draw a blood sample. "Do you want me to step outside while you do that?"

Some techs hated being watched by members of the patient's family while they were drawing blood. It made them nervous.

"No. That won't be necessary," he murmured, his voice muffled by the mask.

"Fine," she said slowly, rising from her chair, suddenly unable to take her eyes off the tech. "But . . . I think I'll step outside anyway—"

The fine hairs on her neck had risen in prickling awareness.

She knew that voice!

It didn't matter that he'd tried to disguise it, *she knew that voice*—and she knew him!

"—go get some coffee. I'll be right back," she mumbled.

She lunged for the door, but before she could open it, he was on her, slamming the door shut with one hand, clamping the other like a vise over her face and painfully squeezing her cheeks until she thought the bones would break.

"No, bitch!" Richard snarled in her ear. *"You're not going anywhere."*

She tried to scream, to breathe through the brutal hand pinching her nose, covering her mouth, but she couldn't.

As she fought for breath, for her freedom, a sizzling shock pierced her side like a thousand tiny needles.

Stabbing.

Numbing.

A Tazer. He'd used a Tazer on her!

"Aah!"

Her arms twitched. Her legs jerked, out of control. She toppled forward, limp as a rag doll.

Still silently screaming, she spiraled down into blackness.

She came around to find herself seated in a rolling cart—no, no, not a cart, a wheelchair.

A hospital blanket had been thrown over her, so that to a casual observer she looked like a sleeping patient.

Beneath the blanket, her wrists and ankles had been tied with what felt like plastic ties, the kind used with garbage bags. The plastic was cutting painfully into her skin.

What the hell was going on!

She forced her eyes to open. Peered out through

the curtain of hair that hung over her face, struggling to remember what had happened, how she'd ended up in this wheelchair.

She drew a deep, shuddering breath.

The reek of old gasoline, exhaust fumes, and cat pee filled her nostrils.

St. Ann's parking lot. Second-floor parking. Oh, God! Richard was there, too. He was just a few feet away, opening the trunk of a car. A big American-made luxury car.

Memory flooded back.

Was this a nightmare? Was she really asleep, and dreaming?

No.

If only it were that simple. That innocent.

This . . . this was real!

She swallowed. Richard was going to put her in that trunk. To take her somewhere. She knew it. And when they got there . . . what then?

Easy.

He would kill her.

No. No! She didn't want to die. She couldn't let him take her anywhere. If he wanted to kill her, he'd have to do it right here. She wouldn't go anywhere with him, wouldn't let him take her away, not without doing her damnedest to fight him off.

Desperate, she threw herself forward, out of the chair, landing heavily on the oil-stained concrete parking lot. She kicked out with her bound feet, sending the wheelchair flying.

Empty now, it rolled rapidly away from her, rattling down the steep ramp of the parking lot like an empty chariot.

If she could just buy some time, maybe someone would come along—

"Cut it out, bitch!" Richard snarled, reaching for her. "If you know what's good for you, you'll keep still!"

"No! Help!" she screamed. "Help me! Somebody! Help!" She tried to kick him off her, to squirm free, but with her hands and ankles tied, she posed no real threat to him, and he knew it. She was just a piece of meat. Disposable. Expendable.

With little effort, he lifted her one hundred and twenty pounds and dumped her into the open trunk like so much garbage. She felt as if he'd dumped her into an open grave.

Another second and he'd closed the trunk, blotting out the dim light, cutting off the air.

Entombed in carpeted darkness, she heard the engine start up; then the car began rolling, taking her with it.

Down one ramp, then another, a moment's pause to pay the parking attendant, then a sharp right turn as he pulled out of the hospital grounds, onto the main street.

Oh, God, oh, God. Where was he taking her? she wondered as she was flung over onto her side by the sharp turn. The cell phone in her pocket dug into her hip. Darkness surrounded her. Tears trickled down her cheeks.

Where?

EIGHTEEN

"I think he turned right at the next corner," Juanita murmured, her words slurred by a hugely swollen lip. The rest of her face was a mess of bruises and scabbed-over cuts.

When Jack went to the motel where the woman rented a room, she'd been afraid to answer the door to him until she heard her friend Louella's voice.

It had been worth the extra twenty to get the statuesque 'Ella to go with him.

"Are you sure it was a right?" Jack asked, eyeing Juanita doubtfully as they neared the next corner. Oriole Street. The battered woman looked barely awake, let alone capable of giving directions to the house that Harper had taken her to. Drugs, or the aftereffects of Harper's beating? he wondered. It was a miracle the son of a bitch hadn't killed her.

"You sure right, honey?" Louella asked, leaning over the seat back.

Juanita nodded. "Yeah. I'm sure."

"Okay. A right onto Oriole it is, ladies," Jack agreed, unconvinced, but making the turn onto Oriole Street anyway. Most of Oriole ran parallel to a strip mall.

The smart offices of Gulf Shores Realty where Liz's mother had worked before her accident were on the corner.

"Where to now, Juanita?"

"When you get to the next stoplight, go left," Juanita supplied.

"She say when you come to the stoplight, you gotta hang a left," Louella's whisky voice piped up like an echo. An irritating one.

"Yeah, yeah, I heard her, Louella. For chrissakes, let Juanita speak for herself, okay?"

"I was just tryin' t'he'p," Louella said. She sniffed. "No need to get so snippy about it, white boy."

It was going to be a long night, Jack thought as he eyed her sulky expression in the rearview mirror. A long and difficult night. He only hoped his supply of cash held out longer than his patience.

How far was he taking her? Liz wondered fearfully.

Please God, let him keep driving, she prayed. *Don't let him stop!*

She knew that when he reached his destination, it would mean the end of the road for her. The end in every sense of the word.

There—that place—was where he would do what he intended to do to her. Where he'd kill her.

In his twisted mind, she'd left him, cheated on him, brought the police to his door, asking questions he didn't want asked. It made no difference to him that she'd left because of the terrible things he'd done to her. He believed that, as her husband, his cruelty was justified.

And, knowing him as well as she did, she knew that dying would be the easy part. Death would be her only escape from whatever games he intended to play first.

With a grunt, she managed to roll over onto her back, then lifted her hips, hoping against hope that her cell phone would slide out of her pocket, into the trunk.

It didn't work. Her pocket was too deep. Too soft.

She wanted to scream in frustration.

Grunting, she brought her hands, still bound together, to her side, tantalizingly close to the pocket, then strained with all her might to touch the SEND key of the cell phone through the soft cloth of the pocket.

Sweat rolled off her face and into her eyes, stinging them. There wasn't enough air.

One key—if she could only press the SEND key—the phone would automatically redial the last number she'd called: Jack's number.

Come on, come on! You can do this. Just another half inch. Reach just another half inch. There. So close! Twist a little farther around. Stretch! That's it. Try just a little harder. Come on!

Do it for Kennedy. Don't you dare give up! Don't you dare let that bastard win! Find the right button . . . There! That's it!

Do it for Kennedy! Do it for yourself!

Just . . . just do it! Do it . . . do it . . .

She pressed the key.

Heard the number dialing . . .

"He turned down all these side streets, then we came out onto a long road. A spooky kind of road," Juanita added with a shudder. "Road had trees and swamp on both sides. Ditches full o' dirty water, too. Looked t'me like the kind of place got 'gators. A place somebody nasty like him would throw a body after he kilt it."

"Think, Juanita. Think! Can you remember the name of the road?"

"Honey, I wish I could. But I cain't!"

"It sound t'me like Old Bayside Drive she talkin' about, but 'course, I ain't allowed t'say nothin'," Louella said with a disdainful sniff.

"Old Bayside Drive? What makes you think that? Wait up. Hold that thought." His cell phone was vibrating. He pulled it out of his back pants pocket. A quick glance at the lighted screen told him it was Liz calling.

"Hi, baby," he began, turning away from the curious hookers, aware that they were avidly listening to every word he said. "Hello? Liz?"

He frowned. *How weird is that?* Instead of her voice, he could hear static, mixed with odd grunting sounds and what sounded like moans, but nothing else. "Baby?" he said again. "You're breaking up."

"Jack! I—Jack—it's me." More clicks. Thumps. "Can you . . . hear me?"

Her voice sounded faint, muffled, as if her mouth was too far from the phone. A lousy connection . . .

"You're breaking up, baby."

"Jack . . . he's got me . . . the trunk of his car."

"What?" The blood drained from Jack's face. The hairs on the back of his neck stood up as he screeched to a halt on the side of the road.

"Liz? Where are you? Tell me! I'm coming, baby! Just . . . just tell me where you are!" he pleaded frantically.

"Can't . . . don't know . . . at the hospital . . . in trunk. I don't know . . . He's . . . me . . . drive someplace . . . far. Oh, God, no! He's stopping Jack! He's stopped. Help me! Oh, my God!"

There was a bloodcurdling scream. Then the line went dead.

Jack swore a blue streak.

"Old Bayside Drive, you said?" he ground out, dark eyes deadly in the rearview mirror as he floored the gas pedal. "I hope to God you're right, 'Nita!" he snarled, meeting Louella's wide brown eyes in the rearview.

"Me, too, sugar," 'Ella whispered, paling beneath her dusky complexion. "Dear Lord in Heaven! This madman gonna kill somebody, way he drive!"

Was Harper taking Liz to a house on Old Bay-side Drive—the same location he'd taken Juanita? Jack wondered, his mind racing, frantic for an answer. Could it be the empty house Laura Scott had intended to show Harper when, according to her notes, he'd posed as house hunter Robert Shaw, the night he ran her off the same road?

It was a long shot, but right now, it was all he had.

The black Explorer shot down Old Bayside Drive like a bullet from a gun. It thundered toward the next turn, tires screaming as it rounded the dangerous curve on two wheels, heading straight as an arrow to the scattering of old Spanish-style villas and small private estates that stood on the very tip of Pelican Point.

Liz's screams echoed through his head as he drove.

NINETEEN

Richard turned down a long driveway flanked by royal palms and mock-orange hedges gone wild, finally pulling the Lincoln onto a circular flagstone driveway before the empty villa's massive Spanish double doors. There he stopped.

The villa was huge, its pale stucco walls ghostly in the gathering gloom. Weathered red tiles capped its roofs. Fanciful wrought-iron grilles framed its windows. Overgrown vines were everywhere.

In the center of the turnaround was a large fountain, a pair of rearing white stallions at its center. The fountain was empty, though. Inoperable. The small amount of water in its basin had been left behind by the violent storm a few nights ago. That water was already green with algae.

He stood there, considering the fountain, the property, for several seconds, imagining it as it could be. As it had once been, long before he'd been forced to make it his bolt hole.

After the little matter in the trunk was done

with, he had a new and very wealthy lady friend waiting to fly down to South America with him. *Serena*. Such a beautiful name for a very beautiful woman. He'd buy a comfortable place like this for the two of them. Perhaps even take on a few surgical cases, rebuild his practice. In South America, there would be many wealthy patients with bad hearts. Patients who could afford to pay for his expertise with a scalpel. But first . . .

Tingling with anticipation, he strode around to the rear of the car, unlocked the trunk, and raised it.

"He's stopped!" she was babbling. "Oh, God, help me! He's stopped!" She gave a piercing scream.

"Save your breath, Elizabeth," he jeered disdainfully. "There's no one to hear you out here. The point is deserted. We can play our little games all night long and no one will hear or bother us! I think you'll like the old place, Elizabeth."

"You're crazy!" she whispered, her smoky eyes dilated with terror in her pale face.

"You really think so?" He seemed to seriously consider her comment as he loomed over the trunk. "Perhaps you're right. You know what they say—genius and insanity are very close to each other. By the way, who were you talking to?" he asked suddenly.

"Nobody!"

"Liar! I heard you. You said, 'He's stopped.' You must have been talking to someone. The detective? Where's your cell phone?" he demanded suddenly.

"What cell phone? Get away from me, you son of a bitch! Don't touch me!" she shrieked as he reached inside the trunk. Reached for her, his punishing hands everywhere as he felt her scrub pockets for the phone. His very touch made her flesh crawl.

When he found the phone, he took it out of her pocket and hurled it into the shrubbery.

As his hated face loomed over her once again, she kicked out at him, aiming her tied legs at his groin, flailing her bound arms at his head as he leaned into the trunk to pick her up. Maybe she couldn't stop him, but she would not go easily.

"Stop struggling, you stupid little bitch! Don't make this any more difficult than it has to be," he ground through clenched teeth, breathing heavily as he tried to get a better grip on her. "You're really starting to piss me off!" he snapped.

"Fuck you!" she screamed, redoubling her efforts.

They both heard the furious squeal of tires as a black Explorer roared up the driveway into the turnaround.

Harper flung around, his face contorted with fury as the car halted. The driver gunned his engine.

"Damn you!" Richard screamed, seeing Jack at the wheel.

Richard stepped away from the Lincoln's trunk, reaching frantically for the weapon tucked in his belt, clearly intending to fire and run.

But before he could draw, Jack roared, "Get

down!" Ducking down himself, he pressed the pedal to the metal. The SUV roared toward Harper as he fired.

The Explorer's windshield shattered with the impact of Harper's bullet as the car struck the shooter, sending him and his weapon flying backward with a loud "thump."

The same round took out the Explorer's rear window as it exited.

Amidst a shower of shattered glass, Louella and Juanita cheered.

Jack leaped from the driver's seat. He dashed over to where Harper, still conscious, had landed on his back. His hand was clawing desperately for his weapon, just a few feet out of his reach.

As Harper hit the ground, a soft chamois leather pouch had fallen from his waistband. It unrolled, scattering several razor-sharp scalpels across the flagstones. The naked blades caught the moonlight, flashing like steel.

Jack's jaw hardened.

Towering over Harper, his Glock gripped in both fists, the barrel angled at Harper's head, Jack stamped on Harper's right hand, trapping it within inches of the fallen weapon.

The long, elegant fingers Harper had prized so highly as a surgeon shattered with an audible snap.

Harper screamed.

"Go ahead! Kill me! What are you waiting for? Shoot me, damn you!" he snarled as blood trickled from between his lips.

"And waste a bullet?" Jack ground out softly. "You're not worth it."

"He dead, sugar?" Louella asked, coming to stand beside him. She looked down at Harper.

"No. Just wishing he was," Jack said heavily as the first police car arrived on the scene, its siren wailing. "This way's better. He gets to find out how it feels to be the victim."

It's over, Liz thought as she waited for them to untie her. The tears began to flow. *Thank God, it's finally over.*

TWENTY

On the second Saturday in September, Liz and Laura Scott held the barbecue they'd planned weeks before.

Jim and Sharon drove down from Orlando. Sharon's face was radiant, and her stomach noticeably bigger, Liz thought as she carried a bowl of potato salad out to the table they'd set up under the awning behind her beach house. That was only to be expected. Her sister-in-law was now in the seventh month of her pregnancy. The baby, a boy, was due in November. Liz could hardly wait to meet her first nephew.

Rob—her only brother with sandy-colored hair, like their mother's—and shy Maria, his girlfriend, had come from Kissimec. Steve flew in from Miami.

The young women made Laura Scott comfortable on a chaise lounge beneath the shade of a striped beach umbrella, a glass of iced tea in her hand, her beloved granddaughter playing with her toys on a blanket nearby.

Liz smiled as her mom held court. She was almost completely recovered from the coma, thank God! The cast on her broken wrist had just been removed. Her facial lacerations had healed almost to invisibility. The purple bruises had gradually faded, except for a faint yellow-green tinge across her cheekbone that makeup would cover until it vanished of its own accord.

All things considered, she had made a remarkable recovery. She planned to return to her realtor position in the near future, just in time to receive her award as Gulf Shore Realty's Realtor of the Year.

"A penny for 'em?" Jack asked, peering at Liz over his sunglasses as he handed her a diet cola.

"Thanks, but I'm not sure they're worth that much. I was just thinking about . . . you know, things."

Jack looked almost himself again, but not quite. Not to her sharp eyes. Despite capturing the fugitive, he'd been different ever since that night when Richard escaped him, and she thought she knew why. It was still bothering him that he hadn't shot Richard when he had the chance. Allowing Harper to get away that night had freed her former husband to come after her at the hospital, Jack had pointed out. It had been a bad mistake on his part that could have had deadly consequences for her.

For her part, she'd forgiven him completely. After all, what was there to forgive? He'd taken enormous risks to catch Richard. In fact, if Richard's gun hadn't jammed, Jack himself would have been killed that night.

Besides, she knew without a shadow of a doubt that Jack would put himself in harm's way before he let anyone hurt her. Knowing that, it wasn't hard to forgive him. Not hard at all. The problem was, he couldn't forgive himself.

"Like what?" he insisted. "You looked miles away."

She popped the soda tab, looking at him thoughtfully as the can opened with a loud hiss. She took a sip.

"If you really want to know what I was thinking," she began slowly, "I was thinking about the night we hid from Richard in the Pecos Visitors' Center. You promised then that you'd tell me about that other woman. The one in New York. But you never did. Will you tell me now?"

"By 'other woman,' you mean Sarah?"

"Was that her name?"

"Yeah."

"Will you tell me now?"

"Sure. What do you want to know?" His tone was reluctant, guarded, despite his words.

"Everything. For a start, did you love her?"

"Yeah." He closed his eyes. "Yeah, I did. But not in the way you think. Not the way I love you." His heart was in his eyes as he said it. She had no reason to doubt him.

"What do you mean by that?"

"Sarah was engaged to my partner, Gino. They

307

were gonna get married that August. I loved her like a—a sister, I guess you could say. Cops look out for each other's families, you know? Like Gino looked out for mine. He always brought my mom flowers on Mother's Day. Kidded around with my sisters, played the heavy with their boyfriends. That kind of thing."

"And? What happened to her?"

He hesitated, wondering how best to begin. "One day, Sarah came looking for me down at the precinct when Gino was at the firing range. She asked if she could speak to me in private. She told me she was thinking about breaking things off completely with Gino. She said she was scared of him. That he'd got this hair-trigger temper, you see? She wanted me to talk to him.

"When I asked her why, she told me he'd been knocking her around, hurting her, and that she'd had enough of telling everybody she'd walked into a door. She even showed me a coupla faded bruises. She said he didn't trust her. That he was jealous and possessive. He checked up on her all the time. Didn't want her hanging out with her girlfriends, didn't want her to work after they were married—the whole nine yards. The way she told it, the guy was a control freak.

"Sarah was a beautiful woman. Smart. Sexy. Funny. Ambitious. She had a good job in the city, too. Hotel industry. Word was that she was on the fast track to a big promotion. I think Gino was afraid she'd leave him behind, you know? He talked a good story, but underneath it all, he was insecure. He told me he didn't want his wife working—that he believed a woman should stay home, have babies, cook, take care of the house, let the man be the man, you know?"

"The Victorian type, huh?" Liz said sadly. The story was painfully familiar.

"I guess so. But hey, I thought I knew Gino better than that. He was like a brother to me. My *partner*, for crying out loud. You don't get any closer than that. We looked out for each other, watched each other's backs. If he was the monster she'd described—a woman-beating son of a bitch, like she said—hell, I would know it, or so I thought.

"I figured maybe she'd found somebody else. Someone she liked better. A guy who was more ambitious, maybe, than Gino. Maybe she was feeding me a line of bull so I'd help her leave him. See, I didn't believe her, Liz. I couldn't believe her. Gino was my friend. I *knew* him—or so I thought. And so—God help me!—I told her no," he explained heavily. "I said I couldn't talk to him. That this was between the two of them."

He took a long sip of his beer. His eyes were bleak and distant as he remembered what must have been a terrible moment in his life. "She looked at me as if I'd hit her—like she didn't even know me! Jeez. I'll never forget that look. Never."

His voice trailed into silence.

She waited a few moments until he'd regained

his composure, then reached across the sandy expanse between their towels and took one of his hands between her own. She squeezed it, her gray eyes soft with love and filled with understanding.

"Nothing you did or didn't do can change the way I feel about you, Jack. I love you. I love you with all my heart. So. Tell me the rest," she urged him gently. "Get it off your chest."

"All right." He nodded. Sipped his beer again. "The next time I saw Gino, he looked like hell. I asked him what was going on. At first, he didn't wanna tell me, you know? But then he says he and Sarah aren't getting along. He thinks she's fooling around with someone else. She'd moved out while he was at work the day before, emptied out their apartment. Now, he says he can't find her. He says it's tearing him up, he loves her so much.

"Hey, I felt for the guy, but I didn't tell him Sarah had come to see me. Maybe I should have. Maybe it would have changed things. I don't know.

"Three weeks later, they found Sarah in a hotel room in the city—the same hotel where she'd worked. She'd been beaten, then shot in the head. The investigators said you could tell by her wounds that her attacker was no stranger. She'd been killed by someone she knew. It was personal.

"Next thing I know, Dispatch radios that there's an APB out on Gino. Word was that my partner had killed Sarah—shot her with his own service revolver!

"I didn't believe it, not for a minute. I couldn't.

It was Gino's night off and I knew where he hung out. He'd been doing some heavy drinking since the split with Sarah. I decided to find him. To ask him if he knew who'd done it.

"I went from bar to bar, looking for him, but in the end, *he* found *me*. He was acting real squirrelly, you know? Not himself. He freaked me out. He said he'd talked to some people, and that they said they'd seen Sarah talking to me down at the precinct house.

"He'd worked it up in his head that *I* was the other guy—the one she'd been fooling around with. He asked me to deny it. Can you believe that? I was his partner, for crying out loud!"

"Oh, my God."

"Yeah," Jack said heavily. "I didn't believe it either. Anyway, we went outside to the parking lot, and Gino starts screaming about how we were partners. That he'd trusted me with his life. What kind of an s.o.b. fools around with his partner's woman? he asks me. Said he didn't want to live anymore, not without Sarah. He'd killed her. He was going to kill me next, then himself.

"I told him he was talking out of his head. Tried to reason with him. But he wasn't having any of it." Jack fell ominously silent.

"What happened then, Jack? Don't stop there. Finish it!"

"Gino drew his weapon. He pulled off a shot. It missed me, barely. I was in uniform, so I was carrying, too. I pulled my weapon and fired back. The round hit him in the chest. He was dead before he hit the ground. I killed him, Liz! I killed my own partner—a fellow police officer. In a way, I killed Sarah, too."

"No, Jack. No, you didn't. Don't think like that. Gino killed Sarah. You shot an armed man who was trying to kill you. Shot him in self-defense. You said yourself, Gino was not in his right mind. What else could you have done, Jack? Think about it. He meant to kill you. He probably *wanted* you to kill him."

He stared at her, amazed by her perception. Her insight. "Yeah. That's what the Internal Affairs shrink told me. That Gino wanted to provoke 'death by cop.' An assisted suicide. He was afraid to 'off' himself, sooo—he forced my hand. Made me do his dirty work for him.

"I took leave to get over it, saw the psych consult, but counseling didn't help much. Neither did being promoted to Detective." He sighed heavily. "I should have believed her, Liz. Sarah, I mean. I should have helped her to get away from him. Found her a safe place to hide. When I think back over it, I did everything wrong. I should have guessed what he was like. I should have recognized the signs."

"Jack, don't even go there. Don't torture yourself anymore. Hindsight—well, it's always twenty-twenty, you know? When these things come up, all we can do is deal with them the best we know how at the time. There's nothing else we *can* do except give it our best shot. You have to move forward, Jack. Go on from here. Put the past where it belongs: behind you. It's time to forgive yourself now."

His story explained why he'd urged her so forcefully to get away from Richard when they met in the chat room. And why he'd taken the huge step of quitting his job in Hawaii in order to find her, to warn her that Richard was coming for her. It had been his way of healing. Of making things right. Of living with himself.

A trauma in a stranger's life had helped to change the course of hers. And in the process, it had brought the two of them closer than she'd ever imagined two people could be.

"How did you get to be so damn smart?" he asked huskily, pulling her under the shade of the beach umbrella. The others were too busy eating and talking to miss them.

"Oooh, I eat a lot of fish," she quipped. "Didn't you know? It's brain food."

"Smart-ass. Come here, you."

She gave herself up to his long, lingering kiss, her arms curling around his neck. "Mmm. Nice. You're a pretty smart man yourself, Jack. You know why? You know what I like."

"You mean that? Marry me, Liz," he urged when he came up for air. "Save my reputation. Make an honest man out of me." He grinned, but his eyes were earnest. Sincere. Brimming with love.

"I don't know about marriage," she teased gently.

"Personally, I prefer living in sin. It gives—you know—*things* an edge." She raised her eyebrows, then nudged him in the ribs and winked. "Ya know what I mean? Hubba hubba!"

"Hubba hubba?" He snorted with laughter. "You're crazy, you know that?" he accused, catching a streamer of her long black hair as it lifted on the gulf breeze. "Crazy—and wonderful." He rubbed the fragrant silky length between his fingers. "Hungry?"

She nodded. "Starving."

"Then let's go get something to eat. Those Hawaiian ribs smell great," he said as he got to his feet.

Pulling Liz up after him, he headed for the barbecue grill, where Jim Scott and his youngest son, Rob, reigned as cookout kings.

Liz hadn't said yes to his proposal, he thought. But then, she hadn't said no, either. Given the circumstances of her first disastrous marriage, it was more than he'd dared to hope for. He understood exactly where she was coming from, too. He was a patient man, and she was worth the wait.

"Up! Up!"

Feeling an insistent tug on the cuff of his khaki shorts, Jack looked down, to find Kennedy gazing up at him. She was standing, hanging on to a fistful of Kona's thick fur with one hand, his shorts cuff with the other.

His dog looked long-suffering and put-upon, but she made no effort to pull away as Kennedy toddled a few steps. In the weeks since her release from the animal hospital, Kona had mellowed. Both dog and baby had grown very close.

"She's walking, Jack! Kennedy's walking!" Liz exclaimed softly.

"So she is! There's my good girl!" Jack praised.

Bending down, he swept the little girl up into his arms, ruffled pink bikini and all. Blowing noisy raspberries against the soft, baby-scented folds of her neck, he lifted the giggling toddler astride his shoulders, holding on to her chubby little feet.

Tiny fingers immediately grasped fistfuls of his hair.

"So. What do you think, kitten? Should Mommy marry me?" he asked her.

After a moment's hesitation, Kennedy nodded her little head up and down.

"Da da!" she squealed, kicking her dimpled feet. "Da da!"

"Aha! Did you hear that? She called me Dada. 'Out of the mouths of babes,'" Jack murmured, eyeing Liz expectantly and smiling.

She laughed. "If I didn't know better, I'd swear you coached my daughter, Detective McQuinn," she accused, her smoky eyes sparkling with laughter.

"Whatever it takes, sweetheart," Jack said with a disarming grin. "Whatever it takes."

Things get hot in
December 2005....

Fade the Heat

Colleen Thompson

a special preview

ONE

"First, you gotta find the perfect bottle," said the Firebug, his voice a rasping whisper that was painful to listen to. "Too hard, and it won't bust when it hits the floor. Too thin, and it explodes on impact with the window, splashing you with fuel mix and burning you to hell."

The visitor leaning over his bed looked down into the noseless face, most of which was mercifully hidden by a thick compression garment. He didn't have to worry that the poor bastard would see him staring because the Firebug's eyelids had been seared off, too, and the burn unit nurses bandaged whatever had been left behind them. Probably something that looked like a couple of freaking chunks of charcoal anyway.

Suppressing a shudder, the visitor asked, "So once you've found this perfect bottle, what do you put in there, other than the gas?"

When the Firebug tried to answer, the resulting hiss sounded like sand blown across a windshield.

"Water?" the visitor asked. Without waiting for an answer, he grabbed a cup from the narrow bedside table and held it, though it made him want to puke to watch the man he'd idolized working the bent straw like a baby at a tit.

When he had finished, the Firebug said, "You want it to flare right up, but it don't do any good if it just flashes and goes out. Works best if you make it sticky, so it won't come off of stuff."

Such as flesh and bone . . . For the first time, the visitor noticed the way the Firebug's hands were bandaged, and realized that he must be missing fingers. Maybe all of them.

"And you gotta mix in something else, too," the injured man said. "Somethin' to keep things cooking for a while. Man can burn a tank that way. That's how they did it in the big war."

"What are you, the goddamn History Channel?" The visitor was itching to get the hell out of this place. It stank, for one thing, smelled like medicine and heavy-duty cleaners overlying an undisguisable whiff of human shit. "I just want the recipe, that's all."

"And I gotta have the details. A-all of them." The voice broke like a wave. "What do—what else do I have to live for? You tell me what you're gonna do, I'll help you. Otherwise—"

"You *don't* tell me, I'm gonna—"

"You're gonna do what? Kill me? Go ahead, I'd welcome it. Just tell me how you're gonna use the thing, for *God's* sake. Let me hear the flames speak one more time. Let me smell the smoke. You know you can trust me. You know I'll never say a word, and I'll tell you how to make the best Molotov cocktail this city's ever seen. Maybe the whole damned state of Texas."

The visitor nodded, forgetting the Firebug's blindness for the moment. "All right, then," he said, moving around to block the closed door with a chair. "I can tell you this much, and I swear I'll come back once it's over and give you every detail."

He heard the Firebug's breathing quicken, wouldn't be surprised if the pathetic son of a bitch was getting hard. Presuming his little mishap had left him anything to stiffen.

Swallowing back the thought, the visitor said, "I'm going to burn a man's apartment. And then I'm going to do the man himself. And he's a doctor, can you beat that? I guess I'm moving on up in this world."

Five-year-old Jaime Perez had taken exception to his vaccination shot. So much so that Dr. Jack Montoya's ears rang and his shin ached as he limped out of the exam room.

Gratefully, Jack closed the door on the boy's howls and silently blessed the poor mother, who was struggling to console him with the roll of stickers Jack had left her.

On his way to his next patient, Jack peeked past the reception counter and into the waiting room.

There, a pack of tiny, dark-haired children shredded outdated magazines while exhausted-looking women pretended not to notice. Old men hawked into folded handkerchiefs, and a hugely pregnant woman was vomiting into a trashcan. Adding to the mayhem, the TV hanging near the water-stained ceiling blared a Spanish-language game show no one watched.

Four-thirty and the crowd hadn't thinned a bit, despite the unseasonably cold October rain rattling against the skylights. Jack cursed the fellow doctor who'd walked out the day before, after he'd been held up at knifepoint in the parking lot at lunch. Jack knew he ought to be more sympathetic, but between the clinic's low pay and the neighborhood of derelict old houses, boarded-up *taquerias,* and rough-and-tumble bars, it could be months before they landed a replacement—if the hospital board didn't nix the position altogether in the latest round of budget cuts.

Hurrying to the next exam room, he grabbed the patient's chart. Before he could read it, the new nurse, Carlota Sanchez, flagged him down.

"Dr. Montoya, it's Mr. Winter—*Darren Winter*—on the line." Carlota's brown eyes were huge, and the hand covering the telephone receiver's mouthpiece shook a little. Twenty-two and fresh from nursing school, she had been flashing Jack flirtatious smiles for weeks, which proved she hadn't been in the profession long enough to absorb the male-physicians-are-scum attitude embraced by so many of her fellow nurses.

This afternoon, however, Carlota was obviously flustered by the media frenzy that had focused upon Jack. "Reporters have been calling here all day, and now he's on the air, *live*. Will you talk to him?"

Jack hesitated, thinking maybe he should take the call—and tell Houston talk radio's most over-inflated ego where to shove his allegations. Or better yet, Jack could describe for the man's listeners the gut-wrenching horror of watching a child die of a treatable disease. Let them hear the details of the parents' pain, their suffering—and then ask *them* for suggestions on how to tell the next kid, "Sorry, it's against the law for me to help you. Your family came from Mexico illegally."

Jack would love hearing the man reporters were calling the next Schwarzenegger spin *that* to his would-be constituency. It probably wouldn't slow the momentum of Winter's listeners' attempts to help him steal next month's mayoral election with a highly-publicized, if unofficial, write-in campaign— but it would feel so good to make the pompous jerk squirm, if only for a moment.

"I'd better not," Jack told Carlota, thinking of the hospital board instead. Since Winter had started his public tirades about the falsified medical records someone had leaked to him, Jack knew his job was on the line. Worse yet, it looked as if the board members might see the incident as the excuse they needed to shut down this chronically underfunded satellite clinic. And leave the kids that he'd been helping completely in the lurch.

Since he didn't have the luxury of venting his frustration, he took the wiser course instead, the one that led to his next patient. But after closing the exam-room door behind him and taking one look at the fair-skinned blonde who'd been waiting inside, he realized he'd been had. The shrewdness of her gaze all but shouted "Press."

"If Darren Winter or one of the newspapers sent you, you can get the hell out of my office," he told his unwelcome visitor, even as he breathed a silent prayer that the papers she held wouldn't prove to be copies of the additional files he'd been praying would stay hidden.

Amusement glinted in her blue eyes, and atop the exam table, she crossed long, jean-clad legs. "Well, Montoya," she said, stifling a dry, constricted cough. "I'm surprised you're not in some fancy private practice, what with that brilliant bedside manner."

A grin slanted across model-perfect features—not that he could see her prancing down anybody's runway showing off the latest styles. Above the jeans, a faded blue T-shirt peeped out from beneath an unzipped and well-worn leather jacket. Her lace-up boots, too, looked as if she'd had them a long time. But no way did she live around here, not with that short, but feminine, precision haircut or the trio of tiny silver rings that ran along each earlobe.

Still, there was something familiar about her, something that reminded him of . . .

Feeling like an idiot, he glanced down at her chart, something he normally did before entering an exam room. His gaze fastened on the name across the top.

"Reagan Hurley," he read. Despite his troubles, he smiled at the rush of memory that followed. He hadn't seen her in twenty years, since she and her mother had left the city. "I was positive by now you'd have married some bean-counter in the 'burbs, where the two of you would live with three-point-two blond kiddies and a nice big dog to chase around the yard."

She laughed. "You've got the dog part right, but you're off on everything else, right down to the bit where I'm a reporter or some sort of spy. What's the deal with that?"

Jack shook his head. "Bad assumption. Sorry. There's been a little misunderstanding. People have been after me all week, and—" *And I'm going to answer for it Monday morning.* He pushed aside the thought, which had nagged at him since his supervisor's terse call a few days earlier.

"Forget it," she said before beginning to cough in earnest.

There was a choked quality to the sound Jack didn't like. But before he could ask about it, she handed him the paper she'd been holding.

"I really came to get this signed," she said. "It's a release for work. Just a formality, you know? Some stupid hoop they make you jump through."

Something in him unclenched when he saw the

323

paper was what she claimed. Maybe nothing more *would* surface. Maybe whichever clinic employee had leaked the information had only found the one discrepancy.

Or maybe today's rash of reporter phone calls meant that someone, somewhere, already had the rest. Though needles of panic jabbed his stomach, he examined Reagan's form.

In the blank beside "Employer," he saw *City of Houston.* "Don't you have a regular doctor? Surely, your insurance won't cover this clin—"

"Don't sweat it. I'll be paying cash today."

Alarm bells went off in his head, and resentment spiked through him at the thought of all the patients—*real* patients—out there waiting, while he and a single nurse practitioner struggled through an endless afternoon.

"So tell me about your pain," he prompted, because that was what such visits invariably came to. A wrenched back, pinched nerves, and a request for drugs to soothe them. He'd seen it far too often, but for reasons he could not explain, he felt especially disappointed this time.

She shook her head. "I damned well didn't drive over here on a day like this to worm some prescription out of you. I'm not in any pain, and I'm sure as hell no junkie."

Her anger sent a meteor-bright image arcing across his memory: that day near the secluded bayou bend when a girl in pigtails had played David, whacking the meanest Goliath their neighborhood—*this* neighborhood—had to offer between the eyes with a smooth stone. With a lump rising on his forehead and a fist-sized rock clutched in his hand, Paulo Rodriguez and his bad-ass brothers might have killed her if Jack hadn't intervened. Still, eight-year-old Reagan hadn't backed down for a second.

Like him, would she carry that terrifying memory forever?

Because whether she'd forgotten it or not, he saw that some of that old spirit lingered, no matter what her current problems.

"Then why were you off work?" he asked as he pulled a stethoscope from the pocket of his white coat. "That cough?"

She shrugged. "It's nothing but a cold. I get them—or allergies or something, especially days like this. But I was sent home because I took a little smoke."

Over the heating system's noisy, if ineffectual, efforts, Jack heard the rasping sound her breathing made. After scanning the vitals recorded by the nurse—all normal—he glanced down at the questionnaire Reagan had filled out. It was the first one he'd seen written on the English side all day.

"You're a firefighter," he noted. "Like your father."

As she nodded, pride and pleasure warmed her features—and took Jack's breath away. He doubted she had any idea of the effect she had on men. Even on one doing his damnedest to remain professional.

"I had to pay a lot of dues first," she said. "Fire science degree, then three years working one of the department's ambulances as an EMT before I made it to a pumper like my dad rode. Only job I ever wanted."

He didn't doubt it one bit, after the way the department had rallied around the Hurleys when Reagan's father died. Jack wondered for a moment how different his life would have been had his family known such support when his own father was murdered in the blazing scrublands of South Texas. Pushing aside the uncomfortable thought, he said, "Let me have a listen to those lungs."

"You don't really need to—" she began, then stopped once he frowned at her. With a sigh, she peeled off her jacket and lifted her t-shirt to make his task easier.

As a physician, it was his job to notice bodies. Hers was lean and well formed. Beautiful, he thought, then shoved aside the unprofessional assessment. Athletic, he amended. Healthy-looking.

Yet, as he'd suspected, the sounds in her bronchial tubes didn't measure up. Now he was certain she'd heard about him on the radio and decided he would be an easy mark.

Scowling, he moved his stethoscope aside. "How many doctors did you go to before you heard about me?"

"I don't know what you mean," she said.

326

He tried staring her down, but she didn't flinch. He might have known.

"Like I said, I get colds," Reagan added, pulling down her shirt's hem. "And when I came across your name in the phone book, I thought I'd throw some business your way."

That remark sounded so implausible, he chose to ignore it. "Do you wake up nights with trouble breathing?"

She re-crossed her legs. "You can save the screening questions. I'll say no to all of them."

"You'll need a lung function test," Jack told her. "Though I suspect you've taken one or two before. At least."

She slid off the end of the table. "So you're accusing me of what?"

"Wasting my time, for starters," Jack shot back.

"I spent two hours cooling my heels in your waiting room, so don't talk to me about wasting people's time."

"You've been diagnosed with asthma, right?" he demanded. "And after what you heard about my problems, you figured I'd be sympathetic. Because you need somebody understanding, someone who won't ask too many questions."

"What kind of bullshit—"

But he wasn't finished. "I'm guessing your lungs are bad enough to jeopardize your job. But you don't want to hear you're finished as a firefighter, so you're shopping for a doctor who'll say otherwise."

Pain flashed over her expression before it hardened into fury. "You're completely wrong about me. Again."

He had no idea what she meant, and he was not about to ask her. "Then take the test. But I'll have to send you over to the county hospital to do it. Neighborhood's gone downhill since you left here. We had a break-in last week. Someone made off with our spirometer."

"Forget it. I've had my fill of waiting for one day, and your bedside manner must be an acquired taste." She stuck her hand out. "If you'll just give me back my form . . ."

He held onto it and looked her directly in those storm-blue eyes. Trying to see past his hurt to the patient who now stood before him, a woman facing fear as well as a disease. "If I'm right about you, there are treatment options," he said, his voice gentler, "specialists to help manage your condition. I'd be happy to refer you to one of the leading pulmonologists in Hou—"

She grabbed her jacket before edging toward the door. "You always were too quick to judge, Montoya—or at least to judge those of us who check the wrong box on the census form."

It took a moment to sink in that this woman was accusing him—*him*—of prejudice. He'd heard such things before, from black addicts looking for their next fix and even from fellow Hispanics who'd told him he wasn't Mexican enough. But hearing Reagan Hurley say it left him incapable of speech.

Now he was convinced that, just as he did, she remembered every detail of that day near the bayou. Even those he wished he could forget.

Before he could recover, she stepped out of the room. Glancing back over her shoulder, she said, "Keep the damned form. I've got others."

"A whole stack of them, I'll bet," Jack finally managed, but he had to say it to her back.

She was already disappearing from his life.

After a coughing jag triggered by the cold rain, Reagan looked up into the on-rushing steel grill of one damned big green car.

"What the hell?" She threw herself against the spoiler of her beat-up blue Trans Am. Heart thudding against her chest, she called after the retreating sedan, "Watch where you're going, jerk!"

Its dented hulk squealed around the corner before it disappeared, giving her only a fleeting glimpse of a guy with a black stocking cap pulled down around his ears. She didn't think to get the license plate until the car was gone.

On shaking legs, she climbed into the Trans Am, brushed the rain from her face, and cranked the protesting engine until it finally caught. As much as she wanted to tear off to get the moron's plates, her old car refused to cooperate, sputtering and dying no fewer than three times before she finally coaxed it from the parking lot.

Let him go, she told herself. Chasing him's not worth the trouble anyway. The cops, she knew, would pay little heed to anything she told them, since the driver hadn't struck her. Besides, she had too much at stake to spend whatever was left of the day filling out a report that would go nowhere.

"Time to find another doctor," she breathed, her words sounding strange and shaky, as if she'd flung them into a spinning fan. She pulled into an empty spot in front of a long-closed gas station. After glancing around to make sure no one was watching, she removed an inhaler from her pocket.

It took three puffs to get her breath back, puffs she'd sworn to herself this morning she didn't really need.

As she waited for the elephant to climb off her chest, she recalled Captain Rozinski—the same captain her dad had worked for—saying, *"I've known you for a lot of years now, kept an eye on you while you grew up. I'm saying this as your friend, not just your captain. Don't keep fighting for a job you can't do."*

Her eyelids burned, and she swallowed past a lump of pain.

"He's right," she said aloud, but the words faded to irrelevance against the images leaping through her brain. She saw herself scrambling onto the ladder truck, still pulling on her gear while lights flashed and the siren wound up; heard fire roaring, breaking above her head as flame flashed over. She soared with the high of hauling in a length of hose, blasting that inverted sea, and smothering the fatal

330

orange waves. But it was so much more than an adrenaline addiction. It was the floodtide of relief she'd felt when an old woman she'd dragged clear of smoke coughed and breathed and lived to hear her grandchildren weeping their relief; the way it felt walking into the station at shift change and knowing she belonged. And it was the sense of connection to the father who had come before her, to Patrick Hurley, the man who had known things as she did. To sever that link, to allow it to ebb away with time, would be like losing him all over again.

Reagan's fingers clutched the wheel so hard they ached. *It can't be finished.* I *can't.*

"You damned sure are if you give up," she told herself, then flipped through the list of family doctors she'd left lying on the seat. Thirty seconds later, she found a listing for an office located off the next exit down the freeway.

She asked herself why not? But a quick glance at the time gave the reason. It was already 5:06 on Friday. She'd never find a physician in the office now.

Anger blasted past self-pity: anger at the doctors, with their banker's hours and their surreptitious glances at expensive watches as they delivered diagnoses guaranteed to trash a patient's life. And anger at Jack Montoya, who was supposed to be some sort of soft touch but had turned into one of their kind just the same, even if he wore a cheap digital instead.

But the fury that burned hottest was directed at herself, for allowing weakness to snatch away her future . . . and her last connection to a job that had become her life.

Using the back of her leather jacket's sleeve, she wiped away the single tear that had betrayed her. Defeated, she decided to drive home, at least for the time being. But as if it sensed the opportunity to make a bad day worse, the Trans Am stalled again.

She swore anew, hating the thought of taking it back to the shop, where her mechanic would joke that she was sending his three kids through college with the Blue Beast, as he called it. He'd advised her several times to put the old Pontiac out of its misery—or, more precisely, out of hers. But she'd had the car since high school, and Reagan got attached to things.

Besides, she didn't have the money to splurge on a new car—not after she'd used every penny she could scrape together for a down payment on her house, a bungalow in Houston's Heights neighborhood around the corner from a place her grandparents once owned. At the thought of her bank account balances, she popped the dashboard hard enough to get the wipers slapping. The blow also started up the radio. Unfortunately, the tuner was stuck on the AM station carrying Darren Winter's drive-time show. Though she ought to know better—he usually said something infuriating every eight seconds or so—she turned it up to hear him over the defroster, which was blowing cold air against the steamed-up windshield.

"If we want our borders to mean anything and our economy preserved," an overconfident male voice urged listeners in major-market cities nation-wide, *"we have to derail the border runners' gravy train. No access to employment. No education for their kids. And for God's sake, no free healthcare when they come down with the sniffles."*

She rubbed at her still-clouded windshield and wished she could funnel Winter's hot air through her defroster. Even though he wasn't an official candidate—apparently, political commentators weren't allowed to keep their jobs if they ran for office—it scared the hell out of Reagan to imagine his listeners succeeding in getting him elected mayor. She only prayed that once he got control of the city's multi-billion-dollar budget, he wouldn't do anything alarming with the fire department's share.

"Like with this Dr. Jack Montoya I've been telling you about," he began, just as Reagan had been about to cut him off. *"Or I should say Joaquín Montoya, the son of a man drowned try-ing to illegally cross the Rio Grande. No need to guess in which direction this doc's sympathies are skewed."*

"Leave his father out of this, you idiot," Reagan growled. "Or at least get your facts straight."

She'd heard around the old neighborhood that Antonio Montoya had been murdered by *coyotes* on his way to visit his widowed mother in Mexico. For years, Reagan had carried an image of a man savaged by a pack of animals, but as she grew older, she'd learned *coyote* was a name given to criminals who smuggled illegals across the borders. Vicious sons of bitches, they often led their charges to the desert, where they killed them for whatever money and valuables they carried.

"But the fact is," Winter continued, his outrage mounting with each word, *"Dr. Montoya of the East End Clinic doesn't have the luxury of setting policy—or ignoring state law, for that matter. Not when he's working for us, the taxpayers."*

Reagan had heard all this before, including the accusation that Jack had falsified a diagnosis so he could legally treat the child of undocumented workers. For asthma, of all things.

Not that it had made him one bit more sympathetic to Reagan's cause. Sympathetic, nothing—he'd been rude as hell. And to think, she'd remembered the guy as a nice kid, the kind of boy who could inspire a younger girl to go squirmy in the stomach and imagine all sorts of stupid things. It just went to show that it didn't take a radio show platform or political ambition to make a jerk of someone; apparently, having a handsome face and an M.D. tacked onto your name could effect the same result.

The loudmouth's voice grew in volume, as if the mix of ego and indignation had pumped up the wattage on her speakers. *"And I think it's high time this sort of bleeding-heart liberal got the message. Since he won't respond to me, I'd like to put you, my Winter Warriors, into action. I'm not telling anyone what to do, of course, but if several concerned citizens were to, say, visit www-dot-America-for-Americans-dot-com on the Internet, they might find personal contact information for a certain physician who has been—shall we say— 'outted' by the fine webmaster, Ernest Rankin, whom many of you know from his frequent guest appearances. To remind Dr. Montoya he is working for you, the taxpayer, and not just any Jose who can swim a river, why not send him a personal message that we're onto him? Again, that web address is . . ."*

What was that reckless idiot suggesting? Reagan sucked in a startled breath, then exploded in another fit of coughing so hard her eyes teared.

By the time the sound subsided, her speakers bleated the cheesy theme music that let her know the Darren Winter show had just returned from its commercial break. Hammering the dashboard to turn off the radio, she shifted the car through its gears and headed toward her house, where Frank Lee, at least, would wag his tail to see her. Her warm, dry, brick kitchen would be waiting, and even in this weather, her windowsill herb garden would provide enough basil and oregano to throw together a kick-ass pasta dish.

If she could force herself to swallow it. Though she'd had nothing but a chalky-tasting energy bar since breakfast, the thought of cooking—and worse yet, eating—left her nauseated.

She tried to convince herself things could be worse. Since her friend, rookie firefighter Beau LaRouche, was working, she could at least enjoy an evening free of his non-stop boasting about his paintball prowess or his ruminations about people at the high school both of them had attended years before. Besides, come Monday, she still had a couple hundred other doctors she could hit up for a signature. And unlike Jack Montoya, at least she wasn't going home to an answering machine that would be shorting out under the strain of irate messages from half the country, thanks to Winter and America-for-Americans-dot-com.

But when she ran inside from her detached garage and scooped up the ringing phone, the voice on the other end blew away whatever smugness she'd managed to scrape together.

"Hurley, hoped I'd catch you home." Captain Joe Rozinski's voice hadn't lost that stiff, official manner he'd adopted since she'd transferred to his station. If anything, he sounded more distant than ever.

As Reagan fended off her white greyhound's slobbery kisses, she wished, not for the first time, that she could have back the old captain, the one who had never forgotten her at Christmas or her birthdays, who had become a father to her since the horrible day he'd watched her own dad die. But hearing the captain call her "Hurley" reminded Reagan those days were gone forever—banished by far more than fear that the rest of the crew would accuse him of favoritism.

"I just had to pick up a few groceries," she said quickly. Technically, while off sick, a firefighter was required to call the captain for permission to leave home. She'd often enough heard Rozinski complain that he had better things to do than play hall monitor to sick firefighters, but Reagan wondered if, in light of their recent disagreement, he would crack down on her today.

"So you weren't at the doctor's, hunting up a signature?"

"Uh, no. I already got that taken care of," she lied, reasoning that by Thursday, when her crew returned for its next twenty-four-hour shift, she would have the issue covered.

"Really? Then you won't mind dropping by the station with it this evening," he suggested.

Cursing herself, Reagan wracked her brain for a suitable excuse. "I would," she told him, her heart doing a quickstep in her chest, "but I had to take my car in to the shop. I accidentally left the form inside. And besides, I don't have a ride right now."

"So how'd you get your groceries?"

Suddenly sweating, she slipped off her jacket. He knew damned well she was lying. The question was, which of them would blink first?

"Peaches took me after we dropped off the car," Reagan said, hoping the mention of her neighbor's name would convince Rozinski to drop the subject. Though the captain had witnessed scores of gory accidents and gruesome deaths during his thirty-two years in the department, he lost all power of speech when it came to Reagan's fun-loving neighbor.

Reagan supposed she should have warned the guys on her shift that despite her traffic-stopping curves, strawberry-blond bouffant, and world-class flirting skills, Peaches had been born James Paul Tarleton of Amarillo. But only days before her neighbor stopped by the station, Reagan's co-workers had amused themselves on a frigid February night by encasing her Trans Am in ice, a mission they'd accomplished by repeatedly sneaking outdoors and misting it with a fire hose. They'd had a good laugh over the gag, but watching them make fools of themselves with Peaches had been worth every minute Reagan spent chipping and thawing her way into the car.

Despite her situation, the memory of their horrified reactions to the truth made Reagan grin.

"If you want," she added, "I'll give you Peaches's number. She'll be happy to confirm it, if she's not out shooting pictures." She waited, praying he would not want to risk the razzing he would take if it got out that he had asked for Peaches' number.

"I'm working a debit day on Monday," Rozinski growled, referring to the extra shift each firefighter worked every three-and-a-half weeks. "Meet me here at the station at (oh-six-thirty)—with the form and no excuses. Either that or I'll assume you're at

338

the transfer office putting in for an ambulance position."

He wanted her to return to her old station, where she would spend the better part of her career ferrying headaches, head colds, and head cases to emergency rooms because the patients lacked the insurance—or the good sense—to visit their own doctors. He'd been after her for months about it, since it became apparent that her "colds" were more than that. And last week, when she had coughed so hard she'd been unable to climb a smoke-charged stairwell with her usual seventy pounds of gear, he had finally shouted at her, *"Go home, Hurley. Go home 'til you can do the job, or damn it, don't come back."*

Stung by the demand that she transfer, Reagan lashed out like a wounded animal. "I joined this department to fight fires, like my dad. I've worked for years to get into suppression. I can handle it."

He struck back with the most devastating weapon imaginable. "Your father would never try to hold on like this, wouldn't respect it either. You're not just dragging yourself down here. You're dragging the crew down. You have to stop this, Reagan, for your own good. You have to understand it's over. You're useless to us this way."

She wanted to shout that she would damned well show him who could do the job. Who was it who'd been known from the start for matching male rookies axe-stroke for axe-stroke—despite her slender, five-six frame—and fighting interior fires with a will? And who was it who'd represented the station in the women's boxing division of the annual clash with the cops the past two years? She wasn't finished, not by a long shot.

"If you don't get this problem of yours under control and you refuse to transfer, I'm going to report you as unfit for duty," Rozinski told her. "You and I both know you'll lose your job entirely if it comes to that."

Before she could protest, she heard an alarm go off at the station. She recognized the series of tones even before Rozinski said, "That's for us. I've gotta run."

He hung up, leaving her to imagine the crew—*her* crew—rushing to pull their gear on, climbing on the apparatus . . . and driving off to do the job without her.

Had she even left a hole when she had gone? Or had they already filled it, with someone whole and strong?

As she set down the receiver, Frank bounded over to the closet where she kept his leash and barked to let her know he'd had enough of waiting. Though she hated going back out into the weather, Reagan responded on autopilot, grabbing an old Astros cap, then leashing the dog and exiting the front door to take him on his evening walk. She'd better cut it short, she realized as the rain rolled off the cap's brim. Though she'd just used her inhaler, she could feel her damned lungs twitching with the insult of the cold, damp air. But her feet weighed her down like anchors as the captain's words replayed in her head a dozen times.

As she fought the asthma's anaconda grip, she thought of her battle against Rozinski, her illness, and the medical community in general. And how, at 0630 Monday morning, the whole damned mess would come to a head.   .

She could cave in now or go down swinging, but Reagan Hurley was looking for an Option C . . . some passage through this firestorm that would help her fade the heat.

KATHLEEN NANCE
Jigsaw

A car following too close, too fast, left Bella Quintera wrecked by the side of the road. The identity of her rescuer confirms Bella's fears. Years before, Daniel Champlain had been her lover, but the relationship was one she strove to forget. The NSA agent's rugged good looks still haunt her—as does his betrayal.

Now Daniel demands Bella listen. She is in danger. He wants to know about her new creation, about its implications for national security. What she's designed is worth killing for; but is a master criminal truly after her—or is Daniel again pursuing his ambition, thoughtlessly flipping her life upside down? The peril is real, no game like the jigsaw puzzles she makes in her spare time. And this puzzle has missing pieces: the ones that show whom she can trust.

EVELYN ROGERS
More Than You Know

Toni Cavender was the toast of Hollywood. But when a sleazy producer is found brutally murdered, the paparazzi who once worshipped Toni are calling her the prime suspect. As a high-profile trial gets under way, Toni herself finds it hard to separate fact from fiction.

When an unmarked car tries to force Toni off a cliffside road on a black, wet night, the desperate movie star hires detective Damon Bradley to find the truth. Someone is out to destroy her. Someone who knows the lies she's told . . . even the startling reality that lying in Damon's arms, she feels like the woman she was destined to be. Yet Toni can trust no one. For she has learned that hidden in the heart of every man and woman is . . . *More Than You Know.*